MURDER
— IN —
ROCK COVE

a novel

Robert B. Stone

Murder in Rock Cove

Copyright © 2024 Robert B. Stone

Produced and printed by Stillwater River Publications. All rights reserved. Written and produced in the United States of America. This book may not be reproduced or sold in any form without the expressed, written permission of the author(s) and publisher.

Visit our website at www.StillwaterPress.com for more information.

First Stillwater River Publications Edition

ISBN: 978-1-965733-13-4

Library of Congress Control Number: 2024921716

Names: Stone, Robert B. (Robert Bailey), author.
Title: Murder in Rock Cove : a novel / Robert B. Stone.
Description: First Stillwater River Publications edition. | West Warwick, RI, USA : Stillwater River Publications, [2024]
Identifiers: ISBN: 978-1-965733-13-4 | LCCN: 2024921716
Subjects: LCSH: Couples—Connecticut—Fiction. | Mansions—Connecticut—Fiction. | Murder— Investigation—Connecticut—Fiction. | Crimes of passion—Connecticut—Fiction. | Connecticut— History—20th century—Fiction. | LCGFT: Historical fiction. | Detective and mystery fiction.
Classification: LCC: PS3619.T675 M87 2024 | DDC: 813/.6—dc23

1 2 3 4 5 6 7 8 9 10

Written by Robert B. Stone.
Published by Stillwater River Publications, West Warwick, RI, USA.

The views and opinions expressed in this book are solely those of the author(s) and do not necessarily reflect the views and opinions of the publisher.

To: Donna

Robert Bailey Stone

For my Family, Friends, and Future Readers

ACKNOWLEDGEMENTS

THIS STORY IS THE RESULT OF A DREAM, AS ARE ALL my stories. This story was originally written down in 2007 and a final draft done in 2009 as is noted on the title page. At that time, I did not feel the story was complete enough to take it to print. At the urging of my wife, Angela, and my principle reader, and another working of the manuscript, I have changed my mind and now present this story for your approval.

I want to thank those who read early drafts of the book and gave constructive and literary criticisms. I wish to express my gratitude to Margaret Skenyon whose guidance and dedication in preparing the final draft of the manuscript is beyond any mere words I could apply. I thank my wife, Angela, for putting up with my attempts to accommodate our lives and still write, and still make her happy. She is my first reader always and can be a tough critic, as well.

Finally, I would like to thank my readers. Your acceptance of my efforts has encouraged me to go back through my notebooks of dreams and begin picking story lines I feel can be fleshed out into full stories. There will be more books coming.

PROLOGUE

THE RAGE SHE FELT WAS BEYOND HER CONTROL. The scream that escaped her throat as she collapsed on the floor had sounded unworldly even to her own ears. Once she regained control over her body, she dragged herself up from the floor, tears streaming from her eyes and, in a blind fury, marched down the grand staircase to the library. Throwing open the door, without regard for the noise it would make slamming against the wall, she crossed the room to the wall display of weapons. She pulled the Colt revolver from its place on the rack and jerked open the drawer below the display. She found the rounds for the revolver and, with increasing rage, filled the chambers of the cylinder, carelessly spilling the shells on the floor. She slid the revolver in her pocket, its weight unfelt.

She was still in her riding habit from her early morning ride and her horse was still tied to a pillar of the porch at the front of the southern colonial. Constance Stanhope threw herself into the saddle with the grace and finesse of an experienced horsewoman. Not only did she know horses, she knew guns as well, and she knew who was responsible for the anger that was consuming her. She dug her spurs into the flanks of her Arabian mare and reined it toward the horse path that ran around the perimeter of the cove. It took less than fifteen minutes to arrive at her destination. Every minute had increased Mrs. Stanhope's desire for revenge. Nothing would stop her from fulfilling her objective. She emerged from the wood thicket beside the cove and galloped up to the rear of the Victorian mansion. She slid from the saddle not bothering to tether the mare's reins. Her horse shied and trotted a few steps away, its muzzle dripping lather. She had been ridden hard as could be seen from the bloody spur strikes in her flanks.

The few people who were about were busily preparing for the festivities that were to take place in a few hours. The porch was festooned with ribbons and bunting. The caterers were setting up tables and chairs on the great lawn. No one paid a great deal of attention to a woman arriving in riding attire and rushing into the house. It seemed everyone was preoccupied with their own assigned tasks. The buzz of a wedding day seems to have that effect.

Mrs. Stanhope entered the kitchen and quickly ascended the back staircase to the second floor. Those she passed would vaguely recall someone coming through the kitchen. When she reached the second floor, she heard chatter and laughter emanating from one of the bedrooms. There was no doubt this would be where she was going to find the object of her rage. Constance Stanhope walked with determination toward that room, the sound of her riding boots muffled by the thick carpet on the hall floor.

She stepped into the room her face expressionless. There, before her, stood the cause of all her anger, the reason for all her grief, and the symbol of everything she despised. The bride was facing away from Mrs. Stanhope but saw the expressions on her bridesmaids' faces suddenly change. She turned to see Mrs. Stanhope standing not five feet from her. She looked at her with surprise.

Constance Stanhope saw Becky Carlisle standing before her in a beautiful white wedding gown: the long lace sleeves, the high necked collar, the full veil. It was the kind of dress her own beautiful daughter would have worn on her wedding day. But now, all she could see was the person who had caused her the worst pain she could ever have felt, the person who had robbed her of her immortality, the person she now hated most in the entire world. Mrs. Stanhope felt the textured grip of the pistol in her hand. She smiled at the bride-to-be, and, without a conscious thought, she raised the pistol.

ONE

IT WASN'T WHAT HE WANTED. IT REALLY WASN'T what she was looking for either. But here they were, James and Carol Day, standing in front of a magnificently kept Victorian style house in Rock Cove, Connecticut, half listening to the constant sales talk of Linda Giuliani of Century 21 Realty.

"It's really one of a kind," Linda was saying. "You are the first people to actually be shown the house. It's just come on the market, and I just knew it was something you would want to see!" James was hearing about every other word the realtor was saying. He was more interested in looking at this edifice before him.

James and Carol Day were the epitome of a twenty-first century power couple. Young, well, relatively so, he at 31 and she at 28, they had tried the fast-paced urban lifestyle of New York City living and done well at it. James had adapted to the hustle and bustle of the Big Apple well from his childhood days in the suburbs outside Cleveland, Ohio. The atmosphere of business suited his desire for success instilled in him by his mother. He and Carol had met in college at Ohio State where James had majored in Economics and stayed for a postgraduate degree in Finance, and she had been a Graphic Arts major. His decision to stay an extra two years at O.S. was in no small measure a result of his love for Carol. Their move into good jobs in Manhattan after her graduation had been considered a stroke of luck by their college friends, most of whom had dropped away after nearly ten years.

Carol had been a gifted artist since childhood. She would spend hours with her finger paints even before she entered school and would create masterful swirls of color and composition. The day she discovered that art and computer graphics could be married into an incredible new art form, Carol knew what she wanted to do the rest of her life. Carol found her way into the booming computer business in New York. She started a small graphic arts business that had grown to have a recognized identity among the computer elite of New York. Carol's down-home Midwestern approach to business and graphics resonated well in the flash of New York. She believed in the tenets of hard work and stick-to-itiveness that had been instilled in her early in her life. Of course, it didn't hurt her business image that she was a five-foot-four-inch stunner with auburn hair and light blue eyes. Her staff of fifteen now kept the day-to-day business running and her need to be on site every day had diminished. And that was fine with Carol. Although her husband's drive to succeed had been adopted by her when he had first captivated her during their college days, Carol was beginning to feel that his love for her was being overpowered by the heady lifestyle and success he was having in New York.

James had made partner in three years with the Wall Street investment firm he had started with after arriving in New York, something unheard of in such a short period of time on "The Street." His business savvy and good looks made him an immediate favorite with the other partners. His six-foot frame betrayed the athlete that he was and his soft, thick hair, appearing to have always just been styled only added to his air of confidence and self-assurance. Success was his opiate of choice, and his addiction was growing. His development of a risk-return profiling criteria for analyzing corporate stock in sideways markets had accelerated the company earnings nearly 30% over that of competitive brokerages and had rewarded him with income and personal recognition among the highest on Wall Street. At this point, he felt he was king of the heap. But he knew something was missing. He knew his wife wanted out of Manhattan and he believed most of his work at this point could be done over the internet. James loved Carol for more than just her success in business. But, that part of him he found difficult to express. He knew if his marriage was going to be more than a convenience of business, it was time to get out of Manhattan.

James and Carol had lived on the upper west side in a nice mid-level apartment for the past five years. When they looked at the amount of money they had spent over those years, they were sick thinking about the amount of waste. Yes, they had lived in the heart of the greatest city in the world in an apartment that anyone in their right mind would want. It was exciting and exhilarating living and working in the whirlwind of Manhattan. Anything and everything, from art to entertainment, was there. But New York was not a place either of them would want to raise a family and Carol could hear her biological clock ticking louder every day.

When the decision to move out of the city had been made, the Days had considered first a place out on eastern Long Island. Many of their friends had gone that route; first, buying the place in "the Hamptons" for the weekends, then extending weekends to four days and fewer days in the office. In fact, the Hamptons were getting just as crowded as the city. Traffic jams on the L.I. Expressway on Friday nights going out to the island meant long delays and frayed nerves just to have the same process repeated getting back into the city on Sunday night. Even the little burgs on the island that had been bypassed in the mad growth of the nineties were now being re-discovered. Carol and James were not concerned with commuting since they both could effectively run their respective businesses over the internet. But living on the Island meant running the gauntlet through the city to get anywhere.

It only took them a long weekend to eliminate the New Jersey shore from consideration. Not only was it pricey, but not easily accessible either. Jersey was just too commercial, even on the shore.

They had considered the vaunted towns of western Connecticut like Greenwich, Darien, and Westport, the so-called gold coast of western Connecticut. These towns offered properties that made the total rental expense the Days had incurred in the last five years look like the down payment that they would need. The property tax alone was a shock to James and Carol. But, more importantly, southwestern Connecticut still held the "feel" of New York that Carol was trying desperately to get James away from. It identified with the metropolitan attitudes of the city more strongly than any other genre.

So, here they were on this brisk October day in eastern Connecticut in the tiny hamlet of Rock Cove looking at this "incredible bargain," according to Linda Giuliani, with a warm southwestern breeze coming off Long Island Sound. Why Rock Cove?

Why not? It held everything that James and Carol Day had not found anywhere else. It was on the water; that had been an important component in their search for a home outside the Big Apple. They had grown fond of the beaches and the water and the smell of the ocean in their years on the east coast. It was far enough east to be out of the influence of New York City. In fact, anything east of New Haven was beyond that influence. There was a definite change in the feel of Connecticut once you passed east of New Haven. Eastern Connecticut was still rural countryside. Even so, it was not isolated. New York was only a couple of hours travel time by car or by rail. Boston was about the same. And exploring Providence, Rhode Island, might turn out to be an interesting diversion. Visiting those friends that had moved east to Long Island actually was going to be much easier. There was a ferry across the Sound at New London. Long Island is shaped much like a fish. The ferry landed at the tip of the northern fluke of the tailfin at a place known as Orient Point, and that meant being able to get to the Island without having to go through New York City traffic.

"The house has been well taken care of externally, "James heard

Linda Giuliani say. "Although, I really don't know what the inside looks like. It's been years since anyone has actually lived here. The taxes and the caretaker have been paid by a trust that the original owner set up years ago."

James and Carol had commented on the freshly painted gateposts and the condition of the lawn and plantings as they had driven up the loose white stone drive from the country lane onto the property.

"A trust? What trust?" said James as he turned with a questioning look to face directly at the realtor. "Who sets up a trust to take care of the outside of an empty house?"

This was not the first time Carol and James had met with Linda Giuliani to look at properties. In fact, this was their third weekend looking at properties in small towns in eastern Connecticut. They had liked her immediately when they first met at her office in Stonington. Carol had felt something down to earth about Linda's pleasant face with soft features framed by her brown hair cut in a pageboy style; it gave no indication of this realtor's skill and success. Her fellow realtors called her a shark. Her small frame with, perhaps, thirty pounds more weight than it should be carrying was dressed today in a business suit that was smart without being too dressy. Even though Linda was surprised by James's question, those green eyes behind the rimless glasses gave no clue to that surprise.

"Well, I really don't know all that much about it. You can probably talk with Stanley Beckwith in Stonington. He was the attorney for the trust and the party putting the property up for sale."

"What do you think, Jim?" Carol said in a low, breathy, almost dreamy voice. "It really is beautiful."

As a slight gust of wind ruffled his hair, James Day turned his attention to the house. It was beautiful if you liked Victorians. The house was obviously built to design, a mix of Queen Anne and Folk Victorian, it held all the charm of the design. A wide covered porch coursed around the bottom floor on the three sides facing the water. A broad front staircase led to the sun-sheltered porch. The railings and banisters were typically ornate. Two large bay windows projected from the front of the house shaded under the porch facing the magnificent lawn that ran down to the water's edge. Two towers rose on either corner of the front of the house ending in turrets three floors up. Windows on the third floor with curved glass would afford a sweeping view of Long Island Sound. The scalloped-edged shingles and roof finials only added to the bewildering excess that was Victorian architecture. With shingles painted a clean white, trim done in a medium blue, and banisters and spindles a lighter blue, the house would stand out against the green of summer even more than it did against the bright foliage of autumn.

Linda Giuliani had shown them an aerial photograph of Rock Cove before they had left her office. The photograph clearly showed the house surrounded by its ten-plus acres sitting on the east side of the cove. The property ran from the inlet of the cove for which the town was named, eastward for just over seven hundred feet of frontage on the Sound, and almost the same amount along the shore of the cove. The view of the water provided by a nearly unobstructed view of better than two football fields was amazing.

James looked at Carol as she intently looked at the house. He could see she was dissecting the features of the house with the eye of an artist. He could tell that Carol was beginning to change her first impression of the house.

"How about we see what we're really getting into," he said looking at his pretty wife. He loved Carol with all his heart. He looked at the realtor and said, "Can we go inside?" Carol looked up at her husband and smiled that dazzling smile that she kept only for him.

Linda smiled and started up the stairs to the ornately carved front door with the beveled lead glass inset. As she mounted the last step with James and Carol behind her, she stepped to the side and turned around facing the water. With typical realtor's flare, she spread her arms and exclaimed,

"I don't think you'll find a better view of the water anywhere."

In the three weeks that Linda had been squiring this young couple around the small communities of eastern Connecticut, she had grown to like them. She could tell that this pretty young woman was engaged in some kind of struggle for the attention of the man she loved. She also knew that Carol's opponent in this struggle dwelt in New York City and was not human. Linda wanted to help Carol win.

She left the Days to admire the view and turned around to open the realtors' key case that hung around the brass doorknob and remove the key to the front door. Carol and James stood with an arm around each other's waist and looked across the lawn at the slate gray water of Long Island Sound in the late fall. The crisp breeze made them slit their eyes and Carol used her free hand to shade her eyes from the sun. The wind-whipped waves spilled into white caps.

The Days heard Linda placing the key into the lock in the door. As she did so, she paused and turned to James and Carol. The bright smile they had become so familiar with was no longer evident on the realtor's face. Instead, they saw a look of trepidation.

"Jim. Carol. I don't know exactly what we are going to find in here," Linda said with a fair amount of gravity in her voice. "I told you this house has been put on the market to be sold "as is." I don't really know what that means. To my knowledge......"

Linda's vision was suddenly distracted. She was no longer looking at Carol and James, but at something beyond them.

"You! Hey, you! Who are you? What are you doing here?" Linda said in a loud voice as she walked past the Days to the banister at the edge of the side porch. James and Carol trailed her and saw the object of her concern.

Standing on the crushed stone path that ran around the house was a man dressed in jeans and flannel shirt and a baseball cap. In his hands was a rake and before him on the path a wheelbarrow. He stopped when he heard Linda's words and looked up at the trio on the porch.

"I'm sorry. Didn't mean to disturb you. Just doing a little clean up. Leaves, you know."

"What are you doing here?" the realtor asked again. "There isn't supposed to be anyone here. This is private property."

"Ma'am, I'm sorry to have bothered you. Call it force of habit. My name is Ben. Ben Allen. I've been taking care of this place like my father did before me for most of my life and it's hard to stop."

Ben Allen appeared to be a simple man, simple in his ways, not in his mind. He looked to be in his mid-sixties and weathered by a life of working outside. His eyes showed the sadness he obviously felt at losing a position he had held all his life. As he looked up at the three people on his porch, his shoulders seemed to droop a bit. He shrugged and started to turn away.

"Sorry to have disturbed you. I'll be leaving now."

James was suddenly struck with a thought, an impulse.

"Hold on a second...Ben, was it?" He called after the man. James crossed the porch in only a few steps to the side stairs and bounded down them two at a time and stood only a few feet from the caretaker.

"If we were to buy this place, would you be interested in continuing as caretaker?" James heard the words tumbling out of his mouth before he had time to even form them in his head. James often gave sway to his impulses. Most of the time, they had proved themselves to be right. In his business, timing was everything and making decisions quickly was often critical.

Ben Allen smiled slightly as he lifted his head and looked questioningly to see if James Day was serious. The intent eyes and bearing that met his gaze assured Ben that James was serious.

"I've got a few more years work in me yet. I'd hate to spend them doing work somewhere else." A small smile crept over Ben Allen's face. James was smiling, as well.

"What's it like inside, Mr. Allen?" Carol had descended the same stairs James had vaulted down and now stood next to her husband sliding her hand around his elbow. She could feel the muscles of his arm.

"I can't really say, Ma'am. I don't think I've ever been anywhere other than the kitchen and that was years ago," Ben replied lifting his head a little further and beginning to study this young couple.

They seemed nice enough. She was the kind of woman any man

would be proud to have holding his arm. Her smile was captivating and brilliant. She seemed to bubble with energy and sparkle with enthusiasm. When she looked at someone, they knew they held her full attention. In contrast, James seemed more reserved, and, in spite of his impulsiveness, he appeared to approach things with a more analytical mindset. His manner was not cold, but more formal.

"But you've been here for so long," Carol said.

"Yes, I have. But Mrs. Carlisle left more than 30 years ago and the rule for my being kept on was to never enter the house. Keep the outside neat as a pin, keep the grass mowed, the shrubs all trimmed, clean up spring and fall, but never enter the house. Don't even have a key. If I suspected a problem, I was to call Mr. Beckwith."

Ben Allen glanced up at Linda Giuliani and realized that she was listening just as intently as the young couple before him.

"Ben, don't you think it just a little strange that you are taking care of a house that no one lives in?" James asked. "I mean, all these years and you mean to tell me no one has been in there?"

"Sir, I'm telling you that no one to my knowledge has been in the Carlisle Mansion since Mrs. Carlisle was taken out of here in 1970. I have been on the grounds almost every day since and I would know if someone had tried to get in," Ben replied forcefully.

James turned his head in the direction of the realtor and asked,

"Mr. Allen called this the Carlisle Mansion. What's that all about?"

Linda Giuliani flipped open the three-ringed binder she had been holding in her arms ever since they arrived at the house. She fought the breeze a bit to find her fact page on the property.

"Yes.... Yes, according to what I have, this property has been referred to as the Carlisle Estate. The house was built by Edward Carlisle in 1904. It has been owned by the Carlisle family continuously since it was built." It was evident that Linda was quickly skimming her notes for pertinent information.

"Mr. Carlisle commissioned it... it may be a Peabody and Stearns inspired design.... approximately 5 bedrooms, formal parlor, sitting room, kitchen, butler's pantry, formal dining room, servants' quarters. Will require some major updating."

Linda stopped reading and looked up from her binder at the Days, who were looking at her intently. With a fragile, almost comical half-smile, she said timidly, "Shall we see what that means?"

James turned to Ben Allen.

"Would you like to join us?" he asked Ben.

"Sir, the rule for me was never to enter the house. I don't see why I should violate that now. If you'd like, I'll wait a bit for you. There are some leaves over by the lilacs I can clean up." Ben smiled broadly at James showing a set of terribly crooked teeth with several missing. James nodded and, taking Carol's hand in his, climbed up the stairs back onto the porch. As they walked around the corner of the house, they saw Linda Giuliani slip the key into the lock and heard the lock turn over.

TWO

THE DOOR FELL OPEN WITHOUT A CREAK OR A groan from its unused hinges. The three forms in the doorway felt a gentle rush of warm air greet their stares, somewhat stale, but not unpleasant. All three noted the thick skim of dust on the floor; unmarked and worn by the hardwood beneath like a fine felt cloth. Hanging immediately inside the door was a chandelier festooned with cobwebs floating in the air, the fire of its crystals dulled long ago by the layer of dust that was everywhere. To the left was an umbrella stand draped in dusted spider webs; its mirror, likewise, covered in dust. Linda Giuliani stepped across the threshold making little toe prints in the undisturbed layer of fine dust and gently moved the cobwebs floating from the chandelier past her head.

"Well, here we are," she said trying to be bright. "It definitely will need a good cleaning."

Carol slipped into the hall and wrapped her arms about herself as she looked at the high ceiling and the wallpaper, its floral design yellowed with age, but still firmly attached to the wall. The hardwood flooring gleamed in polished beauty where her footsteps had disturbed the layer of dust. James stood like a statue in the entrance. His eyes were adjusting to the dimness of the house. All he could think to himself was what a mess.

On the left side of the entry hall next to the umbrella stand were a set of closed pocket doors. On the right was the arched doorway into a huge front parlor. The staircase to the second floor stood at the back of the hall, its broad, wide steps covered in carpeting, the color of which was indiscernible under the layer of grime time had laid down. The stairs were the widest either of the Days had ever seen with an elegant banister leading to a massive newel post at the bottom. A metal figure of winged Victory surmounted the post veiled in cobwebs. Overall, it was the most spectacular entry hall either Carol or James had ever seen.

"Come on, Honey," Carol said as she bounced back toward James and took his hand, pulling him into the hallway.

"Well, I suppose we could turn it into a museum," James said smiling.

"It's going to take some work, I would say," Linda quipped. "Let's look around."

Linda led the way into the parlor. It was immediately evident that furniture was present from the sheets thrown over the forms in the room. Everything was covered in that persistent layer of fine sediment.

Carol went to the bay window and attempted to part the lace sheer curtain to admire the view of the water. It disintegrated at her touch and a small cloud of particulate floated in the air.

"Let me remind you that the sale is 'as is,' so all the furnishings are included in the price" Linda's voice broke the feeling of muffled silence. James looked at the realtor as if to say, "Oh, hold me back! That'll make the sale!"

She carefully drew a sheet off a form near her trying hard not to disturb the dust too much, so it did not become airborne. Beneath the sheet was revealed a beautiful, high backed, upholstered chair. The pattern was bright and richly colored. It probably looked just the way it had the day it was covered some thirty-eight years before if Ben Allen was to be believed.

Carol attempted to duplicate Linda's adept removal of a covering from a form near her with much less success. As the sheet fell to the floor and the dust wafted into the still air, a standing brass lamp gleamed into view. Its shade was yellowed from time, and would need to be replaced, but the lamp itself was beautiful.

"Perhaps we should leave these things covered," suggested Linda. "Let's go look at the other rooms." Linda led James and Carol through an archway behind her into a second parlor.

The huge form covered with a sheet in the center of the room was obviously a table. Carol gently lifted one corner of the covering cloth to reveal the beautiful cherry surface of the table beneath. She could tell from the gloss of the polish that it had been cared for well. Carol was glad that the day was as bright and sunny as it was because the interior of the house was dark.

"Are there any lights in the house?" Carol asked.

"I don't think the power has been turned on," Linda replied, "but, we can try them."

She moved to the wall by the doorway that led back into the hall just before the staircase and felt for a light switch. She felt it under her fingers. It was the old style from when houses were first electrified, a raised half-circle with a lever protruding from it. She clicked the switch.

The two crystal chandeliers over the table delivered a soft glow through the layer of dust covering them. Carol was able to see just how large the table really was. It would easily seat twenty people. Along the wall she saw a row of what had to be chairs, although under their covering sheets, they looked more like soldiers lined up for review. Against the wall next to the window stood a tall object covered by a sheet. Carol suspected it was a China cabinet, but decided it was wiser to find out later.

While the two women explored the dining parlor, James was taking in the grandeur of the rooms. This was the kind of home his mother would have seen as representing success, he thought to himself. There were high ceilings with ornately carved cornices and window framing carved with the same motif. In places, the ceiling paint had begun to pucker and blister slightly, but it was minor considering they had not been touched in so many years. He noted wall coverings that would need changing, windows with thick panes of beveled glass still tight against the elements. He found himself ticking off in his head the value of what he saw before him. Furnishings like these could be auctioned for a fair amount; he was thinking, maybe enough to offset some of the expenses of renovating.

"Come on! "Carol grabbed his hand as she rushed by following the realtor back toward the front hall. He had not noticed they had finished their exploration and were ready to invade another room.

Linda stepped across to the left side of the hallway and half-bent to the handles of the closed pocket doors. Looking over her shoulder in an impish way, she said to Carol like a conspirator, "Ready?"

Linda flipped another light switch on the wall beside the pocket doors, grasped the handles of the doors in her hands and spread her arms sliding open the doors.

James and Carol stood in the doorway of a second parlor much less formal than its twin on the other side of the hall. The forms covered with sheets here were much smaller than those across the way. This was a room where someone could relax and be comfortable. The bay window in this parlor had no shear and Carol was able to look out and see the greenish-gray water of the Sound at the end of the lawn. Another window gave a view of the side porch and through it James could see Ben Allen raking leaves out of some lilac bushes not far from the house. At the back of the room was a door.

"Let's go through there," Linda suggested. She and Carol were really enjoying themselves. Here they were in a house neither of them had any knowledge about. Carol had caught Linda's excitement about seeing the house and learning its layout. As James stood assessing the size of the room and looking through the window at Ben Allen fighting the swirl of leaves caused by the slight wind, he did not notice the women disappear through the rear door.

When he finally came out of his haze of thoughts, he trailed after them into a short hall with a door to the right. He opened the door and found a half bath. The fixtures were not new by any measure, but James was relieved to see that the toilet was at least not an old Niagara system with the fill tank suspended high on the wall. He was sure that the original would have been had it not been updated at some point.

He continued down the short hall and came into a sitting room with an entire wall of windows. This room might have been an early attempt at a Florida room. It faced west and the late afternoon sun would have flooded this room with light even in the dead of winter. James, again, noted Ben Allen making long, determined strokes with his rake moving the brown dead leaves into a drop cloth he had spread on the ground.

"James? Ja-ames? Where a-are you-o-o"

He heard Carol calling him in that playful multi-tone call she reserved for those times when she really wanted his attention. Following the sound of her voice, he walked through a free-swinging door to find himself in the kitchen with Carol and Linda. He felt like he had stepped through a time warp into the 1950s.

Immediately to his left were a couple of steps leading down to a short hall leading to a mud room and the back door. The kitchen ran nearly the entire length of the back of the house. Carol was standing next to the kitchen table at the far end of a room longer than it was wide. It was classic 1950's chrome and red Formica. The red Formica counters ran on either side of the room, broken only by a massive section of gas burners on the left and a double sink on the right. White metal cabinets lined both walls and below the counters. The black and white linoleum flooring and café curtains on the windows made James's time travel complete. Linda Giuliani appeared through a doorway on the right near Carol at the far end of the kitchen.

"Feel like you've stepped back in time?" Linda said half-laughing and smiling broadly. "I can guess that you'll be changing this pretty quick," she quipped.

She turned to Carol and said, "The refrigerator is here in the butler's pantry. It's pretty old, so, you'll want to replace that. There is a counter with a sink and a door leading back into the dining room. I didn't know there was a second set of stairs in the house, but there is!"

Carol picked up on the excitement in Linda's voice. She winked at Linda and the two of them made a silent gesture they both understood. Carol shot a glance at James, and he saw the twinkle in her eye as she was going through the doorway. James could hear them talking in hurried low tones like little schoolgirls as they slowly mounted the stairs.

James walked through the kitchen trying not to disturb too much dust in the process. He entered the butler's pantry and started up the stairs. The stairs were in sets of four with a small landing where the stairs turned ninety degrees to the next flight of risers, and again to a third set of six steps. In fourteen steps, he found himself in the upstairs hallway. Linda and Carol were already at the front end of the hall where a large stained-glass windowpane graced the center window of the three facing the water. James looked to his right and saw another door standing ajar. He opened the door and saw another staircase leading up to the third floor.

"Hone-e-ey," Caroled cried in exasperation, "Come on! Will you keep up? It's the master bedroom," she said with obvious excitement as she pointed into a room at the far end of the hall from where James stood.

"Alright, alright… Coming," he replied, trying to quicken his steps on the thick, dusty carpet beneath his feet.

"Look, Honey," Carol gushed as James entered the room. The room was huge. The wall facing the front of the house had three large windows and a door leading onto a small balcony. The corner of the room ballooned out in the shape of the tower; more windows on the adjoining wall beyond and another door leading to a separate balcony gave a tremendous amount of light to the room. The ceiling was at least fourteen feet high, and the room had to be thirty feet across. Even James was stunned by the dimensions.

Linda was leaning against something covered with a sheet that might have been a dressing table, a makeup table, or something similar just watching James's reaction to what he saw. He caught her looking at him and just shook his head. Did she know his thoughts? Did she realize how much this house was proving his beliefs about love and success? His mother was right: love was important, but success, and the cold, hard cash that came with it, were what allowed love to have a place to live in.

Carol came back into the room having explored the far end of the bedroom.

"James, there's a dressing room for you and one for me and a full bath with a nice shower and a bath…"

He could tell that Carol was really taken with the house. It was grander than anything she had ever lived in. Before he could respond, she went out of the room and off to explore the other rooms on the second floor. Linda was smiling to herself and making some notes in her binder when James asked her very matter-of-factly,

"What was the asking price for this place? I want to make sure I heard you correctly."

"The entire property, house, garage, ten-plus acres is $650,000."

She could see the puzzlement on James's face. Linda couldn't always read James as she could most people. Carol had told her how James had taken her breath away in college because he was so sure of his future and how to attain success. Carol was sure he loved her even if his business personae seemed to be more dominant to those who did not know him.

"It truly is a once-in-a-lifetime opportunity. And that includes everything in the house," she quickly stated trying to allay his obvious confusion.

"I don't get it. I just don't get it, Linda," James looked at Linda with total and complete disbelief. He knew that the going price for an estate like this on the water, even in this part of Connecticut, was two to three million.

"Why so little? Why now? Who is this Beckwith guy?" James said to Linda.

Linda shrugged her shoulders.

"James, I can't answer that. All I can tell you is that this property at that price won't last a week on the market. Even if you came in and demolished the place and started all over, it would still be a steal. My thought for the two of you would be that the price leaves you plenty of money to do the modernization this place needs. Even if you decided just to fix it up and then sell it, you would STILL make a killing!"

James knew that Linda was right on all points. The price was obviously a steal. He felt like a mark waiting for the other shoe to drop. There had to be a catch. As he thought about it, he glanced out the window and saw Ben Allen turning the corner of the house still with rake in hand.

"How much more of the house is there to see?" he asked Linda.

"Well, I guess Carol is looking at this floor right now. There are three more bedrooms. They're all a little smaller than this. I think a nursery and two more full baths."

James nodded his understanding.

"Then, there is the third floor. That has a storage area and servants' quarters. I'll bet there's a full bath up there too."

At that moment, Carol came bouncing into the room with excitement pouring out of her.

"Oh, Linda! James! Come, come look! It's a nursery!"

She could not contain herself. She grabbed each of them by a hand and fairly pulled them into the hall. She quickly led the way to the door at the far end of the hall next to the door leading to the staircase up to the third floor. She stood in front of the door and gazed lovingly up into James's eyes as she silently turned the doorknob and pushed the door open using the weight of her body against it. She smiled her best smile at him.

There stood a painted wooden rocking horse, long stilled, and covered with the patina of dust and cobwebs that covered everything. Shelves along one wall held all manner of toys covered in a gossamer coating of dust: balls, wooden trucks, dolls, jacks, stuffed animals. James noticed in particular a stuffed lion placed on a shelf, so he appeared to be rearing up; his impending pounce now held back by the thin threads of spider webs. The windows brought in plenty of light and made the room one of the brightest they had seen in the house. Against the wall next to the door stood a child's bed, perhaps three-quarter size; on the far wall a crib stood.

Carol watched James's face closely. She was hoping she would see that look of understanding that she needed to see. She had made it clear to James that a child was important to her; it would complete her, she felt. He had told her that he thought he might be ready for a child, as well. James had always been the more practical, pragmatic one of the couple. He felt it was more important to have a place to raise children than to have the children. Well, now, to Carol, having a child was more important than anything else. She looked but did not see a reaction. She was hurt. Her happy smile fled from her face.

"Let's see what there is on the third floor," Linda broke the awkward silence. She had seen Carol's expression change and could guess pretty easily why. Linda had really grown to like this young couple, although she certainly felt closer to Carol than her husband. James led the way to the third-floor stairway and Linda put a comforting arm around Carol as she closed the door to the nursery. Linda gave Carol a slight hug of understanding and smiled at her as she lifted her face to look at Linda.

The staircase to the third floor was narrow and not meant to accommodate traffic of two abreast. James led the way up the stairs to a landing at the top. As he reached that landing, there was a small hall leading into a sitting room. As he walked down the hall, he noticed it was paneled in solid wood planking from floor to ceiling. About halfway down the hall, the wall on the right side was stepped out about an inch. He would probably not have even noticed it if he had not hit his shoulder against it as he passed.

"That was clumsy of me," he said absent-mindedly, as he rubbed his shoulder. "That's something that will need to be taken care of."

They entered the small but comfortable sitting room. It occupied the area of the tower under the turret on the opposite side of the house from the master bedroom. The windows afforded an uninterrupted view of Long Island Sound to the west and Fishers Island Sound directly in front of the house. On a clear day like this, you could see the shoreline of Fishers Island about two miles offshore.

James noted the full bathroom and the large closet. He then went back to the hall and opened the door that was there to the unfinished part of the floor. In reality, the servants' quarters had been finished out of the attic storage area. He walked the length of the house and satisfied himself that there were no leaks in the roof. He was actually just buying himself some time.

He knew he had really blown it this time. He knew that his wife had expected some positive reaction when she had opened the door to that nursery. He knew he had let her down. Now, he felt like an ass. He loved Carol with all his heart and could open his heart to her when they were alone. But, as soon as there were others present, he covered that tender part of his being, and he did not know why. His business personae became dominant. Once again, Mr. Practical showed the ice water in his veins. He really did not want to face her right now. He needed some time to figure out how he was going to fix things, so he wandered about for a few minutes not really concerned about what he was looking at, just trying to formulate a plan. He loved her dearly, but there were times he was dumb as a rock.

Carol sat in a chair that faced out the windows. She didn't bother to remove the sheet that covered it. She didn't care about the dust any longer. She was angry at herself. She was angry with James. She knew she couldn't expect him to change overnight. She knew he had to warm to the idea of a child. He had gotten used to life being just the two of them. Even though he had said it was time to start a family, his actions sometimes still betrayed his reluctance. She knew he was afraid, and she knew she had to allay those fears. She loved him to distraction, and she knew he really did love her.

Linda quietly approached Carol as she sat in the chair and, sitting on the windowsill facing her, she said quietly,

"He'll come around, Sweetie. Once you get him away from the city and here with you, he will decompress. He's like a lot of men. He just needs you and time."

Carol looked up into Linda's warm, loving eyes and held back her tears. She nodded in agreement and mumbled a thank you. Linda put her arms around Carol and just held her for a long moment.

James came back into the room just as the two women released their embrace. He was rubbing his right shoulder with his left hand.

"I did it again! Darn!" he spoke. "I don't know why that wall jogs out like that, but I hit it again. We're definitely fixing that."

Carol froze. She looked at James with surprise.

"You mean......" was all she could utter.

James shrugged his shoulders, then smiled and nodded.

"Oh! JAMES!!" Carol fairly screamed as she flew across the room and wrapped her arms around her husband. All her disappointment of moments ago was forgotten. She hugged this man she loved with all her strength. She felt him wrap his arms around her. She kissed him gently on the ear and felt him kink his neck in excited response.

"I love you, my passionate man," she whispered in his ear.

Linda was taken aback by the sudden and unexpected announcement by James. She looked at the couple embracing before her and caught James's looking at her and smiling. He nodded affirming that he was serious. Linda smiled; outwardly showing her appreciation of love, but inwardly checking off another sale made.

THREE

THE TRIO DESCENDED THE BACK STAIRCASE TO the butler's pantry and spilled into the kitchen. Carol was babbling enthusiastically with Linda Giuliani about changes they needed to make and who she knew in the area that could do renovations. James looked casually out the window and saw Ben Allen standing near the garage with a cigarette hanging from his lips. He was standing so the garage shielded him from the wind that now had more bite in it as the warmth of the sun began to fade in the late afternoon.

"Linda, will you write up whatever needs to be done to get the house off the market and I'll sign it," James said suddenly. "I'll be back in a few minutes. I need some air."

Carol and Linda hardly took note of James leaving the kitchen and heading out the front door. They were absorbed in the heady excitement of discussing a new home, a new way of living. Carol could hardly believe what James had done. He never arrived at a decision on the spur of the moment – well, almost never - outside of business.

"I am so happy right now," Carol said. "I need to get us out of New York so we can start a family. Jim has been so dedicated to his business

I feel I am losing part of him." Carol looked suddenly like she felt she might have said too much, but the look in Linda's eyes allayed her fear."

"Carol, he's only working hard to give you everything you want," Linda said in a comforting manner.

"All I want is for him to make me more important to him than his work," Carol replied with determination in her voice.

Then her mood seemed to lighten as she said, "When we first met in college, he was so sure of what he wanted and how to get it. I admit, I really thought it was what I was looking for also. But, my parents gave me love and I know James can do that too."

"I just feel that if I can get him away from the lure of New York...." Carol said, resuming a more intense tone.

The two women lost all sense of time as they found some dish towels in one of the kitchen drawers and dusted off two of the kitchen chairs and half of the red Formica table so they could sit and complete some papers.

As James closed the heavy front door behind him, he heard the solid metal clank of the latch catching. He turned to his right on the porch and headed for the side stairs, the same stairs descended earlier in the day when he had first spoken with Ben Allen. Turning the corner of the house, a blast of cold wind hit him squarely in the face. The sun was perhaps an hour from setting. He had not noticed how long it had taken to tour the house. He was glad that the caretaker had found enough to do to stick around.

James descended the stairs with a bounce in his step and heard the sound his shoes made on the loose white pebbles of the path as he walked toward the side of the garage where he had seen Ben Allen sheltering. As he heard the crisp crunch of the loose stone beneath his shoes, he smiled to himself. He had made his wife happy. Very happy. He had rarely seen her as happy as she was at that moment. He had felt it the moment they pulled onto the property that Carol would want to live here. It was everything Carol never had growing up. James had met her parents just once after they were married. Her father was a clerk in a small bank and had struck James as a man of small stature with an even smaller concept of success in James's opinion. Carol's parents emphasized family and love. It was good for them to do so because they had little to show for years of work. Had Carol not won a national computer graphics competition for a scholarship, she might never have made it to college. The thought of that made a chill run down James's spine. After all, if she had not gone to college, they would never have met, he would not be standing where he was; his entire life would have been different. He pulled his fall coat just a little tighter around his trim body.

Ben Allen heard the sound of footsteps on the loose stone, too. He knew that someone was approaching even before he saw James. He wasn't sure what to think of this couple. They seemed very nice and down to earth; not at all what he would have expected in someone from New York. He was usually suspicious of anyone who came into the place he had lived all his life. Now he might be depending on one of those people to continue to have a livelihood. He knew everyone in town and had grown up with many of them. Many more had moved away. And, if they returned after experiencing the world, they seemed strangely changed by the experience. The people of Rock Cove saw themselves as not bothering the world and didn't want to be bothered by it. But, Ben had a good feeling about these people.

James came around the corner of the lilac bushes at the end of the stone path and saw Ben standing in front of the open door of a small tool shed next to the garage proper. He was just putting away his rake and drop cloth.

"Ben, I'm glad you were able to wait," James said. "I'm sorry we were so long, but I'll renew my offer to you about continuing to take care of the place."

Ben Allen turned to face James Day. He was taking the measure of his prospective new employer. He liked this young man's attitude. He liked that he came right to the point when he spoke. He was about to answer when James continued.

"I don't know what your pay has been, but let's just say I'll increase it by ten percent to start. There may be a lot more to be done when the renovations start. Lots of people are likely to be about, so, you'll be earning that extra pay."

"So, you're going to buy the old place?" Ben finally was able to say. He felt like a tremendous weight of worry had been lifted from his shoulders. James gave a reassuring nod that brought a smile to Ben Allen's weathered features.

"Are you sure you don't want to speak to Mr. Beckwith before you go increasing my check, Mr. Day?" Ben let the question hang in the air.

"I'm sure I'll be talking with Mr. Beckwith, Ben. And it's James or Jim. Mr. Day was my father. And your pay is raised regardless," James responded with a smile.

"Mr. Day, I mean, Jim, it may take me a while to get used to that, but I will try." Ben Allen extended his hand and James Day grasped it. The two men stood for a moment and knew they had reached an understanding.

"I would like to ask you a couple of questions about the place though, if you don't mind," James then asked.

"Well, I'll answer them if I can," Ben replied.

"You said something about your father having worked here?"

"Yes sir," James's eyes widened at the address, "I mean Jim, sorry," Ben corrected himself with a little embarrassment.

"My father came to work for the Carlisle's in 1910. He was only twenty-one when he got the job with Mr. Carlisle," Ben said with a fair amount of pride.

"He took care of this place for fifty years. Did most of the repair work himself and taught me how to do it too. Even after the '38 hurricane came through and ripped things up pretty good on the grounds, the house needed only minor repairs. She was built to last.

"I can't speak about the inside, but the outside has been painted every few years and shingles on the siding and roof have been replaced as they were needed. Gateposts were painted this summer just before Mr. Beckwith told me the place was going up for sale."

James could see Ben looking past him at the mansion with great pride. It was his life's work, and he was proud of it. He looked back at James.

"I took over from my Dad in about 1960. He was getting a little frail by then with some arthritis and such. He lived only a couple of years after that. Heart attack. No warning. I think he went the way he would have wanted. Quick, you know? My mother didn't do well after dad died. Yeah... well, they're together again." Ben looked at James and gave him a wry little smile.

"They took Mrs. Carlisle out of here about ten years after I started working. She wasn't in good shape when they did. People said she was going a little senile, but I never saw it. She just couldn't take care of herself anymore and there were no more good housekeepers around."

Ben shook his head as he looked at the loose stones his shoe was moving around.

"She was a fine woman, Jim. Real classy. But, she had some strange ideas. My dad told me that after Mr. Carlisle died in 1912, she lived on here, but she never wanted anyone in the house; wouldn't let anyone in the house except her maid."

Ben was still moving stones with his left foot when James interrupted his thoughts.

"She never had any children?" James asked. He was thinking of the nursery he had just seen.

"Oh, there was a daughter," Ben replied with a reassuring nod of his head. "I never knew her. My dad told me she was a pretty thing. Died very young. On her wedding day. Right here in the house," Ben related with a nod toward the house.

James's jaw dropped.

"You mean she died right here in the house?" James showed his obvious alarm. "Linda never said anything about somebody dying in the house!"

"Nobody talks about it anymore," Ben said in a very unconcerned tone. "It happened. It was a long time ago. That was a different time."

"What do you mean 'nobody talks about it anymore'?" James tried to hide his growing concerns.

"Well, it was before I was born," Ben Allen gave a nervous little laugh. "But my Dad told me it was the worst scandal to ever hit Rock Cove. I guess Mrs. Carlisle never really recovered, so they said."

James knew the ride back to Linda's office was going to be very interesting. He now had some questions he wanted answered. He was standing quietly digesting what Ben Allen had just told him, letting the little gusts of wind that whipped around the corner of the garage buffet his form.

"You're still serious about buying the place, aren't you, Sir?" Ben's voice showed his concern that he might have just torpedoed his own continued employment. "I haven't said anything to change your mind, have I?"

James broke from his thoughts and gave Ben a grimace.

"Sorry, I meant Jim. It's going to take me a while."

"We're committed to it, Ben." James knew that there were deaths in lots of homes. People still lived in those houses. If this house was what his wife wanted, he would figure out a way to tell her so she would not be upset over it.

"Let's not say anything about that to the Mrs. just yet. Let me figure out when to tell her," James said in a low conspiratorial voice.

"Why don't you give me your cell number and I'll call you tomorrow to let you know what is going on. I'll need it once the workers start on the house, too, so we can keep up to date as to how the work is going," James said as he reached into his pocket and withdrew his cell phone.

"I don't have one," Ben said, "I mean a cell phone. Never really felt the need for one. I'm always here if anyone needs me."

James stood in mild shock. He thought to himself, yes, it really is a different life out here. He had been married to his Blackberry the same as everyone else he knew and had migrated to the latest iPhone.

He could not imagine what it would be like to be out of touch and unreachable to people.

"Alright. Well, I'll see you tomorrow after we meet with Linda at her office and before we head back to New York," James said, hiding his surprise as best he could. "You're sure you will be here?"

"You are figuring about noon or so?" Ben said. "I'll be here."

As the two of them stood sheltered from the wind by the garage, the crunching of stones alerted them to the approach of the two women. They were strolling arm in arm and were chatting away like old friends as they came into view. Even though Linda was a good fifteen years older, they had found common ground in the form of the house and were exuberant in their conversation.

"We're done," announced Linda cheerfully. "She's all locked up."

Linda extended her hand to Ben Allen.

"Thank you, Mr. Allen. It was a pleasure to meet you. Sorry I didn't know you were still here." Ben Allen took the realtor's hand and smiled broadly showing again his need for dentistry.

"Ben will be staying on, actually," James interjected, "I've hired him back." James was smiling at himself.

"Oh.... Wonderful! That was very good of you, James." Linda seemed a bit surprised by the news.

"I am glad you are going to stay on," Carol bubbled. She passed by the hand that Ben extended to her and gave him a hug that startled him with its familiarity.

"It's getting late, James. We should get back to my office." Linda started walking along the loose stone drive in the direction of her car. Her short-heeled shoes made walking a little difficult on the loose stones. Ben Allen walked up next to the realtor and offered his arm in assistance. Linda smiled at him and said something that was lost in the wind and took his arm.

James and Carol stood for a moment looking at their new acquisition. Carol ran her arms around James's waist and buried her head against his chest. It was warm there and her head was sheltered from the wind. James put his arm over her shoulders.

"What do you really think, James?" Carol's voice was mellow and soft.
"Honey, if it's what you want...."
She looked up at him smiling.
"It wasn't when it was first described to us, but now... there's so much we can do with it!!"

Linda Giuliani started her car around the circle of driveway in front of the house. Carol had slid into the passenger side of the front seat when she had run ahead of James as they had walked toward the car with their arms about each other. She, laughing, had reached the car ahead of him and wanted to sit with Linda in the front seat. It was alright as far as James was concerned, actually. It might be easier to ask the questions he wanted answered from the back seat.

Carol and Linda picked up their chatter right where they had left off before arriving at the garage. James sat quietly for several minutes just listening to the happy, light conversation between the two women about the changes to this and the alterations of that, and the way things could be changed and suggestions about who could be used to make the changes. But, he was really hoping that Carol would stop and take a breathe so he could intervene. Until his opportunity came, he looked out the window at the bare limbs of the trees.

Rock Cove was the antithesis of New York City. There was little traffic and fewer people. The trees were in the last stages of color with many having already dropped their brightly colored leaves so the ground was a patchwork of yellows, reds, and browns. To see that in Manhattan required a visit to Central Park. The air in Rock Cove had a quality about it that made James recall his childhood. it was wonderful to breath that memory again and think about his mother and fall in the Midwest.

He had a lot of questions floating in his thoughts; some half-formed, some fully formed. It was very clear to him that he had just agreed to buy a house that his wife now desperately wanted, in which someone had died years ago, and he had not yet told his wife that one little fact. Then again, it was a house that no one had lived in for over thirty-five years but had been cared for externally by some trust. Suddenly, he became aware of a lull in the front seat conversation.

"Linda," he started, trying to choose his words carefully, "what do you know of the history of Rock Cove?" He thought he would start with a good, safe question.

"Well, as you know, I'm not a native of the area, really. I mean, to be considered a native by the local people, you need to have been here when the Indians were around. I mean the real Indians." The humor of her answer made Carol giggle.

"I'm not the one you should talk to about the real history. Attorney Beckwith would probably be better suited to give you history. What I do know is back in the 1890's and early 1900's there were certain places up here that the rich and famous came to get away from the cities."

"You mean like Newport," Carol chimed in.

"That's right," replied Linda. "Another was Watch Hill just across the border in Rhode Island. A third one that no one remembers was Rock Cove."

"You mean there were mansions here like in Newport?" Carol asked.

"Well, not exactly," said Linda as she skillfully drove down the narrow country lanes leading back to her office. "The research on the area I did for you two showed me only one other estate was in Rock Cove. It was owned by a family by the name of Stanhope. It was on the opposite side of the cove and was wrecked in the tidal surge in 1938."

"Are storms something we need to be concerned about," Carol asked with some gravity.

"I don't think so, my Dear," Linda said smiling as she looked straight ahead. "The 1938 storm was a very unusual storm and forecasting has gotten much better since then. Your property sits on the higher side of the cove inlet. The cliffs down to the water are about twenty-five or thirty feet above the water. The side where the Stanhope mansion stood is much lower to the water. Next time we are out to the house – I mean out to YOUR house," Linda smiled broadly as she looked at Carol, "I'll show you where it stood. There are two or three houses there now."

Linda looked in the rearview mirror and saw James sitting in the middle of the back seat thinking deeply.

"I can arrange for you to meet with Mr. Beckwith, if you'd like, James," Linda offered. She saw James arouse out of his thoughts.

"Yes, please, Linda. As soon as possible really," James knew that Linda could not answer his questions. Perhaps this Beckwith person could. James had a feeling he would still need to do some research of his own in addition to whatever the attorney could tell him.

As they turned onto the main street of Stonington, James suddenly said to Linda, "Can you stop here a second, Linda?"

Linda pulled the car into one of the diagonal parking slots. Carol returned Linda's look of confusion as she slid the shift into park.

"I'll only be a couple of minutes," James said as he slid out of the car. In three strides of his long legs, he was across the sidewalk and had entered the Verizon Wireless store.

FOUR

JAMES LOOKED ACROSS THE DINNER TABLE AT HIS wife. She was in the middle of devouring her baked scrod. He sipped his beer and tried to pace himself through his own dinner of sea bass. They had both been starving when Linda dropped them off in front of her office. They had spent the entire day with her. Other than a muffin and coffee, neither of them had eaten all day.

"The first thing we need to do is get some people in to clean the place," said Carol between forks filled with fish. "Linda said she thought she knew someone who could tackle a big job like this." James nodded in agreement.

They sat in a corner of the Dogwatch Café in Dodson's Marina in Stonington. It had been suggested by Linda as a good place to eat and she was right. The sun had set long ago, yet there were still wisps of faint light low in the west that allowed the mare's tails clouds to still be visible. Soon the lights of the marina would be the only illumination beyond the windows.

"I want to throw open all the windows and give the house a good airing," Carol was saying. "And those rooms! Oh, James! We could invite all our friends from New York for the weekend and STILL not fill the house!"

James was listening to his wife bubbling with enthusiasm. He liked it when she got so totally involved in a project. It was how she ran her business too. He pushed his empty plate toward the center of the table and leaned his elbows on the table. He smiled at her.

"You know this is going to take a little time to do, don't you?"

"That's alright," she said smiling back at him. She had a small flake of fish just below her lip. James smiled and took his napkin, reached across the table, and gently plucked it from her face. Carol quickly took his hand and held it close to her cheek. She kissed the back of it softly.

"Thank you, Honey," she said looking with deep affection in her eyes.

They finished their meal quietly exchanging glances and talking softly. When they had finished their coffees and asked for the check, they were the last ones in the restaurant. They said goodnight to the waitress who smiled at them. She knew James had been very generous with his tip.

The air was crisp and smelled of the sea as James opened the door of their rental car for Carol. The moon was nearly full and cast a glow on everything. As James settled himself behind the steering wheel, he said to Carol,

"Well, I guess we'll need to get one of these now. Do you have any idea what kind of car you'd like to have?"

Maintaining a car had been one of the things that living in Manhattan did not require. But, living in Rock Cove would make it a necessity.

"I hadn't thought about it," Carol said vaguely. "I liked that little SUV I saw the other day, though."

James turned the key and guided the car out of the parking lot and onto the road that led to the interstate. It would only take them a few minutes to reach their hotel in Mystic. They were to meet Linda at her office at ten the next morning, but, right now, their stomachs were full, and they were too exhausted to think about that. Carol started to doze. James could feel the need for sleep too. He needed to make a list of things he wanted to ask Linda in the morning, but he knew he needed a clear head for that.

James pulled the car into a parking space at the hotel and sat for a moment. He looked at his wife, now sleeping in the passenger seat, her legs drawn up and her head cradled by the headrest. James turned in his seat and looked at her lovingly. He softly called her name. When she stirred, she looked at James with sleepy eyes.

"Come on, Honey," James said softly, "Let's get to bed. Tomorrow is going to be another busy day."

"James," Carol said, placing her hand on James's left breast as if she wanted him to wait. "We really are going to do this, right? I mean, I didn't dream this, did I?"

James shook his head to say no and left the car. He came around the car before Carol got out and put his arm around her as he closed the car door. Carol slid her arms around James's neck and kissed him tenderly. James held her close. It was warm standing there in an embrace.

"Come on, Baby," James said softly. "It's cold out here. And I know where there's a nice warm bed.

Carol smiled at James still with her arms wrapped around his neck. She could see him clearly in the pale moonlight. She gave him a final peck on the lips and released his neck. She ran her hand down his arm and met his hand as they walked to the door of the hotel and took the elevator to their room without stopping at the front desk. Tomorrow would be here soon enough. Right now, all they wanted was sleep.

The phone on the night table next to the bed let loose with a short, measured ring that cut through the haze of sleep. Carol felt James move in the bed and heard him fumble with the receiver and say thank you in a desultory tone to no one. He rolled on his back and quietly asked,

"Are you awake, Honey?"

Carol had been lying on her side, her back to James. She now rolled over and put her arm across his bare chest. His eyes were closed, but he smiled at the feel of her skin. Carol knew that James loved her, but he tended to be discreet in public. It was times like this that she knew the depth of his love for her. She could have stayed there the rest of the day.

"We need to get up and get going," he said sleepily.

"Alright," Carol droned in reply. She threw back the bed covers and sprinted into the bathroom shutting the door behind her. James heard the shower start and knew he could stay in bed a few minutes longer. But he knew he wanted that list of things to discuss with Linda. With a final groan, James sat up on the edge of the bed and wiped the sleep from his eyes. He pulled on his pants that were hanging over the back of a chair and sat down at the desk in the room. He pulled a pad from the drawer and picked up a pen and started to write.

James wrote the first few lines of his list without hesitation. Utilities needed to be turned on. Building inspection had to be completed. Someone needed to be hired to do a thorough cleaning. He stopped for a minute and settled back in the chair, his pen raised to his lips and rotated between his fingers. After a few moments of thought, he wrote two more entries: ask about rentals in the area, and second, get contact information for Stanley Beckwith.

The door to the bathroom opened. James had not heard the shower turn off he was so lost in thought. Carol stood in the doorway wrapped in a towel and using a second towel to dry her hair.

"Did you leave a towel for me?" James said jokingly. Carol looked at him knowing he was kidding.

You better get showered," she replied. "As it is, we'll have to pick coffee up on the way."

James slowed the car and pulled into the parking lot next to Linda's office. Carol and he had been discussing things they wanted to talk to the realtor about this morning. Carol agreed with most of James's list.

She added a couple of new items to the list: who would Linda use to do the renovations, and where could she find information about the history of Rock Cove? They lifted their coffees from the holders in the car and walked to the door of the real estate office. It was 10:05 and Linda's car was already in the lot.

The office was located in a two-story commercial building on the main road through what passed as the commercial crossroad of Rock Cove. Linda was coming out of her office as the Days came through the front door.

"Good morning," she said brightly as she approached them. "Hope you slept well?" She led them to a meeting room where she had papers arranged on the table and motioned them to the chairs set at the table.

"Before we get into signing anything, are there any questions you have for me?" Linda asked.

James covered the first few topics on his list. The utilities were something Linda could assist them with, as well as getting the inspection done. Then Carol said, "You mentioned yesterday that you thought you knew someone who could do the cleaning?"

"Yes. I called them this morning. Since this is Saturday, they are normally not in the office, but, they said, if we called them when you were done here, they would meet you to talk about it or you could call them on Monday." Linda made a note on a pad at her right side and tore off the top sheet and handed it to Carol.

"I have some other questions," James said, "but, they can wait until we're done with the paperwork."

Linda opened her folder and proceeded to review the purchase and sale agreement she had typed up for the Days. She pointed out the total sale price, the "as is" statement, and the provision showing that all furnishings and contents of the house were a part of the purchase price. She had left blank the portion showing the amount of money to accompany the agreement as a binder. She showed James that the usual provisions regarding the house passing its physical and mechanical inspections had been left out of the contract since the sale was an "as is" condition, but still thought it a wise move to have the inspections done anyway. It would certainly give them an idea of what would need to be done. The provision regarding his ability to obtain financing was still included in the binder even though Linda knew there would be no problem with that... She asked James how much of a deposit he wanted to give with the purchase and sale.

"Would $50,000 be sufficient?" James asked. "The financing is not a problem. I've already been approved for a mortgage of up to $1.7 million."

She passed the purchase and sale agreement to James and Carol for their signatures. James turned his head to look at Carol. A knowing look passed between them. She smiled and gave him an assenting nod. James picked up the pen Linda had laid next to the form and signed it with his bold signature. He then passed the pen to Carol and turned the paper so she could sign. James pulled his checkbook from his pocket and wrote a check to Linda's firm.

It was done. Linda congratulated the Days and came around the table to give Carol a hug and shake James's hand. Carol was excited and shaking like a leaf. James felt strangely elated. They had now purchased a house larger than either of them had ever lived in. Would it become the home that Carol wanted?

"Is there anything else you need from us?" James said to Linda. "If not, I have a couple of other things I'd like to ask you."

"Certainly," replied Linda.

"I would like to speak with Mr. Beckwith about the property. I know that is probably a little unusual since he is the seller. But he is also an attorney, and I would like to know what he knows about the property."

"Well, you're right. It is a little unusual, but then, everything about this property has been a little unusual. I will be presenting your offer to him, and I will ask if he would be willing to talk with you," Linda replied.

"When will you be presenting the offer?" asked Carol.

"Well, I called Mr. Beckwith's office this morning and told him I expected a good offer on the property today, so he is planning on seeing me this afternoon. I thought I might see him while you were meeting with Paul Murray."

"Paul Murray?" James repeated the name.

"Yes. He's the person I spoke to you about doing the cleanup of the house."

Linda handed James a business card for Murray Renovations: Architectural Design, Historical Restoration, and Renovation.

"Paul's office is in Pawcatuck just a little east of here. Because of the restoration work, he has the equipment and the people to do an expert job of thoroughly cleaning the interior. I've seen his work, and he is very good." Linda spoke with an assurance that Carol and James trusted. "If you're going to be looking for someone local to do renovations, I can think of no one better than Paul. Do you want me to give his office a call and see if he can meet with you?"

James nodded. He had known Linda long enough now to trust her judgment. She had delivered everything their first meeting had promised. He was comfortable with the way she conducted business.

Linda disappeared for a few moments and reappeared carrying a soft covered portfolio she offered to Carol.

"I found this of some interest when I was reading up on the property. Maybe you'd like to look through it," said Linda.

Carol laid the book on the table in front of her. James leaned over her shoulder. The title on the cover read "A Brief History of Rock Cove by Ellen Perry."

"Whose Ellen Perry?" asked Carol.

Linda stopped dialing the phone long enough to say," She's a librarian who retired to Rock Cove a few years ago. She worked in the Bieneke Library at Yale for years."

A small piece of paper protruded from the top of the book several pages into it where something had been marked. Carol opened the book at that page and immediately saw a picture of the Victorian, their Victorian, she hoped. The picture showed an old car pulled up in the circular driveway in front of the house. A man in what looked like livery sat in a front seat without a roof. Carol noted his cap and the goggles that sat on the rim of it. An older gentleman stood beside the enclosed passenger compartment holding the door open for a woman who appeared to be some years younger. The caption read: Mr. & Mrs. Edward Carlisle and the chauffeur posed outside their lovely mansion c. 1910.

"Look Honey! I don't think it's changed at all since then," Carol said turning to James and pointing at the picture. "She looks so young in this picture." She bent closer to the book to study the picture.

Linda hung up the phone.

"Paul Murray can meet you in about half an hour at his office. That's more than enough time for you to get there. I can give you directions if you like?"

"No need," James replied. "GPS in the rental." James made a motion with his thumb toward the car in the parking lot. Linda smiled and handed him back Paul Murray's business card.

"I guess we better hit the road," James said looking at Carol who was engrossed in the book. She looked up.

"Can I take this with me?" she asked Linda.

"Oh, of course, Carol," Linda said. "Keep it as long as you like. I know where you'll be living." She gave a slight laugh.

"I'm heading out right behind you to present your offer to Mr. Beckwith," she continued picking up her pocketbook and a soft leather briefcase bulging with files.

"I'll call you as soon as I have an answer. I hope you like Paul Murray."

FIVE

THE GPS LED JAMES AND CAROL INTO THE COMmercial center of Pawcatuck, such as it is. Near the river that separated Pawcatuck, Connecticut, from Westerly, Rhode Island, the voice of the navigation unit calmly announced they had reached their destination. They found themselves in front of an old mill of natural brick that backed up to the river. It was easily over a hundred years old and had now been rehabilitated into space for small businesses. Over the door hung a wooden sign ornately carved that announced, "Paul Murray Renovations."

Carol had been talking the whole time they had been driving about her ideas for changes to make in the Victorian. All James had said was the occasional, "MMhmm...... Oh, yeah.... "Uh-huh," in response to Carol's enthusiastic soliloquy. As they left the car, he finally said, "Well, this may be the man who can tell you if what you think you want to do is possible."

They entered the mill building and heard a bell ring somewhere in the back of a room with large tables and a wall of long thin drawers. A high counter stood just inside the door and a small area to the right had a couple of chairs and a table with *Modern Architecture* magazines piled on it. From an office somewhere in the back of the building, a high, thin voice called out, "Be right with you!"

Carol and James could see blueprints spread out on one of the large tables. The room was bright from intense ceiling lights. The brick walls, high ceilings and the wide plank floors made the office have a unique feel to it: an architectural design business in an architecturally significant building. It fit.

Carol and James saw a slightly built individual appear from an office.

"Come on in, Folks," he said motioning them to come around the counter and through the short swinging gate by the waiting area. He walked toward them at the same time. Carol noticed he wore a pair of half-rimmed glasses down on his nose and a pencil was stuck over his right ear. The thinning hair on his head was made up for by the lush goatee on his chin. He was dressed in a plaid flannel shirt and jeans and walked toward them in quick, short steps.

"Mrs. Day? Mr. Day? Paul Murray, here. Nice to meet you both," he said in that unusually high voice as he extended his hand in greeting. "I understand from Linda you're buying the old Carlisle Mansion?"

"We've put a bid in," James replied. Paul Murray was a good eight inches shorter than James, but his open, friendly manner made up for any lack of physical stature.

"How can I be of service?" Paul inquired.

"Well, the first thing we need to have done is have the place cleaned," said Carol, "Thoroughly!"

"That is something we do a fair amount of," Paul Murray said with a smile. "Because of the seasonal nature of many of the larger residences here and in Watch Hill, we have a crew of cleaners that are very thorough and very quick." He showed obvious pride in his business.

"Do you know the property?" Carol asked.

"I'm not familiar specifically with it, but we have the equipment to clean and restore virtually any structure after any type of loss."

"This isn't a seasonal cleaning we're talking about," James picked up on Carol's initial statement. "This house has not been occupied for over thirty-five years. It has thirty-five seasons of crud to be cleaned. Oh, and it is also furnished."

Paul Murray looked a little stunned by what James had said. He had been told by Linda when she had called this was a big job. He had expected the usual need to clean out trash and do a general cleaning. But, this was going to be a challenge and Paul Murray liked challenges.

"The furniture has been in the house the entire time?" Paul asked. His question was answered by a nod from both Carol and James. "Do you want that cleaned also?"

"We don't really know what's there," answered Carol, "so, I guess the answer would be yes." She looked at James for a sign of his agreement. He nodded in agreement again.

"Linda mentioned the house is about 7,800 square feet not counting the third floor and the unfinished basement. Does that sound about right?" Paul opened a drawer under the large table they were standing next to and pulled out a legal-size pad. He removed the pencil from his ear and started making some notes. "Normally, we have a charge by the square foot, but to be honest. I would be interested in seeing the place. I understand it's a beautiful Victorian."

"Actually, Mr. Murray," James said, "my wife wants to ask you some questions about updating the place. Nothing has been done in years and we think there are a lot of things that have to be done and could be done with it."

"Well, I would be happy to work with you on some design possibilities." Paul Murray smiled at the couple. "The restoration and cleaning keep the bills paid, but the architectural design is my specialty."

"We haven't heard on our offer yet, but we would like to try to get the cleaning started as soon as we know we have the house," James said. As James finished talking, he felt the vibration of his cell phone in his breast pocket. "Excuse me a moment," he said, as he pulled the phone from his pocket, turned around, and walked a step or two away from Carol and Paul.

Carol's eyes followed James's movements for a few moments and then she turned back to Paul Murray.

"Is it possible to architecturally change the interior of a house without changing the outer appearance of it?" she asked Paul Murray, softly.

"Oh, certainly," he replied. "Other than weight-bearing walls, almost anything can be done." He smiled warmly at Carol. She was sitting now on a stool drawn up to the table on which Paul was writing. "If you have an idea of what you want, we can pretty much make it happen."

James finished the call and slid his phone back into his shirt pocket as he turned back to the table.

"Well, it looks like we have a house," he announced looking at Carol. She jumped into her husband's embrace and squealed in delight.

"Congratulations!" They heard Paul Murray say.

Carol turned to the architect beaming her happiest smile.

"Mr. Murray, will you clean my house for me?" she said trying to contain her joy. "And, while you're at it, I would like to talk with you about making some changes to it!"

"First things first, Honey," James chimed in with his own excitement evident on his face. He looked at Paul Murray. The excitement of the news was contagious and even getting to him. "Paul, can you give me an estimate as to what it will cost to bring the house at least up to code?"

"Certainly," he said. "I'd be happy to."

As James and Carol settled back in their car, Carol could hardly contain herself. She was the proud owner of a magnificent house, a place where she and her husband could begin to raise a family. She turned in the passenger seat and gave her husband a deep kiss.

"Did Linda say anything else," she asked James. He was, himself, smiling about their good fortune. He was really beginning to like the area and the people he had met. He could feel the joy he had brought his pretty wife.

"We're heading back to meet with Linda. There was something I forgot to talk with her about. It was on the list, but we got sidetracked with the book and forgot about it."

"Oh! The book!" Carol exclaimed. She reached into the backseat and retrieved the bound manuscript. "I forgot all about it!"

As James started retracing their drive back to Stonington, Carol opened the cover of the manuscript. She noted the dedication:

To my new neighbors and friends, I dedicate this
Brief history of a place I have only recently come to.
Love as much as all of you.
—Ellen Perry 2002

Carol turned the page and started to read. As James drove, she read excerpts of the pages to him.

"The village of Rock Cove has a long and quiet history. It has survived on the rocky coast of eastern Connecticut since 1768 as a quiet village of artisans and independent fisherman who have plied the waters off its shore for its bounty."

"During the American revolution, Rock Cove was used as a major landfall for delivery of arms and supplies that were then transported to the siege of Boston...."

"Until the end of the 19th century, the community was fairly unremarkable. As railroads began to crisscross the northeast in the 1800s, Rock Cove was bypassed ...."

As she turned the pages and read on, she was approaching the page marked by that little piece of paper.

"Toward the end of the 19th century, Rock Cove experienced a brief, but spectacular moment of notoriety when it was identified by the "Four Hundred" of New York's socially elite and wealthiest patrons as an acceptable place for a "summer cottage". Newport was getting overcrowded and was farther and more difficult to travel to from New York. The consolidation of smaller independent lines by J. P Morgan, the elder, into The New Haven Railroad made Rock Cove accessible and requiring less travel time than getting to Newport."

Carol turned the page and there was the picture of the Victorian – now her Victorian.

"Listen to this, Honey," she said to James as she read on.

"Rock Cove was the site chosen by two of Connecticut's most successful families to build their gilded age mansions. These two estates were located on the two points on opposite sides of the entrance to the cove. The Stanhope Mansion was a Southern Colonial design structure on the west point of the cove. It was noted for its stunning two-story columns across the front of the house...."

Carol's voice trailed off as she skimmed ahead. "Here we go," she said.

"The Carlisle Estate to the east was built as a magnificent Victorian. Its higher elevation gave it clear vistas of the waters of the Connecticut shore. It was praised when it was built in 1901 for its unique blend of several Victorian designs and the layout of its gardens...."

Carol smiled at James as he drove the car.

"Keep reading," he said smiling at her.

"Okay...Mmmmm, let me see. Okay."

"These two families were among the wealthiest of the era and their attempt to bring the world of the socially prominent and the elegantly fashionable to Rock Cove met only limited success. Their wealth and proximity to New York made for their inclusion in Mrs. Astor's elite group of "Four Hundred" by Wade McCallister, self-appointed doorkeeper to high society. With occasional visits to the Stanhope and Carlisle mansions by Vanderbilts, Astors, Oelrichs, Belmonts and others of elite New York society, Rock Cove was considered next in order to Watch Hill and Newport as a summer retreat of the wealthy. The coming of society's elite to Rock Cove came toward the end of the Gilded Age and lasted only a few brief years. A rivalry developed between the

Carlisles and the Stanhopes as to which was the more socially prominent in Rock Cove. Just as they were responsible for Rock Cove gaining notoriety among the wealthy and becoming a footnote in the history of a notable age, they were also to be responsible for, perhaps, what was the saddest and most tragic event Rock Cove has ever experienced."

Carol looked at James. Her expression was one of confusion and concern. Her joy and pleasure at reading about the place where they were going to live and the house they had just purchased had ceased.

"So, what else does it say?" James asked her somewhat concerned himself.

Carol started turning the pages expecting to see something more, looking for an explanation of what occurred. There was nothing more to be found.

"Unfortunately, only the Carlisle Mansion is still in existence to be admired for its beauty. The Stanhope Estate fell into disrepair during the 1930s and was totally destroyed in the storm surge of the great storm of 1938.

"That's all it says," Carol said in frustration. "What does it mean, James?"

"I don't know, Sweetie, but I think we're going to have a few more questions for Mr. Beckwith on Monday. I think we need to talk with this Ellen Perry, too, if she's still around."

They passed a few minutes without saying anything to each other. Carol stared out the side window lost in thought and not really seeing anything. She was thinking about the book. How accurate was the author? What events was she writing about? Did Linda know anything she had not told them? She was generating all sorts of questions about everything. This house that she wanted now so very much to be hers, was there really a problem they were unaware of? Is that why it was so cheap? Who held the answers to her questions? Was James having the same questions?"

When she realized the car had stopped moving, they were in the parking lot at the real estate office. James was sitting behind the wheel looking into space.

"Do you think Linda knows anything she hasn't told us?" Carol asked tentatively.

"No. No, I don't," James replied. "I think if she knew anything she would have told us about it. Remember, she's not a local."

The young couple exited the car feeling a little deflated and confused. Linda Giuliani was standing at the door and saw them approaching. She expected to see them excited and smiling. What she saw made her worried. She had seen those looks from other couples after making decisions on real estate. Buyer's remorse was a powerful feeling.

"Is everything alright?" Linda asked as James closed the door. "Mr. Beckwith was very happy with your offer. He is looking forward to meeting with you on Monday. Nine thirty, James, if that is convenient?"

James nodded and continued to look distracted. Carol looked similarly concerned.

"Hey, you two, what's happened?" Linda asked, trying to cheer them. "You have the house.... Isn't that exciting?"

She took Carol by the arms and tried to get her to look at her. Carol reluctantly complied and Linda could see the concern her eyes held."

"What happened?" Linda asked with caring concern in her voice.

"In the book you gave me," Carol said. Linda could see the tears welling in Carol's eyes, "it says something happened between the Stanhope's and the Carlisle's. But, it didn't say what it was. Do you know?"

"I don't, my Dear. If I did, I would tell you," Linda replied, wrapping Carol in her arms. "It's going to be alright." She was still sure it was buyer's remorse.

Linda held Carol for a long moment. When Carol indicated she was alright, she stepped back from Linda and asked, "Do you know if Ellen Perry is still in the area? Do you know anyone who could tell us what this event was?"

Linda thought for a moment.

"I believe Ellen Perry still lives in Rock Cove. You might ask Ben Allen if he knows where she lives. As for what this event was..." Linda thought for a moment, her hand fisted and rubbing her chin with her index finger, "I would definitely ask Mr., Beckwith. It's my understanding that he has been the Carlisle family attorney forever."

"What about asking Ben Allen?" James interjected, "He's worked on the estate his whole life. He must know something." Linda nodded.

Well, not to change the subject, but I put together what you asked me to, James, when I got back to the office," Linda said as she handed a manila folder to James. "I put them in order of what I think is most desirable to least. All these rentals are within ten miles and are ready for immediate occupancy with short leases. I'm sorry I am tied up tomorrow with that open house, but you have all the addresses so you can see them tomorrow on your own. Call me if you decide or have any problems."

James tucked the folder under his arm. He was feeling a little better. He wasn't so sure about Carol. She had a look in her eye he had seen before. He thought he recognized intense determination. He had no idea how accurate he was.

SIX

JAMES ROLLED OVER AT THE SOUND OF THE PHONE ringing. He responded to the wakeup call with his usual alacrity. He turned to wake Carol and realized that she was sitting at the desk by the window in their hotel room reading something on her computer. She was dressed only in her bra and panties. He lay for a moment admiring the smooth curves of her body accentuated by the sunlight streaming in the window. He took pleasure in how beautiful she was. She never moved when the phone sounded or when James moved. Carol was intent on what she was reading.

"Good morning," James said with a slight question as he looked at Carol.

"Do you know where the Carlisle's and Stanhope's made their money?" She asked him without taking her eyes off the computer screen.

"Actually, that was one of the things I had planned to ask this Beckwith guy tomorrow," James replied rolling his feet onto the floor and wiping the sleepers from his eyes. "I should have guessed you would Google it sooner or later."

"Well, let me tell you what I have found out." Carol sat back in her chair and looked at James with a cat-that-caught-the-mouse smile and that intense, penetrating stare James had seen yesterday in the car. "It seems that Lord and Lady Stanhope were locked in a real game of one-upmanship with the Carlisle's," Carol began.

"Lord?" James said looking quizzically at Carol. "You mean they were English?"

"He was," Carol replied. "She was an American that hit the jackpot of her time in social climbing. She got herself a Title."

"I don't understand," James said looking puzzled. He put his hand, palm up, in front of him. "I have no doubt you're going to tell me, but, let me brush my teeth first."

He got up from the bed and made his way to the bathroom. As he flushed the toilet and squeezed some toothpaste on his battery powered toothbrush, he heard Carol begin to speak.

"In the "Gilded Age," the height of achievement for every matron of society was to get a title either for themselves or for their daughters. It was some kind of instant identification of having made it. That was why so many of the super-rich of the Age traveled to Europe and did tours of the Continent. They were shopping – probably more like trolling – themselves and their daughters before the peerage of Europe! Do you believe they did that to get a Count, or an Earl, or a Baron?"

Carol was sitting back in her chair with her foot on the edge of the desk looking at James standing at the door of the bathroom, toothbrush buzzing in his mouth. She was thinking how good he looked in his boxer briefs. Even though he was over thirty, he still had the tight body of an athlete and the best legs Carol had ever seen on a man.

"Charles Augustus Stanhope, pronounced more like 'Stannup,' was the 8th Earl of Harrington. He was landed gentry and a blue-blooded member of the English peerage. The title went all the way back to the 1680s. He was heavily into banking, as well, and like all good British Peers of the realm, he served in government."

"Sounds like the lady hit the jackpot, alright," James said after rinsing the last of the toothpaste from his mouth. "She got her title and money, too."

"Not like she needed it," Carol continued with a wry smile. "Lady Stanhope, formerly Constance Gildersleeve of Portland, Connecticut, was second daughter to shipbuilder John Edward Gildersleeve."

"Never heard of him," James said looking at the ceiling comically.

"Well, you know all those ferries around New York and elsewhere? Guess who developed the directional propellers for those?" Carol said with the assurance of knowing the answer.

"So, it was a match made in heaven, eh?" James said as he started dressing.

"I'm not so sure," Carol said, dropping her leg and leaning back toward her computer screen. "It says here, Lord Stanhope was born in 1844. Constance was born in 1880. They were married in 1900. That would make him fifty-six and her twenty."

"I'd say that Lord Charlie got the better half of that deal," James said laughing at the thought as he finished buttoning his shirt. "It sounds like he was really robbing the cradle."

"Hey," Carol said, "Let's remember who was after whom? Seems there was a daughter born in 1901... Sophia, named after the maternal grandmother."

"Doesn't sound like the old geezer wasted any time with his new, young bride," James said as he circled around behind Carol's chair and looked at the screen.

They read together the information on Carol's computer screen. Lady Stanhope had split time between England and America and had built a summer residence in her beloved Connecticut. Lord Stanhope had died suddenly in England from a heart attack as he was leaving Parliament in 1912. Lady Stanhope had then made her Connecticut mansion her principal residence with occasional trips to the Continent in season with her daughter. Trips to England to meet with her solicitors were infrequent and ceased completely after the untimely death of her daughter, Sophia, at the age of twenty-six. She was unmarried at the time of her death and, therefore, this line of the Stanhope family died out.

The Title of Earl of Harrington had passed to Charles Stanhope's nephew upon his death in 1912. However, the assets of the earldom did not devolve to the 9th Earl until the declaration of Lady Stanhope's death several years later.

"I'll bet the 9th Earl could have cared less about a mansion in Connecticut," Carol said with some disgust.

"Well, if he didn't own it until after Lady Stanhope died, who knows how things had changed." James said with a shrug. "What about the Carlisle's?"

"I left that for you," Carol said. She stood and casually walked toward the bathroom. James followed her with his eyes. She gave him a playful look over her shoulder as she unclipped her bra and let it drop on the floor. She gave a little laugh and disappeared behind the bathroom door. James crossed the hotel room in only a few strides and slowly opened the door to the bathroom. The room was filled with steam from the running shower.

"Want some company?" he said as he closed the door behind himself.

James sat in the chair and bookmarked the page on the computer screen. He was sure they would be referring to it again. He clicked on the icon to get to the home page and typed in a new search. After narrowing his initial search, James was rewarded with an entry for the Carlisle he wanted.

Edward Thomas Carlisle, born 1860, first son of Thomas Ellington Carlisle (1830 – 1881) founder of the Red Ball Packet line in 1849. Before the advent of the contiguous railroad system, freight and passengers wishing to travel in New England often did so by coastal packets. These were ships of varying sizes that sped people and cargo along the coast of New England from New York to many of the seaports all the way to Boston and the seaports of Maine.

There were several packet lines that vied for the passenger service between New York and Boston, most notably the Fall River Line. These ships grew in size and grandeur with the advent of the steam engine. By 1893, the *Priscilla* was the epitome of the mammoth "palace" steamers of the era. She was 440 feet long and made overnight voyages from New York to Fall River on the Taunton River in southeastern Massachusetts. From there, passengers boarded the Old Colony Railroad and completed their journey to Boston's South Station.

While most of the competition was for the passenger service business, Thomas Carlisle concentrated on capturing the freight business. His Red Ball steamers were the fastest on the water and had a reputation for safety and being on time. Long before Commodore Vanderbilt and the likes of Daniel Drew were battling each other for supremacy in the emerging railroad industry, they were competing for control of the waters off New England. Until the small regional rail lines were finally brought under the control of Jim Fiske and J. P. Morgan, the elder, the steamships of the coastal packet lines flourished. Eventually, they were all controlled by the powerful New Haven Railroad: all except the Red Ball Line. J. P. Morgan knew that the freighting business was more important to his control of commerce in the New England corridor than was the passenger business. Thomas Carlisle knew it also.

Unfortunately, Thomas Carlisle did not live to see the full success of his enterprise. In 1881 while at a meeting with the Board of Trade in New York City, he contracted a cold that worsened into pneumonia. At the age of fifty-one, an American original millionaire was dead, leaving one of the largest and most successful transport businesses in existence to his twenty-one-year-old son.

Edward was not unfamiliar with the business. At fifteen, he had gone to sea aboard one of his father's packets as a cabin boy. He had learned the business from the bottom up and was ready to take the reins of control when the time came. He was also a shrewd businessman and could see the handwriting on the wall. Although the coastal packet passenger business would continue through the first third of the twentieth century, Edward knew that the railroads would prevail in capturing the freight business more quickly than anyone believed. In the first decade after the century changed, Edward Carlisle finally sold the Red Ball Line to the J. P. Morgan controlled New Haven Railroad. The price paid by Morgan made Carlisle among the ten wealthiest men in the United States.

In 1904, Edward purchased land on a point east of Rock Cove in eastern Connecticut and began construction of a mansion later known as the Carlisle Estate. He married the following year, and the Victorian style home was given as a wedding present to his new bride, the former Edith Masters. She had been a childhood friend of Edward and was, actually, a distant relation. The newlyweds arrived at their new home and nine months later were the proud parents of a baby girl named Elisabeth.

James was still reading when Carol emerged from the bathroom and began dressing.

"Find anything interesting?" she asked as she quickly dressed.

"Well, I've discovered that you and I got married way too young," he said with mock gravity.

"What do you mean," Carol said with increased interest. "Back then, I would be verging on being a spinster at my age." She laughed.

"Well, maybe you were too old to marry, but I was definitely too young!" James playfully replied. "These guys were marrying much later in life. And marrying young chicks to boot!"

"Remember, Honey, women died young back then. Childbirth was really dangerous. Children didn't survive either. "Carol was now being serious. "They had no antibiotics and medical care was abysmal. It was common for men to marry more than once."

"Let me finish what I'm reading while you finish getting dressed, "James said. He looked back at the computer and scrolled down.

The last couple of paragraphs before him provided the information that Edward Carlisle had, in retirement, become a serious art collector. His collection was so highly regarded, it had been on permanent loan to several museums. It was in pursuit of additions to his art collection that had led to Mr. Carlisle's demise. He had been on a buying trip in Europe and was in a hurry to return home. Edward had reservations aboard the RMS *Celtic* for his return to the United States, but, at the last minute, he was able to switch his passage to the newest liner of the White Star Line. She was faster and would cut a minimum of three days off the crossing. Best of all, she was unsinkable.

Edward Carlisle's body was recovered from the frigid waters of the North Atlantic on the morning of April 15, 1912, several hours after the RMS *Titanic* had gone to the bottom of the ocean after striking an iceberg. It arrived in Halifax, Nova Scotia two days later. His body was then shipped to New Haven and was buried next to his father and mother in the family plot in New London, Connecticut after a private funeral service.

James sat back in the chair. He knew about the *Titanic*. Everyone knew the name even if they did not know what happened.

"Honey? James?" He suddenly became aware of Carol calling him. She was standing by the door ready to leave dressed in tailored slacks of tweed and a brown ruffle necked sweater with three-quarter length sleeves and short boots.

"Yes, yes, I'm coming," he replied absent-mindedly.

"You can tell me what you discovered over breakfast," Carol said taking his arm.

Breakfast had been busy. James related all he had learned about the Carlisle family and the Carlisle Estate to Carol. She was astounded that Edward Carlisle had been aboard the RMS Titanic. She was disappointed that James had not found out what had happened to Mrs. Carlisle after the death of her husband. Even more interesting might be what had happened to the daughter.

As they finished their coffee, James and Carol mapped out the list of rental properties they wanted to see that day. They had decided that it would be foolish to try to renovate their new home while they were still living in New York and the solution was to rent a property in the area under a short-term lease. Carol could certainly monitor her business by computer and James could reduce his need to physically be on Wall Street to two or three days a week. Carol was hoping it would be a chance for James to begin transitioning to their new way of life.

It was now late morning. As James entered the address of the first rental property on their list into the GPS, he and Carol prepared themselves for the unenviable task of looking at rentals for the next few hours. Their only hope was to have enough luck to find something suitable for their needs quickly. In any event, James definitely wanted to get out to the estate before the sun went down. They would be closest to it between the third and fourth stops on their list.

James turned off the lane and into the loose stone driveway leading onto the estate, his Estate. They had lucked out in their search for a temporary residence. It had only taken three hours. The place they had settled on was only about four or five miles from the Estate. It was a home with an in-law's apartment that had recently been vacated by an elderly couple. Nursing homes become a necessity when the elderly can no longer function on their own. It was available immediately and the rent was very reasonable. Best of all, it was wired for internet and the owners seemed very nice.

James drove slowly up the driveway swinging halfway around the circle in front of the house. It was another glorious late fall day. James and Carol exited the car and met in front of it looking toward the water. It really was a magnificent view. Carol ran up the front stairs to the porch and sat on the railing to get an even better view. She tried to imagine what it must have been like when the Red Ball Line ships were sailing offshore. She wondered if it was the same view that Edith Carlisle had enjoyed a hundred years before. The late fall sunlight reflected brightly off the water and the warmth of the sun felt wonderful. James, looking up at her and raising his voice in the slight breeze, said, "I'm going to walk around and see if I can find Ben."

Carol nodded her understanding as he started to walk around the corner of the house. James did not know if he would find Ben Allen, but he had said he was always around, so he felt the chances were good. He walked down the path toward the garage. He passed the tool shed and cornered the building.

The garage was large with three stalls for vehicles and a second floor that was as large as the first floor. Each car bay had its own set of double doors. A door to the bay farthest from James was standing open. James walked toward the door knowing that the loose stones had warned whoever was inside of someone's presence.

As James looked inside the darkened interior of the structure, his eyes needed to adjust to the reduced light of the interior. He saw a figure standing in front of a workbench built across the back wall of the garage working on the engine of what looked like a leaf blower.

"Ben? Is that you, Ben?" James called out.

"Yeah, it's me," Ben responded. He turned to see who was calling him. He saw James standing in the doorway looking at him. "Just trying to get the idle right on this." He spoke almost to himself.

James walked over to where Ben was standing and settled on a high stool to Ben's right in front of the bench. He could see the caretaker knew what he was doing. His hands moved with a deftness that came as much from understanding as from experience. James had his back to the open door and did not know that Carol had appeared in the doorway.

"How's it going, Ben?" said James trying to initiate conversation.

"Oh, it's going," replied Ben Allen in his normal tone and with a slight smile.

"I was hoping to find you here to let you know we are not going back to New York right away. We've found a place to rent for a bit so we can at least get the renovations on the place started," James continued in a friendly manner. "I also wanted to give you this."

James removed a brand-new cell phone from his jacket pocket and placed it on the bench in front of Ben. Alongside it, he placed the instructional booklet for the phone.

"I figured we'd get you into the twenty-first century, Ben. I'm used to being able to reach people."

Ben Allen continued to inspect the engine part he held between his grit-laden fingers. He did not seem to acknowledge the phone sitting on the bench. He paused in his inspection of the part he held and wiped the fingers of his left hand on a rag sitting on the bench. He reached into his own coat pocket and placed an identical cell phone on the bench next to the one James had placed.

"I kind of took the hint the other day," Ben said as he returned his attention to inspecting the engine part he held.

"But I appreciate your thoughtfulness. Oh," he continued, reaching into his pocket again, "here's my number and I put my email on there for you, too."

James took the rebuke of his gift in the manner that Ben intended it. He was not hurt as much as he was surprised at his own stupidity. Just because this was not Manhattan did not mean these people were ignorant or unfamiliar with the latest technology of the day.

"Sorry, Ben," James said as he sheepishly retrieved the proffered phone.

"That's alright, Jim. I think we're going to get along fine," Ben said looking at James. He smiled broadly.

"Can I ask you a couple of other questions," James asked, smiling himself. Ben nodded for him to continue.

"You mentioned the other day that you had never been anywhere in the house but the kitchen. Why?

"When I was a kid and Mrs. Carlisle was already an old woman, she loved to have the kids from the neighborhood play on the great lawn. She would sit in one of the big rockers on the porch and watch us kids run and tumble and fly kites on windy days. I had a lot of fun here as a kid." James could see the sweet smile of remembrance come over Ben's face as he spoke.

"The one restriction for all of us was no one was allowed in the house. Even my Dad was not allowed in the house until just before he retired.

'Course he didn't care to be inside anyway," Ben said. He continued to reassemble the parts that he had laid out on the workbench in front of him as he spoke.

"There must have been someone in the house with her," James said. "She couldn't have been living all alone in a house this size."

"Oh, she had a maid for a number of years," Ben said reassuringly, "more of a housekeeper, really. I think her name was Cassie. Never heard her speak, come to think of it. She was totally devoted to Mrs. Carlisle. She's the one who finally forced Mr. Beckwith to put Mrs. Carlisle into a nursing home. Cassie was no young chicken either and it got to a point where she just couldn't care for her alone any longer."

Where was her daughter, Ben?" Carol had been standing in the doorway listening quietly the whole time. James and Ben both turned to see her silhouetted in the doorway. Ben looked at James. He could tell from the look James was giving him that he had not told Carol about Elisabeth's death.

"She was...uh, she had already died, Mrs. Day," Ben stammered. Carol walked toward the two men.

"What do you mean?" Carol asked.

"Honey, I didn't have time to tell you. The daughter, Elisabeth, Becky is what they called her, she died on her wedding day," James said in an attempt to rescue Ben from having to explain. "It happened here, at the house."

"You knew? You knew and you didn't tell me?" Carol looked at James in disbelief. Someone had died in her house? She found it hard to believe that James had not told her. She turned to Ben Allen.

"Why were you not allowed in the house, Ben? Is it haunted? Is that it? What haven't you told us?" Carol was beginning to fire questions at Ben without giving him a chance to answer.

"I didn't say that," Ben said almost cowering under Carol's onslaught. "My father used to say he had heard noises once in a while years ago, but I've never heard anything. Mrs. Carlisle once told my Dad that the house had a spirit that she had to take care of and that's why she

65

wouldn't consider selling it, but she was an old lady when she said it, and everybody thought she was a little off."

"You said noises," Carol said looking right at Ben, "What kind of noises?"

"I don't really know, Mrs. Day. My Dad didn't really explain. He said he had occasionally heard what he thought was wailing. You know, someone sobbing. But that was years ago when he first started working here." Ben's voice trailed off as Carol's gaze told him she was focusing on her thoughts more than what he was saying.

"What happened to the daughter, Ben?" James asked softly.

"I swear I don't know the whole story, Jim," Ben said, now wondering if he might already have said too much. "It was her wedding day and my Dad never really spoke about it. All I know is it was a very violent day, and she was killed."

"Killed?" Carol looked intently at Ben. "You said she died. You never said anything about her being killed!" Carol turned to James almost in a panic. "I have to know what happened to her," she said to James with a note of desperation.

James looked down at his wife and he knew she would not rest until she knew what had happened here so many years ago. James looked at Ben and said, "What year did this happen?"

"It was 1927," Ben replied, "late summer. I swear to you, my Dad never wanted to talk about it, and I never pressed him about it. I know it was reported in the papers because she wasn't the only one who died that day."

Carol and James looked in astonishment at Ben because of this revelation while Ben, for his part, did not realize what he had just said.

"You mean there was more than one murder here?" Carol asked. Now she was frantic for information.

"No. No, that wasn't what I said!" Ben was now choosing his words very carefully. "From what I've heard from the older people in town over the years, the same day that Mrs. Carlisle's daughter died, the Stanhope daughter, Sophia, also died."

Carol felt weakness in her legs. She sat heavily on the stool James had been sitting on previously. Ben's revelations were almost more than Carol could manage. Was it possible they had just purchased a house with a history marred by violence and murder? What scandal had exploded here? Carol was feeling faint.

When she opened her eyes, she felt the cool cloth on her forehead. James was standing over her. She was lying on the back seat of their rental car feeling a little disoriented and dizzy. She heard Ben Allen's voice filled with concern.

"Is she alright, Jim?" he was saying. "I don't think I've ever seen anyone just drop like that. Scared me half to death."

Carol had gotten her bearing enough to swing her legs out the open car door and sit up on the seat.

"Are you feeling better, Honey?" Jim said with his voice laced with concern.

"How did I get here," Carol said in a detached voice.

"You fainted, Mrs. Day," Ben said anxiously, "Jim caught you and we brought you out to the car for the air. I hope it wasn't something I said."

Carol gave a faint smile to Ben Allen and assured him it was nothing he said. In reality, it was everything Ben Allen had said. As Carol's mind cleared, she made a silent promise to herself. She was going to find out what had happened that summer day in 1927. The answer was somewhere, and she was going to find it.

SEVEN

"FEELING A LITTLE BETTER?" JAMES ASKED AS HE drove the car to the hotel.

Carol nodded. She was now sitting in the front seat of the car with her coat pulled up around her. The sun was setting, and the glare of the dying light made her squint.

"James, I want to know what happened in 1927 at that house," she said at last.

"So do I," James replied. "I've already been thinking where we could look for more information. I think our first source is Mr. Stanley Beckwith tomorrow morning."

"I want to talk to Ellen Perry," Carol said in a voice that seemed far away. "She wrote that manuscript. She stopped short of saying what happened, but she has to know."

"I think we should go back to the newspapers, as well," James added. "Ben said it was in the papers." He glanced at Carol and saw her shading her eyes with her hand. "You know, you scared him half out of his wits with your fainting act."

Carol looked at James with a look of disgust and said, "It was no act."

There it was again. A smart remark that could either be a return of the cold, unfeeling James Carol was trying to make go away or an attempt at humor that fell terribly short. Carol wasn't sure which it was. She pulled her coat closer and turned to look out the window.

By Carol's reaction, James knew his attempt at humor had fallen flat. He wanted to say something more, but decided it was better to just let it go.

They had reached the exit for Mystic on the interstate. James took the exit and drove to the hotel. Carol was feeling much better, physically, by the time James had parked. They walked into the lobby and stopped at the front desk. Carol asked the desk clerk if she happened to know Ellen Perry and showed her the book she had under her arm. In that effusive manner that all hotel desk people seem to share, the clerk said she did not know her, personally, but she would see what she could find out for Carol.

The Days got in the elevator and punched the button for the floor of their room. Carol was feeling drained. It had been a long day. She leaned into James in the elevator. She could feel the tiredness in him from the way his body relaxed. As soon as they entered the room, Carol sprawled on the bed and was soon drifting into sleep.

James stripped off his jacket and sat in front of the computer. He opened the laptop and turned it on. He used his search engine to look for newspapers in southeastern Connecticut and western Rhode Island. His first results showed a list of about thirty publications, some daily, some weekly, and some biweekly. Some, like *The Hartford Courant*, he recognized immediately while others were complete mysteries. James decided he was only interested in papers that had been founded prior to 1927. That limitation cut his search results to a handful: *The Newtown Bee*, *New Haven Register*, something called *The Day of New London*, and, of course, *The Hartford Courant*. James bookmarked the site.

Then he had a thought. What if there was a newspaper that had been in operation in 1927 that was no longer in existence? James clicked the icon to start a new search. Newspapers that were no longer being published took a little work to find, but, after about twenty minutes, James was rewarded with a list of four extinct publications that met his criteria of having been actively publishing in 1927. Two had circulations in the western counties of Connecticut. One was restricted to the northern tier counties of the state. The last one, *The New London Times*, had reported news from southeastern Connecticut and western Rhode Island.

The New London Times had been founded in 1881 as a family business. The founder had learned the business as an editor of a major New York daily and, as a result, *The New London Times* immediately had a reputation as a good paper. It had flourished until the 1970s when the last member of the founding editor's family had died. Within a year or two, the paper met its own demise.

James felt he had hit pay dirt. He could search online the papers that were still publishing; their archives had certainly been scanned into their internet sites. James knew that finding the archives of a newspaper that had ceased publication so many years ago, prior to the computer age taking off, would be tricky. But, something told James that those archives held the information he needed.

He was pleased with the success of his searches. He was smiling to himself as he looked at his wife sleeping soundly on their bed. She was so beautiful. He closed the computer top and quietly joined Carol on the bed. He slid his arm under her head, and she rolled her body against his side. She made a little noise.

"Hey, sleepy," James said softly, "You need to wake up and have some dinner." Carol made her little noise again. "Alright, half an hour more and then room service. Okay?" Carol made a little contented purr and cuddled in closer to her husband.

Morning arrived before either James or Carol was ready for it. Their late-night dinner had been filled with conversation about what James had learned on the computer. Carol agreed with him that not only was it going to be difficult to find the archives of *The New London Times*, but they certainly could hold the answers to many of their questions.

James and Carol were hurrying through the lobby of their hotel when the clerk at the front desk called to Carol. James told her he would get the car while she saw what the clerk wanted.

Mrs. Day," the desk clerk called, "you were asking about an Ellen Perry?"

"Yes," Carol answered, "Have you found out where she lives?" She turned to look out the front door to see if James had pulled the rental car up.

"I believe the Ellen Perry you asked about lives at 31 Barnett Lane in Rock Cove. I've written her telephone number down and the address for you."

The clerk handed Carol a piece of note paper folded in half. She thanked her and headed out the door where James was waiting in the car.

"What was that all about?" James asked Carol as she settled in the car.

"They found Ellen Perry," Carol said smiling at James and holding up the folded paper. She pulled her cell phone out of her pocket and dialed the number written on the note.

"Hello?" James heard Carol say after about half a minute. "Is this the Ellen Perry that wrote a manuscript on the history of Rock Cove?"

James was now trying to watch Carol while he was driving. He saw her look up at him and nod her head enthusiastically.

"My name is Carol Day. I read your book on the history of Rock Cove, and I really enjoyed it. I have some questions, though. Would it be possible to meet with you in the next day or two to talk about the book?"

James saw Carol nodding excitedly. He did not need to ask the answer she had received.

"Tomorrow? At one o'clock? Oh, that would be lovely. May I bring my husband along?" Carol gave a little laugh after her question. "Thank you, Ms. Perry; we'll see you tomorrow at one. Bye." Carol was ecstatic. She was sure they were getting closer to finding out what had happened on that terrible day in Rock Cove all those years ago. She sat back in her seat with a bounce and started to enjoy the scenery as the car moved along.

James had programmed the GPS in the car while he had been waiting for Carol in front of the hotel. They were now turning down a street that would have to be considered the commercial center of Stonington. James slowed down the car as he and Carol looked at the neat shops and stores that lined the street. Some of the buildings had obviously been built for commercial use. These blocks were interspersed with older style, freestanding store fronts and businesses that were operating from converted homes.

As the GPS announced, "You have reached your destination," James and Carol found themselves parked in front of a ranch style house. An unpretentious small wooden sign hanging from a wooden post by the front walk read:

Stanley A. Beckwith II Esq.
Attorney at Law

The house was old, but well maintained. The walk leading to the front door was made of slate pieces set in cracked stone. A white-painted railing lined the small porch before the front door.

Carol entered ahead of James and saw a pleasant middle-aged woman seated at a desk to her left. They introduced themselves and the woman asked them to take a seat as she picked up the phone and announced their arrival to Mr. Beckwith. She then came around her desk and led Carol and James down a short hall and rapped lightly on a closed door at the end. She opened the door and ushered the Days into the office, then quietly closed the door behind them.

The office had probably been converted from the master bedroom of the house. In one corner was a small conference table with four chairs set around it. A massive wooden desk stood on the other side of the room. It was made of dark wood, the grain of which was difficult to identify because of the mountains of folders and books piled on its writing surface. As James looked around the room, he noticed boxes filled with files everywhere. He guessed that Stanley Beckwith was either an extremely disorganized lawyer or had not converted effectively to the computer age.

Carol saw a man passed middle age pull his heavier-than-healthy mass up from his desk when they were shown in by his secretary. He was dressed in a white shirt in desperate need of ironing with sleeves turned up once or twice and the collar unbuttoned. His tie was pulled down loose around his ample neck. His pants showed creases and wrinkles. A pair of glasses was shoved up on a head of thinning short gray hair accentuated by male-patterned baldness. He smiled at James and Carol and extended his hand in welcome. This was Stanley Beckwith.

"I apologize for the clutter. Believe it or not, we are finally beginning to put everything on computer," he said smiling broadly. "I guess it isn't the passing fad that my father said it would be." His friendly and open manner immediately put James and Carol at ease.

"I understand you two are buying the Carlisle Mansion," He continued. "Beautiful old place. I know it needs a lot of work so you're getting a good buy on it." James's first impression of Stanley Beckwith was changing. Where the clutter and stacks of boxes and his less than perfect attire at first indicated, perhaps, a less than competent practitioner of the law, James was feeling Mr. Beckwith was actually very shrewd. His voice was friendly enough, but his habit of dropping his chin to his chest when he spoke and looking up at the person he was addressing as if he were wearing his glasses on his nose gave him an almost impish quality.

"Mr. Beckwith, my wife and I have a few questions we'd like to ask you since you have been connected to the estate for so long," James said sitting forward on his chair. "I guess the biggest question we have is why is the house being sold now after all this time?"

"I can understand your concern over that," the attorney said leaning back in his chair and touching his fingertips together in front of him. "It would be a concern to me. It might make me think that something was seriously wrong with the house that was not evident." Mr. Beckwith looked at Carol and James for confirmation of his statement. He saw the Days nodding in assent. After a few moments of thought, he leaned forward in his chair and placed his elbows on the writing surface.

"Nothing could be further from the truth. So, you can rest easy about that," he said smiling at them both. "Let me go back a little and explain what happened here with the property. That will probably answer many of your questions."

Stanley Beckwith shifted back in his chair making the springs of the tilt mechanism give out a slight groan. He leaned his head onto the high back of the leather chair. He paused for a moment before he began, as if to order his thoughts about what he was going to relate.

"The business relationship of our family and the Carlisle family started with my father and Mr. Carlisle about 1910. Mr. Carlisle came to my father and asked him to construct a trust that would provide for Mrs. Carlisle and their daughter, Elisabeth, 'forever.' In the event of his death, Mr. Carlisle gave Mrs. Carlisle control over the trust to the extent that she could redirect the benefits from it as long as she remained a widow. If she remarried, the trust ceased any benefit to her. She would be paid a set amount from it and the remaining corpus would be held to benefit his daughter upon her marriage. His daughter would receive an inheritance directly from the trust at the age of twenty-one or, if married before attaining age 21, upon her marriage with the agreement of Mrs. Carlisle and the trustee."

Mr. Beckwith could see that Carol was having a problem with some of his terminology, James, less so because of his financial background.

"I'm sorry," he said, looking at Carol, "I'll try to be more careful with the terms, but it is difficult not to use the jargon. To continue, I have to assume you have already done a little research about the Carlisle family and home just because I know you are both intelligent and curious and because, if I were in your position, I would be doing that too." He saw the nods of agreement from James and Carol.

"So, you probably know that Edward Carlisle was lost on the *Titanic* in April of 1912. Am I right? And, you probably know that their daughter died in 1927 on the day of her wedding."

"We heard she was killed," Carol said. "That's a slightly different connotation as to what happened, don't you think, Mr. Beckwith? I want to know what happened."

Stanley Beckwith showed a moment of surprise as he leaned forward and put his arms on his desk.

"Mrs. Day, I am sure you are going to find out. It is a matter of public record, and I am sure you are resourceful enough to locate the information. Obviously, I was not here in 1927, as most of those who were, are long gone. My father kept a pretty tight lip about the events of that day in 1927, but I can tell you what I know from what he told me. Granted, that may be somewhat slanted, but you have to remember that my father was the attorney who was intimately involved in what was going on. Along with that, he was the trustee of the Carlisle fortune.

"In Rock Cove in the early years of the last century – still seems odd saying that – there were two families who were attempting to bring Rock Cove into the same social status as Newport and Watch Hill, Rhode Island. The Stanhope and the Carlisle families built mansions on either side of the cove and Mrs. Stanhope and Mrs. Carlisle were in a constant battle for social leadership in Rock Cove. If one held a party, the other had a bigger one. If one had two horses, the other had to have four. That rivalry was instilled in their daughters by these women. Sophia Stanhope and Elisabeth Carlisle, who was called Becky by everyone, were being groomed to carry on the war. Sophia was a few years older than Becky.

"Here you had two wealthy widows with young, attractive daughters locked in this warfare for social prominence, after the heyday of their time, in a town that never really made a name for itself as a playground for the super-rich like Newport did. Pretty sad, really, but that was the situation." The attorney shook his head in recognition of the futility of the situation.

"Anyway, the idea of marrying someone who was socially connected was still a big deal to these women and, with that in mind, they went hunting for someone with a title. If one was tracking a Count, the other would be hunting an Earl. Thing is, Sophia, being older, was passing what was considered her prime and verging on spinsterhood in her mother's eyes and the eyes of her society friends. She had failed to make a 'good' marriage." Mr. Beckwith paused.

"But she was only, what? Twenty-six?" Carol questioned. "That isn't' old."

"Back then, it was," Mr. Beckwith smiled knowingly. "You have to remember; Connie Stanhope had been married at twenty and had Sophia within a year. Same was true for Edith Carlisle; she was just twenty-one when she married Mr. Carlisle and had Becky right away."

"Anyway, Sophia Stanhope finally snags herself some Baron on one of her trips and he's supposedly fallen for her hook, line, and sinker. He shows up in Rock Cove and there's big news about Sophia's pending nuptials. The engagement is announced, wedding plans are well underway, and Mrs. Stanhope is in her glory. Everything is going swimmingly. Then, all of a sudden, the engagement is off. Mrs. Stanhope is furious; Sophia is broken-hearted and in seclusion. Seems this "Baron" has changed his mind and, even worse, has decided to marry Sophia's biggest rival, Becky Carlisle. "

James and Carol looked at each other with disbelief. Stanley Beckwith saw them exchange looks and continued, "Yes, it was the ultimate insult to Mrs. Stanhope, her daughter being jilted for the younger Becky Carlisle."

"It was more than Mrs. Stanhope could stand. The wedding plans were now being made for Becky Carlisle and Mrs. Carlisle, her bitter social rival, was now in her glory."

"What happened the day of the wedding, Mr. Beckwith?" Carol asked with some emotion. "We know something happened. Elisabeth was killed."

"I want you to understand that there are varying reports of what happened, but I will tell you what my father told me. The day of the wedding was a beautiful summer day. The sun was shining with a light breeze off the Sound. There had been a storm a few days before, and the surf was pounding against the rocks along the point."

"The wedding was to be out on the lawn of the house. Becky was upstairs getting dressed in her wedding gown. The guests were arriving. As the time for the ceremony drew near, Mrs. Stanhope was seen arriving even though she had not been invited. It appears that she entered the house and found her way up to the second-floor bedroom where Becky was dressing. She apparently entered the room, smiled at Becky, drew a loaded Colt revolver from her pocket and shot Becky Carlisle through the heart."

Carol and James sat immobile. They were thunderstruck. Carol thought to herself, how anyone could be so cruel. Carol had never experienced anything so violent in her life. In fact, she had been shielded to a great extent by her parents, first, and now by James, from the unpleasant things of life.

"Several shots were heard coming from the mansion before Mrs. Stanhope exited the house and calmly walked to the edge of the cliff. They say she threw herself off the rocks into the water." Mr. Beckwith paused and looked down at his desk. "It was tragic. But, what was even more tragic was later that afternoon, when the police went to the Stanhope mansion to inform Sophia of her mother's death, they found her. She had hanged herself in her bedroom. She had been dead for some hours."

Carol began to cry softly. James sat completely still, almost in shock.

"She took her own life," James said shaking his head in disbelief. "So, that's what drove Mrs. Stanhope over the edge. Terrible, just terrible."

"That's what the inquest decided. Instead of Becky Carlisle's wedding being the social event of the year in Rock Cove, her funeral was. Mrs. Carlisle went into seclusion for some time, but she always maintained that strong exterior for which the Victorian Era socially elite matrons were noted.

"What happened to the groom?" Carol asked after gaining control of her emotions.

"The Baron?" Mr. Beckwith replied. "Oh, he turned out to be a fake, some guy with a fake accent. He was only interested in the money these two girls would come into upon marriage. No one is quite sure what happened to him. Some said that Mrs. Stanhope found him in the house and shot him too. Others say he just disappeared. In any event, he was never heard from again."

"No wonder Ellen Perry said it was the worst day in the history of Rock Cove," Carol said looking at James. He nodded in agreement. "It cost both of those young girls their lives because their mothers had to play a silly society game of who was better. And it cost one of those mother's her life, as well."

"And don't forget the groom," said James. "He was never found either."

"He wasn't the only one," Mr. Beckwith said quietly. He had been sitting quietly with his hands folded in front of him on the desk listening to Carol and James digesting what he told them. "They never found Mrs. Stanhope either. They searched for several days up and down the coast and in the cove before they gave up. They decided the undertow had taken her out or she was stuck somewhere under the rocks. Either way, she was gone. She wasn't the first to ever be lost in these waters and never found. Since her daughter was the last member of the Stanhope line, there was no one left. Mrs. Carlisle saw to Sophia's funeral arrangements. I always thought that strange, but, who else was left to make arrangements? A lot of people thought well of Mrs. Carlisle on seeing that Sophia was laid to rest. They felt it was very classy of her to not hold the actions of the mother against the daughter. After that, the Stanhope Mansion went into ruin and the house was demolished by the tidal surge that hit here in the 1938 hurricane."

"Thank you for telling us what happened in 1927," Carol said with a sad smile. "I needed to know, sad as it was."

James looked at the attorney and said, "You still haven't explained why the house was being sold now? And at such a reasonable price?"

"I will be more than happy to explain that, but let's say we go have a bite to eat," Mr. Beckwith suggested, rising from his desk, "on me, of course! There's a lovely little café down the street and it'll be my treat. Besides, there is much more to tell you."

EIGHT

THE TRIO DONNED THEIR LIGHT JACKETS AGAINST the chill of another nice late fall day. Mr. Beckwith smiled at his secretary as he passed by her desk and told her he would be back in an hour or so. He ushered the Days out the door and started walking toward the more commercial buildings of town. As they walked, the attorney asked Carol and James about themselves. They talked about their Midwestern roots and life in New York. When he asked them about their moving to Rock Cove, Carol smiled and told the attorney it was time they got away from the lifestyle of the city and became a real family. He liked what he learned from them, and he wanted to be as honest with them as he could be.

They reached the café after a short walk and settled into a booth along a side wall. The waitress greeted the Days cheerfully and the attorney with familiarity. It was obvious he was a regular. James and Carol looked at the menus she handed them and ordered simple fare. Beckwith merely said, "The usual, Betty." They were more intent on pursuing their discussion with the attorney.

"So, Mr. Beckwith, why ARE you selling the house now?" James asked.

"When the trust was originally set up, the original corpus of the trust would have provided for Mrs. Carlisle and her daughter for their entire lives and still had money left over. When Mrs. Carlisle's daughter died, she requested my father alter the trust so after her death, the trust would continue to pay all the expenses connected with the maintenance of the estate, including the property taxes, the employment of a caretaker at good wages, and any repairs that were needed. However, the house was to be left vacant and no one was to enter it. It was not to be rented or occupied by anyone and not to be sold until the funds in the trust were exhausted."

"So, the trust is exhausted?" James questioned.

Stanley Beckwith nodded. "The amount the trust was originally funded with should have lasted forever. Unfortunately, neither Mr. Carlisle nor anyone else of his time foresaw things like income tax, the 1929 crash, the miserable recession of the seventies, or Mrs. Carlisle going into a nursing home for nearly a decade. Still, the trust held up for nearly eighty years."

"Why sell it for so little," Carol wanted to know.

"At this point, there is no money left to pay any taxes or upkeep. My Father never charged the trust anything but minimal costs for all his time and effort. When I took over, I did the same. I am looking at the sale of the property as finally receiving the fees that are due us for having faithfully served the interests of our clients, the Carlisle family, all these years. The price of the house was arrived at by me as fair compensation for our work all these years. Secondly, I believe Mrs. Carlisle never intended that my father or I should ever be saddled, personally, with expenses connected with the house. Any expenses at this point would be ours to bear."

The waitress arrived at the table with their lunch. Mr. Beckwith deftly changed the subject by asking what plans James and Carol were making for the house. They chatted pleasantly through lunch telling Mr. Beckwith about Paul Murray's firm. He was actually familiar with his work and asked if they were going to use him to make architectural changes. Carol had said she had asked him to make some suggestions.

As they finished eating, James asked the attorney, "How well did you know Mrs. Carlisle?"

"Well, when I started practicing in 1966, Mrs. Carlisle was already advanced in years. She would sit on the big porch and watch the water with her housekeeper and tell the caretaker what needed to be looked after. She was a character; always proper, almost regal in her manner. She would greet me when I arrived as if my coming was an honor, the most important event of the day for her, and I got a kick out of it too." Attorney Beckwith spoke with no small amount of pride.

"Did you meet with her often at the house?" Carol asked.

"Oh no," Stanley replied, "only in summer or when the weather was warm enough to have our meeting on the porch. She used to say the house had ears; that the spirit of the house didn't need to know what was being said. Other times she would come to the office, but that was a rarity."

"Didn't you think it was odd that you never were in the house?" asked James.

"I didn't say that did I?" Attorney Beckwith said with surprise. "Just before we had to remove her from the house, she had my father and me out to the house for a meeting. That was when she wanted to be sure the house would not be sold and would be kept. That was late 1969 or early 1970, I think".

"Was that the last time you were in the house, Mr. Beckwith?" Carol asked.

"I was there once after Mrs. Carlisle was moved to the nursing facility when the furniture was covered. She wanted all personal property removed from the house. She meant things like photographs, records, doodads, and knick-knacks, her very personal things. They were packed up and put in the second story of the garage. As far as I know, they are still there and are now owned by the two of you!" The attorney gave a slight chuckle and glanced at his watch. "Oh dear, we've been a bit longer than I expected. I do have another appointment, but now that you know where I am, feel free to see me any time."

Beckwith waived to the waitress to get her attention. "Put this all on my tab, Betty," He said to her, "and give yourself a generous tip." He smiled with a wink at Betty, and she returned a smile.

The threesome walked briskly back to Mr. Beckwith's office where they parted company. James and Carol thanked Mr. Beckwith for their delicious lunch, but even more for his information. They got into their car feeling they had a better understanding of the Carlisle and Stanhope feud that had destroyed what should have been the happiest of days for one of the victims and had resulted in three (or four?) deaths in that one day.

Carol could not help feeling sorry for Sophia Stanhope. Abandoned by a suitor who then attempted to marry your rival; her devastation must have been total. She could see in her mind's eye Mrs. Stanhope finding her daughter, a suicide, an action that would be the ruin of their social standing. She thought about Becky Carlisle dressing for her wedding, marrying what she thought was the man of her dreams. She would never learn of his deception. How surprised must Becky have been to see Mrs. Stanhope appear in her room? Did Becky have the chance to say anything before a gun was leveled at her? Did she even understand why it was happening?

And then there was the grief of Mrs. Carlisle. How does one withstand the loss of their only child by violence, especially on a day that should have been so full of joy? How does one rise above the need for revenge when there is no one to take that revenge upon? Should it be considered strange that Mrs. Carlisle lived for over sixty years as somewhat of a recluse, guarding her privacy carefully? Was it any wonder she spoke of the house as filled with a spirit that she had to guard? Could anyone have been expected to keep their complete sanity after all she had lost and living alone all that time? Carol was lost in her thoughts until she realized that James was pulling into a Lexus dealership.

"What are we doing here?" Carol asked.

"Well, I guess we ought to look at a car, don't you remember?" James said, smiling at Carol. "I remembered the SUV you liked. There's one sitting out front. Shall we go look at it?"

Carol returned James's smile. Her dark thoughts vanished in an instant. She jumped out of the car and grabbed his hand as they met at the back of their rental car. They walked into the dealership hand-in-hand.

"Hello, Folks! Welcome to Bryant Motors'" said the salesman who opened the door to the showroom for them. "Looking for a car today?"

James looked at Carol and then at the salesman. "This is going to be the easiest sale you've ever made, my friend," James said smiling broadly.

"Who is this person that you've become," Carol said as they got back in their rental car. "I've never known you to be as impulsive about things as you have these past few days. First, the house and now this? A Lexus?"

"At least it's a hybrid, honey!" James said almost laughing.

Carol was looking at the brochure for her brand new fully loaded Lexus RX400H, Bamboo Pearl exterior with black interior. It would take a little time to get used to the voice-activated navigational system, but it was all hers. The salesman had been totally (and pleasantly) surprised when he called James's broker in Manhattan and set up the wiring of money for the full price of the car. Nothing like that had ever happened to him before. When he was asked to have the car ready by the next day, there was no question it would be prepped and ready by 10:00 AM.

As they drove toward the hotel, James knew he needed to check in with his office. The week of vacation he had requested when they had found the house was quickly slipping by and he knew a trip to New York City was in the offing. In addition to that, he knew that Carol and he both needed some things from their apartment in New York for their temporary residence. As he was trying to broach the subject of going to New York with Carol, he heard her say, "I need to check in with my office." They thought alike.

"Suppose we check out of the hotel and head to the city?" James suggested. "It's during the week and traffic shouldn't be too bad. We can spend the night in the apartment and leave early tomorrow."

"We need to be here by one tomorrow. We are meeting Ellen Perry tomorrow at one," Carol reminded him. "We should also get back to Paul Murray to see when he can start cleaning."

"We can't leave New York tomorrow until I see the bank about the mortgage. I think I have almost everything from Linda about the appraisals and the comps. The aerial photo pretty much says it all as far as the property is concerned," James smiled at the thought of the acreage. "If I can meet with the bank tomorrow morning, we could have Paul's company start cleaning by the end of the week."

He smiled at Carol knowing that it would please her to see the house finally opened up.

"Oh, James, we can't go tonight," Carol said with a start. "What about the car?"

James pulled out his cell phone and had Carol read the dealership phone number in the brochure. He asked for the salesman by name and needed to take a minute to assure him he was not calling to cancel the sale because of buyer's remorse or anything like it. He actually wanted to know if there was any way the car could be prepared and delivered by this evening. The salesman took only a moment to assure James that the car could be and would be ready by 7 tonight. He thanked the salesman and assured him the survey he was going to receive would reflect the fine quality of his and Bryant Motors service. James looked at Carol as he closed his phone.

"Problem solved. In fact, we can drive it into the city if you want?"

"Let's," Carol said happily. "We can take the rental car back if you don't mind driving in together. Then we don't have to worry about getting it back later."

We don't need to worry about getting it back. I can drop it off at any one of their rental offices," James said. "We can drive in together and I can be the passenger!" He laughed knowing full well that he would be behind the wheel.

"No, my dear," Carol said dryly, "You're driving and I'm reading the emails that have been piling up on my computer."

"We had better get back to the hotel. We need to get our stuff packed up and get checked out," James said. "Oh, and we'll need to stop by the apartment and pick up the key since we'll be staying there from now on until the house is ready."

Promptly at five minutes to seven, the keys to the Lexus were deposited into Carol's waiting palm. It was the first time she had ever owned a new car. In college she had only been able to afford secondhand cars that never ran right and only lasted just so long. She would be content to just sit in it for tonight and let James have the fun of driving it. As they settled into the luxury SUV, the smell of the new car was almost overpowering. Carol ran her fingers over the dash and the console. She looked at James with a look that conveyed how pleased she was.

They thanked the salesman again and returned his friendly wave as they pulled out of the dealership and headed for the southbound ramp of the interstate. They would be in their apartment in New York City in less than three hours and still be able to have a good night's sleep before driving back to meet with Ellen Perry. If everything went as planned in the morning, they would make that meeting with time to spare.

NINE

IT WAS A MAGNIFICENT AUGUST MORNING THAT greeted Becky Carlisle as she opened her eyes. The sun was streaming into her bedroom and the breeze off the water carried the salty scent of the sea into the room. It would be a warm day made comfortable by that gentle ocean wind. It was going to be a glorious day for her wedding on the great lawn. It was the day she would marry and gain a title.

A light rap on her bedroom door announced the arrival of her maid, Marguerite, with her morning tray. Becky stretched beneath her imported French percale sheet and let out a little groan.

"Good morning, Miss Becky," Marguerite said with a lilt in her voice. She set the tray she was carrying on the small table by the window and moved to open the thin summer curtains covering the windows even wider. It took little strength from her slight body to move the curtains aside. The light coming into the room exploded with intensity.

"Good morning, Marguerite," Becky said sitting up in bed. "It really IS a wonderful day, isn't it?"

"Yes, Miss! Your bridesmaids have all been up for at least an hour and the house is all a buzz! Cook is busy in the kitchen already, but she took time out to make a nice tray up for you." Marguerite turned to retrieve the tray from the table where she had set it and placed it beside her young charge.

Marguerite had been a member of the Carlisle staff for nearly a decade. She had cared for Elisabeth all that time as if she were her own child, comforting her through the little hurts and celebrating her triumphs. And today, she saw her smiling little princess grown to a beautiful, confident young woman, preparing to take a major step in her life. She watched Becky pull her blond hair back with one hand as she raised her cup of morning tea with the other; her firm young body not yet betraying any hint of her greatest secret. Marguerite could feel the tears of pride rising in her as she looked at this radiant bride-to-be enjoying her morning toast.

"Your gown is hanging in the back bedroom, Miss Becky. The hairdresser will be here in about twenty minutes." Marguerite was fussing about the room just to be busy while she talked. She turned and saw Becky sitting in her bed lost in thought. She came toward the side of the bed. "A penny for your thoughts, Miss?"

"Oh. Sorry, Marguerite," Becky said in a detached manner. She turned to face her maid fully. "Am I making the right choice?"

The question took Marguerite back.

"The right choice, Miss?" she responded. "You love him, don't you?"

"Well, I think I do," Becky said with a slightly puzzled look on her face. "At least, I think I do. I mean if he was going to be good enough for Sophia, then he should be good enough for me. Right?" She looked at her maid with an expression that wanted confirmation.

Marguerite looked at her ward with all the sincerity she had and said, "Miss, what does your heart tell you?"

"My heart?" the young woman said thoughtfully. "My heart tells me that I will be a Baroness and that I will be happy to be so!"

She looked at Marguerite with that beaming childlike smile she saved for her very best moments. With that, Becky pulled the bed covers aside nearly upsetting the breakfast tray and danced in circles in the sunlight streaming through the windows in her silk chemise. Marguerite grabbed the tray just in time to stop it from flipping over and watched Becky dance. She remembered her doing the same thing as a child whenever she was excited and happy. Marguerite set the tray back on the small table by the windows. As she did, Becky grabbed her by the arm. Joining hands, the two of them frolicked around the room.

After several minutes, they collapsed on the floor in mild exhaustion. Becky and Marguerite looked at each other as they caught their breaths with an expression that showed their affection for each other.

"How do you like my bridesmaids?" Becky asked her maid.

"Oh, they are lovely," Marguerite fairly gushed with enthusiasm. "They will certainly be overshadowed by the bride, though." She laughed and so did Becky. They lay on their backs on the carpet enjoying the warm sunlight for a few minutes, each with their own thoughts.

"I suppose we should start getting ready," Becky said finally. The two women helped each other from the floor and Becky headed into her bathroom.

He entered the room with all the bearing of a high society don. Although it was early in the day, his grooming was perfect, not a hair out of place, his jaw well shaved and scented. His dressing gown, neatly cinched around his trim waist over dark pants with a razor crease down the legs, completed this image of English social elegance.

"I am glad you decided to meet with me," Edith Carlisle said coldly.

"I took your invitation as a delightful order," he responded with a smile. "Was there something you needed to see me about?" He seated himself in one of the chairs near the wall of windows and straightened his attire, so it fell perfectly. If nothing else, he was a study in fashion.

"Is there something you wanted to discuss, Mother, if I may be so bold as to address you as such?" The grin on his face when he finished speaking made it difficult for Edith Carlisle to control her anger.

"Listen to me," she began, looking directly at him and masking her disdain. "You may have others fooled, but I am not." Her blunt statement brought a look of innocent denial to his face.

"Why, whatever do you mean, my dear woman?"

"You can drop the act, Baron," Mrs. Carlisle said coldly. "Did you think I would not have you looked into? I am not Connie Stanhope. I know who Lord Alethar was and he has no son Richard Albert."

The man sitting across from her showed no outward sign of concern although internally, he was in a panic. He sat frozen in place calmly looking at his accuser.

"If you are concerned that I will expose you for the rake you are, I have no such intentions," Mrs. Carlisle reached for her cup of coffee that was sitting at her right side. "Whatever the case is, my daughter seems to be deeply in love with you, so much so that she has given herself to you. Because she is young and inexperienced in many things, I will do anything to protect her." She was watching him intently and was not surprised to see little reaction to what she was saying. She thought to herself what a cold, calculating cad.

"I do love her, you know," the Baron finally said with all the sincerity of the wolf smiling at grandmother in Little Red Riding Hood.

"Oh PLEASE!" Edith said with disgust. "Don't insult me and act more foolish than you already appear. You love no one and nothing but the wealth my daughter could bring you. I said I would not reveal you as the fortune hunter you are, but, in return, I have a plan you will agree to follow. It will afford my daughter the opportunity to carry on her life without the scandal that having a child out of wedlock would bring and will allow you afterward to find another pigeon to pluck."

The Baron leaned forward in his chair and placed his elbows on his knees. All signs of his cultured airs had evaporated in an instant.

"I am listening," he said coldly, his English accent suddenly missing.

"You will marry my daughter today, as planned." Edith spoke with the full force of her masked anger. "You will reside here or anywhere that I so desire you to for the next year and will play the doting husband.

I am sure you can do that well," she said with a note of sarcasm. "You seem to be good at carrying off roles."

"After a second year, you will quietly and mutually agree to a separation from my daughter and leave for Europe. Your wife will quietly obtain a divorce on grounds of irreconcilable differences, and you will never see her, or the child, again. Do you agree?"

"What's in it for me?" the Baron said with all the coldness attending a business negotiation.

"If you agree to what I have proposed, I will support you and my daughter in a reasonable style for the next two years. Upon your departure and the granting of the divorce decree, I will see you have payment of $50,000 wired to an account of your choosing in any European bank."

The Baron sat back in his chair. His regal posture was now replaced by somewhat of a slouch as he considered the proposal. It was evident that he was trying to decide if two years of his life were worth the stated price.

"What if I refuse your offer," he suddenly said.

"Then, it is quite simple. You will have a very unfortunate accident." Edith looked, with steely resolve, directly into her opponent's cold eyes with all the primal fury of a mother protecting her young. "I will kill you, myself, before the sun sets."

The level of joyful cacophony rose and fell in the room at the end of the hall. The laughter of young women can be so infectious. The six young women making all the chatter and occasional outbursts of laughter were all from prominent families. They had been carefully selected by Becky's mother for their social prominence from a larger list given by her daughter. All of them were products of the smart set that spent summers in Newport and sported New York, Philadelphia, and Boston addresses the rest of the year.

As their personal maids dressed them and a swarm of professionals did their hair and makeup, they talked of this summer's activities and who had been at what party or who was going to the next one. Their gaiety was just another part of a perfect day.

When Becky slipped into the room wearing her wedding gown, the conversation changed to gasps of wonderment and phrases of praise for her beauty. Her hair had been shortened and was styled into the latest fashion of finger waves. It fell just to the edge of the high neck of her gown. The gown itself was floor length with a short train. The cream white satin it was made from fell flawlessly from an intricately embroidered bodice. The full-length sleeves with pearl buttons to the elbow formed a "V" over the back of her hands.

Marguerite quietly entered the room without being noticed by the group. She held Becky's veil in her hand. She stood for a moment watching the happy group bubbling with conversation. The effect of her white gown amidst the pastel colors of her attendants' dresses was brilliant, Marguerite thought to herself.

Becky, seeing Marguerite standing in the doorway, broke through the ring of her friends and came toward Marguerite smiling broadly. Marguerite held the veil out to Becky.

"Oh, put it on," cried the group excitedly.

Becky looked back over her shoulder coquettishly at her friends. She turned back to Marguerite and presented the veil back to her.

"Will you help me put it on?" she asked her.

As Marguerite took the veil from Becky's hand, she beamed with pride. Becky turned and, keeping a straight back, curtseyed so Marguerite could easily reach her head. It took but a moment to position the veil and fix it in place with hairpins. Marguerite touched her shoulder to indicate she was done. Becky then stood and turned to face her. She smiled at her life-long friend and gently kissed her on the cheek. She gave her a final smile and wheeled around to rejoin the group in merry conversation. Marguerite, smiling brightly, quietly left the room.

A few moments later, the excited level of conversation from the group suddenly dropped and Becky noticed her bridesmaids' attentions had focused on something behind her. She turned to see what had captured their interest. With a smile still on her lips, she was surprised to see Mrs. Stanhope dressed in her riding attire standing before her. Becky saw streaks from tears on Mrs. Stanhope's expressionless face. Mrs. Stanhope began to smile....

TEN

PAUL MURRAY WAS A LITTLE SURPRISED AT RECEIVing a call so late in the day from James Day. He had expected it would be a couple of weeks before he heard whether the sale had been finalized or not. He would know then whether he had the job to clean the Carlisle mansion. But James had been pretty clear on the phone that he wanted the cleaning to begin by the end of the week – and here it was Monday.

Paul suspected that Carol Day was going to ask him to make some major changes inside the mansion. He also knew he needed to find a set of plans for the house if they existed at all. If not, he would need to make them himself. He decided, first thing Tuesday morning, he would stop by the town offices just on the off chance that the original plans were on file there. He knew it was highly unlikely, in which case, he was going to stop by at the estate and take some outside measurements.

If the target date for cleaning was to be Thursday or Friday, Paul had to get his crew ready. He spent the remainder of his Monday on the phone lining up his crew of workers. This was an unusual time of the year for them to be getting a call from Paul. It was usually in the early spring he contacted them, when the "snowbirds" were expected to return from down south. Normally, Paul would set them up into teams of two or three to work, depending on the size of the property. This time he was planning on using the entire crew. Of the dozen people he normally employed in cleaning, all but two were available for Friday. He made sure they were going to be able to work an entire week. He felt confident ten people could complete the job in that time. He had no idea how wrong he would be.

Ellen Perry was startled by Carol Day's call. No one had so much as mentioned her efforts at being a historian about Rock Cove for a long time. When she said she had read it, Ellen was suspicious. She knew there were only a limited number of copies that had been produced back when it was written. These had sold sparingly and, other than the copies she had offered to local libraries, there were very few copies available.

In spite of her initial reservations, Ellen was more than delighted that someone wanted to speak with her about a project she had considered so minor and of such limited interest. Carol sounded like someone who was obviously well-spoken and young. Ellen Perry missed that when she had retired to Rock Cove. She thought being in a quiet seaside community would give her the peace she would enjoy in retirement. Instead, she discovered she missed the excitement of the college community. She had been a librarian at Yale University for nearly forty years. She had grown fond of the constant exchange of ideas and the vibrant, lively conversation that took place on a college campus and in her library every day. Working with college students had kept her mind quick and her life full. She might never have retired had she not reached the mandatory retirement age. Now, she spent most of her days at the senior center in Stonington playing bridge or mahjong, except for the two days a week she spent as a volunteer in the Stonington Library. In fact, that was where she had arranged to meet Carol Day tomorrow at one.

Linda Giuliani had done all she could to smooth the way for the sale of the Carlisle Estate. She had provided James with everything a bank would need to facilitate a closing. She had faxed copies of other properties that had sold in the area as comps to his bank as requested. Realistically, there were no comparable properties for the estate. It was truly a one of a kind property that would appraise out at four or five times the selling price. One look at the photographs of the property and no bank in its right mind would refuse a mortgage based on the sale price.

Linda had been a realtor for some time, and she knew it was never a good idea to become too invested in any one property, especially one that had been on the market for so short a period of time. But there was something about the old Victorian and the circumstances of the sale that intrigued her. She had dealt in the past with many of the attorneys in town including Stanley Beckwith. She was honored that he had contacted her when the estate was going to be sold. She took it as a sign of his regard for her ability as a businesswoman to get his price for the property and find a buyer quickly.

At the time the property had been listed, Attorney Beckwith had requested a meeting with Linda in his office to explain how he wanted the property shown. This had made Linda curious, but the rules she was required to agree to in showing the property really raised her interest. Mr. Beckwith did not want the house opened until the prospective buyers were absolutely qualified. Anyone could view the grounds, walk all around the property, see the garage, but not the interior of the house until Linda felt they were serious as buyers – and qualified. Mr. Beckwith had emphasized he wanted the property sold quickly. Linda assured him that the asking price would have one of two reactions: either something was radically wrong with the property, or something was happening that was going to affect the future value adversely. Either reaction was sure to raise questions that would need to be addressed. But, Stanley Beckwith had been adamant that he wanted the property priced to sell quickly. He was prepared to answer any questions regarding the property from any serious buyers. At the price he was asking, Linda had assured him there would be no problem.

She had no doubt there would be all kinds of interest in the property. It was only luck that James and Carol Day had been working with Linda at the time and she knew they were not only qualified, but overly so. She and Carol had grown close over the few weeks they had known each other, and Linda felt the mansion was somehow right for them. She felt she understood how important this house had become to Carol. It was her best chance at getting her husband closer to her and away from New York's "modus vivendi." She wanted Carol and James to get the property.

When she received the call from Stanley Beckwith on Monday afternoon, she was expecting to hear praise from the attorney for her quick sale. The ink on his listing had not even been dried when Linda had sold the property. Instead, she heard a very cold, malevolent voice asking if she was available to meet immediately. She had shelved everything else on her calendar for the rest of the day and driven to the attorney's office. She was now parked in front of his office trying to think of what could possibly be wrong. Nothing came to mind.

She got out of her car and braced herself for what she was sure was trouble, but she had no idea about what. She opened the door to the office and saw no one about. She walked quietly down the hallway and saw Stanley Beckwith sitting at his desk with a short glass in front of him. She rapped lightly on the partially open door.

"Come on in, Linda," Stanley Beckwith said in a slight slur without turning away from the window he was looking out of blankly. He was still wearing the same wrinkled dress shirt he had been wearing when he met with the Days, perhaps a bit more wrinkled than earlier. His tie had been removed.

"What's wrong? Have I done something wrong?" Linda said with concern in her voice as she sat in one of the two chairs positioned in front of his desk.

Stanley Beckwith turned to face her. She could tell from the flush on his face that he was not happy and the glass in front of him, although half full now, had been in a full condition several times prior to her being present.

"Who did they talk to," the attorney said to her in a low menacing tone as he looked over his glasses. "Who told them about what happened at the house?"

"They saw Ben Allen when we went out to the house," Linda said feeling the cold stare of Stanley Beckwith's eyes.

"What was he doing out there?" Beckwith said. "Hell, I fired him a month ago! DAMN!" the attorney exploded as he pounded his fist on the writing surface and stood abruptly. Everything on the desk jumped erratically. "Why didn't you stop him? I want to be rid of this millstone of a house!"

"I didn't know he was there. I swear. He just appeared from around the corner of the house," Linda replied in desperation. "I don't think he did any harm to the sale. The Days really liked the house, and they would have found out about the history eventually."

"He wasn't supposed to be there at all." The kindly, jovial Stanley Beckwith, who had met with the Days, had been transformed by drink into the mean-tempered brute addressing Linda Giuliani.

"Well, he'll be there for the time being. James Day hired him back on as caretaker," Linda replied with force.

"If he has said anything that stops this sale from going through...." The attorney was searching for words to continue.

"I don't think he knows anything more than anyone else. And, maybe even less," Linda replied offhandedly.

"You'd better be sure he doesn't screw things up."

"They knew more than I thought they would. They knew more than I think Ben could have told them."

. "Who did they talk to, Linda!" Beckwith turned and glared at Linda.

"Don't you threaten me," Linda said coldly as she stood and placed her hands on his desk. "I found you a good buyer. I did everything you asked me to. If you have skeletons in your closet, that is not my concern. Maybe it's time they came out. But, if I were you, I'd stop worrying and stop drinking until the sale is final. Drinking makes you very unattractive, Stan."

Linda stood completely erect, braced her shoulders, straightened the jacket of her business suit, and marched out of the office without looking back.

Stanley Beckwith stood very still for a moment, as if someone had hit him between the eyes with a two-by-four. He heard the front door slam and sat down heavily at his desk and looked at the half-filled glass of brandy. He carefully lifted it and set it aside. He folded his arms on the desk and laid his head on his hands.

Linda slammed the car door. She sat behind the steering wheel fuming over the way she had been treated by Stanley Beckwith. In all the years she had been a realtor, she had never been treated in such a manner, especially when she had done such a good job. She had found a good, qualified buyer and gotten the client's price. That was all she was required to do. If her client had something to hide, it was none of her affair. Besides, if what she had shared with these prospective buyers was enough to quash the sale, perhaps the seller needed to disclose something more beforehand.

Linda didn't like people who drank. She had never seen Stanley in that state before and she was sure it might be quite some time before she would ever have any other business with him. Once this business was concluded, she would attempt to steer clear of Stanley Beckwith.

ELEVEN

CAROL WAS ENJOYING SITTING BEHIND THE WHEEL of her Lexus SUV. She told James it fit like a glove. James, for his part, was sitting in the passenger seat smiling and only occasionally searching for the imaginary passenger side brake pedal. They had changed positions at a service area on the interstate just beyond New Haven and were steadily approaching Rock Cove a half hour ahead of schedule. James had driven them out of the city. Rightly or wrongly, he had more confidence in his own driving ability in the heavy traffic of New York City.

Everything had gone well in New York that morning. James had been at his bank right at nine and been able to cut through most of the red tape to get the mortgage all set. He had walked out of the bank at nine forty-five with a check in his pocket for the full amount required for the closing.

James had spoken with his office before he had gone to the bank. He arranged to attend a couple of conferences via the internet and another week out of the office. Other than weekends, James had never been out of the office for more than one occasional day in five years. Now, he had been away over five business days and was taking another week. It felt strangely easy to be able to carry on business without being physically present. He left his new forwarding address in Rock Cove with his secretary and left a message for his partners asking for a meeting to talk about his new work schedule being implemented.

Carol had preferred to meet with her staff when they reached New York the night before. All of her key staff had worked late to be there when she arrived. She caught up on all the current projects and got a report from each of the design teams and was done by midnight. She had been able to sleep a little later than James in the morning, but in reality, spent the time packing more "essentials" for their temporary country residence. The suitcases, soft bags, gym bags, and other paraphernalia were now piled in the back of the SUV. James had made the comment to Carol that, had he bought her a monster SUV, she would have found even more essentials to fill that too.

James was noticing they were creeping up on the rear bumper of a little sedan in front of them and started reaching for the phantom brake pedal again just as Carol veered around it and into the passing lane. He visibly relaxed in his seat.

"What?" said Carol without showing any real concern. "Oh, come on! That wasn't even close!" she continued when she saw James's response.

"That little lever on the left side of the wheel in your hands activates something called a turn signal, sometimes called a blinker, Honey, remember?" James said trying to feign being serious. "You are supposed to use it when you're driving. So, humor me and the other people on the road and let us know what you are planning to do?" He could see he had gotten to Carol and started chuckling, thinking himself very clever.

"I'm a good driver James Day!" Carol said in her best hurt voice. "I just need some practice." She began to smile.

They continued bantering as they passed over the Thames River Bridge in New London and James thought about the newspaper archives he needed to find. Before long, they would be at the Lexus dealership, picking up the rental car they had left there the night before. From the dealership, they would head for their apartment and unload the SUV. They would leave the rental car there and drive to the Stonington library for their one o'clock meeting with Ellen Perry.

The Stonington Free Library was an edifice that had been constructed by the town in 1914, as was proudly proclaimed by a carving of that date in the lintel over the front door. Built of dressed native stone, it was a substantial structure. An extension built in more recent times on the rear of the original structure took nothing away from its impressive appearance.

The information and circulation counter stood immediately inside the front door slightly to one side. Ellen Perry usually sat near the door behind the counter so she could be sure to monitor books that might be leaving without having been checked out. The flow of people in and out of her library here in Stonington was miniscule in comparison to what she had experienced when working at Yale. Most were regulars who were always greeted with a friendly smile and hello. It was unusual to see strangers coming into such a small library. So, when a younger couple entered that Ellen Perry did not recognize as the clock above the door read precisely one o'clock, Ellen Perry could assume with a good deal of assurance that this was Carol Day and her husband.

The young woman approached the information desk smiling as she approached.

"I'm looking for Ellen Perry," she said softly.

"You've found her," Ellen replied returning a smile. "You must be Mrs. Day?"

"Is there somewhere a little more private where we could speak?" Carol asked in her best library voice.

Ellen nodded and walked to the other end of the counter where another woman was quietly reading in a chair. Ellen leaned over and whispered something to the woman, and she nodded. Ellen looked up at

Carol and James and smiled. Ellen stepped out from behind the counter and waggled a finger in the direction she wanted them to follow. She led them to the door of a small room. Ellen looked through the pane of glass set in the door to make sure the room was vacant then quietly swung the door open for Carol and James. The room was very small, perhaps eight feet square, and had a small wooden table and four chairs spread around it. As the door slowly closed and latched, Carol sat in a chair on one side of the table. James sat in a chair against the wall to Carol's right. Ellen Perry sat in the chair opposite Carol at the table. Carol reached for the bag she was carrying and placed Ellen Perry's "brief history" on the table between them. Ellen smiled at the sight of it.

"Where did you happen upon this?" Ellen said. "I wrote this several years ago when I first retired and moved to Rock Cove. Other than the copy here in the library and the few I still have; I don't think I know of another copy." Ellen touched the cover with her fingers.

"Ms. Perry, we have purchased the old Carlisle estate," Carol began, choosing her words carefully, "So, we are curious about what is going to be our new home here in Rock Cove."

"Well, I guess it's normal to want to know the history of an area you're going to live in," Ellen said looking up at Carol.

"Well, I thought it was very well written," Carol said in a complimentary tone. "I think you did a wonderful job of explaining the early history of Rock Cove. But I did have one question," Carol held a note of puzzlement in her voice and her face.

James was impressed by Carol's tact.

Carol turned the book around and began turning to the page where she had placed the paper marker. She opened it and turned it for Ellen Perry to see. It was the page with the picture of Mr. and Mrs. Carlisle by their motorcar.

"I'm not sure you understood what I meant earlier," Carol said. "I want to know about the Carlisle mansion. Specifically, what happened there in 1927".

Ellen Perry visibly stiffened.

"I'm not sure I know what you mean, Mrs. Day," Ellen stammered slightly. "There was a tragedy as I have said."

"We know the Carlisle's daughter, Becky, was murdered by Mrs. Stanhope on her wedding day," James said, thinking he could ease Ms. Perry's concerns by telling her something of what they already knew. "We know that Sophia Stanhope committed suicide the same day."

"We have also been told that Mrs. Stanhope threw herself off the cliffs after she killed Becky," Carol said anxiously, "and it was all over some fake baron. No one even seems to know what happened to him."

"Well, it seems you have most of the story as it has been passed down over the years," Ellen said with a shrug. "What did you expect me to add?"

"We think when you were writing your manuscript, the research you did, told you something more about that day." Carol leaned lower toward the table. "Please Ms. Perry, please tell us. It's going to be our home."

Ellen Perry looked with kindness into Carol Day's eyes.

"I don't really have anything but a few unexplained questions of my own," she said sweetly to Carol. "I can have you meet one source I found interesting when I was researching. She had some strange things to relate, but I couldn't substantiate any of what she told me, so, I just glossed things over in the writing. If you'd like I can arrange for her to meet us here. I work here again on Thursday."

"That would be wonderful!" Carol smiled excitedly. "Should we plan to meet about the same time?"

"I think so," Ellen replied. "Was there anything else I could help you with?"

"Where would I find the archives of a newspaper that is no longer in print?" James suddenly said from his seat.

"What was its name?" Ellen asked, now assuming her librarian's voice.

"The *New London Times*," James replied.

"Let me see what I can find out. Would I be wrong if I guessed you wanted editions from August 1927?" Ellen said smiling at James.

Carol and James came out of the library into the bright sunlight feeling ebullient. Everything seemed to be moving so quickly. They felt they were getting closer to answering most of their questions about the history of the mansion and its saddest day. It was time to finalize the sale and move ahead. Their next stop should have been to Linda Giuliani's office to arrange the closing on the Carlisle property. James did not want to be carrying the check in his pocket any longer than was necessary. Besides that, they had already hired Paul Murray to begin cleaning on Friday.

James pulled out his phone and dialed Linda's office number. After a few rings, it went to voicemail. James left a short message to tell Linda they had been to New York overnight and were back in Rock Cove and he wanted her to arrange the closing with Attorney Beckwith. He finished by asking her to call him when she got his message.

His next call was to Attorney Beckwith's office. After a single ring, the phone was answered by a clear, matronly voice announcing the attorney's office had been reached. James asked to speak with Mr. Beckwith and was informed that he had called in sick for the day. He left a message with the secretary to tell Mr. Beckwith he wanted to schedule the closing as soon as possible and definitely by Friday. After being assured the message would be delivered just as soon as he came in, James thanked the voice on the phone and hung up. James turned to Carol.

"Well, it seems everyone is MIA. What would you like to do?"

"Can we go out to the house?" Carol said expectantly.

James pulled away from the curb and started driving to the mansion. As they drove along, Carol started feeling better and better about the house they would turn into a home. It certainly was not the fault of the house that its history was marred by the events that occurred within it. The people who perpetrated those actions were certainly at fault and, in any event, they were long gone.

"Do you think houses have souls?" Carol suddenly asked James. "I mean, do you think houses pick up the feelings of events that happen in them?"

The question took James by surprise. "I never really thought about it," he replied, uncertain what Carol was thinking.

"Do you think they can heal like people do?"

"Well, I suppose so," James said. He was stealing glances at Carol trying to figure out why she was asking these questions. "If what you are thinking is true, the mansion has had a lot of years to heal, Honey."

"It was just a silly thought," Carol said as she turned to the window and was lost in her thoughts again.

It was not long before they saw the gateposts come into view at the entrance to the estate. James slowed down the SUV and turned into the drive. The "For Sale" sign next to the gatepost was now covered with a diagonal "SOLD!" sign. James tried to remember if there had even been a sign there when they had first come to the estate. He smiled at his inability to remember and began driving up the driveway. As they rounded the last curve of the driveway and the house came into view, James was surprised to see a white utility van parked on the part of the driveway that led to the garage. Across the back doors was lettered: Paul Murray Renovations.

On the near side of the house, James saw Ben Allen standing at the edge of the driveway circle in front of the house motioning to him. He stopped the Lexus next to Ben and rolled down the window.

"I was just going to call you," Ben said leaning toward the window slightly. "I was down by the water and when I walked back to the house, I saw the van and this guy walking around the house. He says you hired his firm to clean the house?"

"Yes, we did, Ben," James said sheepishly. "I should have called to let you know. But, he wasn't supposed to start until Friday."

"Oh, he hasn't done anything yet. He's just been taking some measurements and pictures of the outside," Ben said reassuringly.

Ben stepped back from the car as James opened the driver's door. Carol had gotten out of the passenger side and the three of them began walking around the front of the house. They found Paul Murray, digital camera in hand, taking pictures of the exteriors of the house.

"Hi, Mr. and Mrs. Day," Paul said brightly as they appeared from around the corner of the house. "I hope it was alright to come out and take some pictures. Never been here before and you were right. It's a beautiful Victorian." Paul's demeanor made it clear he was excited about the house. "Any chance I can get inside for a few minutes? I tried to find the original floor plans at the Town Hall this morning, but they don't have them."

"We don't have the keys yet, Paul," James replied with chagrin.

"But we were inside just the other day, Mr. Murray," Carol volunteered. "I can give you an idea of the rooms."

"Well, with the measurements I've taken and the pictures I've taken, if you can tell me how the rooms are laid out, I can probably come close enough to a floor plan to start working on any changes you want to talk about making," Paul Murray said smiling at Carol. "Let's go to the truck. I've got some graph paper there we can use."

Carol and Paul turned toward the van and continued talking enthusiastically as they walked away from Ben and James.

"I think we're going to close on the house tomorrow, Ben." James said. "Then, you'll be officially on the payroll."

"Mr. D..., I mean, Jim," Ben caught himself, "I'll do anything you ask me to as long as it isn't illegal." Ben smiled his broadest smile and shook hands with James."

James shook Ben's hand thinking to himself how odd it was for the caretaker to use a phrase like that.

"All I ask of you, Ben, is to always tell us the truth."

James and Ben walked around the front of the house and continued to talk about the property; what had been done recently, what still needed to be done before winter, anything Ben needed to get in the way of tools or supplies. James confirmed with Ben that Paul Murray would be starting the cleaning job on Friday if the closing on the property could be done on Wednesday. He asked Ben to lend Paul's crew any assistance he was asked to provide. James could see from the look on Ben's face something was bothering him.

"Jim," he finally asked, "does that include going inside the house?"

James could read the concern in Ben's face, the nervous fidgeting in his demeanor.

"Is that still a problem for you, Ben?" James asked with understanding. "Mrs. Carlisle hasn't been here for a very long time. Her rules are no longer in effect. I expect you to feel free to be in the house during the cleaning and renovations and I suspect you will be needed, as well."

Ben nodded his agreement. "Okay, Jim. It may take me a while to get comfortable about that. I've been around her a very long time, but not inside. You probably have a better understanding of the inside layout than I do right now, but I know every inch of the outside of this lady." Ben looked up at the front of the mansion with a smile of appreciation on his weathered face.

TWELVE

IN THE CENTER OF THE ROOM THAT PASSED FOR the living room of their rented apartment was a pile of duffle bags, gym bags, suitcases, and the other "essentials" packed in a couple of plastic bins that Carol had confiscated from the New York apartment. James looked at the pile and started hefting the bags into their bedroom. The bedroom was large and had plenty of bureau drawers and a large walk-in closet that James was sure would still not accommodate all of Carol's clothes. She did love her clothes. He staked his claim to the drawers of the smaller of the two bureaus for his clothes.

Meanwhile, Carol was starting to put away the few groceries they had purchased at the small market in Rock Cove on the way to their apartment. The bare essentials of milk, coffee, eggs, bread, cereal, sugar, etc., were not going to make a dinner tonight, but breakfast would be possible.

After a half hour of putting away clothes, checking what pots and pans were available in the kitchen, and setting up their laptops, Carol and James headed to the Dogwatch Café for another good dinner. Their day had been long and interesting. In fact, everything that had happened over the last two days had been exciting. Now, they just wanted a few minutes to relax and talk while enjoying a quiet meal.

Even though their meals were delicious, it was impossible to keep the events of the day out of their conversation. James wondered what Ellen Perry had up her sleeve. She seemed to know so much more than what she was telling. Carol was excited about her conversation with Paul Murray. They had spent a good half hour together in his van making sketches and discussing possible changes.

"Paul thought we could take the bedroom behind the master and turn that into a bigger dressing room and bigger closets and would let us put a Jacuzzi in an enlarged bathroom, and still add some more footage to the bedroom, itself," Carol was blithering on. "Oh, and for the third floor? We could rebuild the rooms up there and make them much more functional, maybe add a guest suite, and we could each have our own office space, connected if you want." Carol gave James a kittenish smile. "Oh, and in the basement? Paul said, depending on what he finds when he gets there, we might be able to put a sauna and hot tub there and a wine cellar and wet bar. Turn it into a regular party room for when we have our friends visit from New York."

James was listening while his brain kept track of the numbers that were quickly adding up in his head. They made good money and they had saved heavily for the last five years, but there was a limit. It wasn't like they needed to make the changes all at once, anyway, and, if he let Carol look at all the changes she wanted to make, at least he would know how much total money it would take to make his wife happy in their new home. He still did not understand he was the one thing that would make her happiest. If she could just get him to express his affection for her....

It was getting late, and James had not yet heard from either attorney Beckwith or Linda Giuliani. There was certainly plenty of time to contact them in the morning and arrange the closing. For tonight, James just wanted to settle in the apartment. Even though he could feel tiredness creeping over him, Carol was strangely energized and excited. James finished his coffee and placed the car keys on the table in front of Carol.

"Your turn to drive tonight," he said to her just as a yawn contorted his face.

The aromas of fresh coffee and toast permeated the air of the bedroom. Carol thought she was going to be sick to her stomach again. She had been up in the night losing her dinner. James had awakened to find his wife bent over the toilet; her body being shaken by the heaving spasms. It was at times like this that James realized how helpless one could feel. There was nothing he could do for her except put his hand on her forehead and try to calm her with his voice. When the involuntary spasms finally stopped, James had gotten her back to bed and cleaned up the little mess left in the bathroom. He couldn't help thinking if his new landlords might have heard the commotion in the night and what they might now be thinking of renting to this youngish couple from New York.

Carol felt the side of the bed slowly depress and the smell of coffee became stronger, and she felt her stomach roll.

"Good morning, sleepy," James's voice was soft and warm. "Got some coffee for you."

Carol pulled the covers off her face and turned her head to see her husband sitting on the edge of the bed holding a steaming cup toward her. The picture of her husband sitting there made Carol realize just how much she loved this man and how important he was to her. She sat up and put her arms around his neck and hugged him.

James moved his hand with the coffee cup to the side to avoid Carol's lunge. "Hey, hey!" he said gently. "Careful of the coffee, Sweetie."

After a few moments, Carol released her grip and took the coffee cup from James's hand.

"You must be feeling better this morning," James said looking at his wife with a little smile. "You sure ate a bad "something" last night. I'm calling the Dogwatch today to let them know."

"I don't know what it was. Maybe one of the clams, although they tasted alright," Carol said as she blew across the top of her coffee cup and took a small sip.

"Feel like some breakfast?" James asked. "Toast is made, and I can fry up an egg for you in a minute, if you'd like?"

Carol was taking another sip of her coffee. She handed the cup to James and threw back the covers on the bed. "Okay," she said. "Just let me brush my teeth."

Breakfast had been simple fare, quickly prepared and quickly consumed. A phone call from Linda Giuliani had propelled the Days through dressing and getting on the road. She had reached Attorney Beckwith and arranged a meeting to close on the property at eleven. Since her call was received at nine-thirty, they did not have a lot of time to play lovingly, which Carol appeared very inclined to do this morning. James knew it would take them a good fifteen minutes to get to Beckwith's office and he did not want to be late.

As they were driving to the meeting, Carol's phone rang. It was Paul Murray asking if they had time that afternoon to stop by his shop. Carol told him they were on the way to close on the property, and they would be able to stop by after that. As she hung up, Carol looked at James with affection.

"He said he has some preliminary designs ready," Carol said, hardly able to contain her excitement.

James pulled the SUV to the curb in front of Attorney Beckwith's office and parked behind a car they both recognized: Linda Giuliani's Mercedes. Carol's excitement was beginning to infect James. They fairly bounced up the walk and opened the office door.

The same secretary they had seen on their last visit was sitting at her desk intently looking at something on her computer screen. She glanced up from the screen and smiled at the Days.

"Go right in," she said pointing toward the hall. "They're waiting for you. I'm just downloading some forms."

James and Carol both returned her smile and walked down the hall to find Linda seated at the small conference table across the room from the attorney, who was sitting at his desk. Linda was busily removing papers from her briefcase and arranging them in front of her. The attorney was reading several sheets of paper he was holding in his hands. Both of them looked up when Carol and James entered the office.

Good morning," Stanley Beckwith said cheerfully. "I guess today's a big day for the two of you."

James crossed to the desk and extended his arm to reach the attorney's extended hand. Carol approached the table where Linda was seated.

Linda looked at Carol as she approached and gently touched her forearm. "Are you excited," she said softly. Carol smiled broadly and nodded enthusiastically in the affirmative. Linda looked beyond Carol and said to Beckwith and James," Why don't we get started on these papers"?

Carol took the seat to Linda's left and James sat next to Carol. As Linda presented each form in her stack, she explained its purpose and the reason it needed to be signed. Anyone who has purchased a house would not have seen anything unusual in the blizzard of forms, but Carol was feeling overwhelmed, and James was slowing the process down by reading every paragraph. This was a new experience for him, and he wanted to understand everything that was involved. It demonstrated to everyone that he was new to this, and, besides that, it was his nature to read everything before he signed it. To fill in the boring stretches of time while James was reading, Carol and Linda talked. Stanley Beckwith sat quietly looking out the window appearing lost in thought, but, actually, listening to every word intently.

The closing could have taken less than an hour, but James's overly thorough inspection of all the papers dragged it out nearly forty-five minutes over that. Linda and Carol had covered every subject from James' and Carol's background, which they had spoken about before, their careers since college, their plans for the house, the changes they were talking about with Paul Murray, their hopes to start a family, their dreams for the future. It was just a light, happy conversation. The only time Stanley Beckwith seemed to take an interest in what was being said was when Carol was talking about the renovations she wanted to make to the house.

"Are you planning to change the exterior?" Attorney Beckwith asked.

"We're hoping to keep the outside just as it is," Carol replied. "We love the look of the house and Ben Allen has really done a wonderful job of taking care of it. Paul thinks we can do what we want without changing anything on the exterior."

At the mention of Ben Allen's name, Stanley Beckwith returned to silence. James finished his review of the final form and signed the bottom of the last page. He reached into the inside pocket of the sport jacket he was wearing and removed the check from his bank in New York.

Linda gathered the last of the forms and presented Attorney Beckwith with a copy of each and the check that she retrieved from the table. Attorney Beckwith smiled at James and Carol and shook hands with them.

"I congratulate you both on making an excellent purchase," Stanley Beckwith said somewhat somberly. "I have had the responsibility for this property my entire professional life, as did my father before me. You'll pardon me if I am a bit melancholy over its sale, but it is also a relief. I feel the two of you will bring the property back to being a wonderful home and a happy place after all these years."

Carol sat in the car looking at the keys to the Carlisle mansion that she held in the palm of her hand. Stanley Beckwith had handed them to her with no small amount of ceremony. There were six keys on a ring. She was immediately curious as to what doors they opened. She couldn't wait to try them.

James was driving to Paul Murray's shop in Pawcatuck. He was looking at Carol caressing the keys in her hand almost reverently. "A penny for your thoughts?" he said.

"You know," she said still looking at the keys, "it isn't the Carlisle estate any longer. It belongs to us now." She sounded almost contrite.

"We don't have to change the name, you know," James said. "I think the 'Carlisle Estate' is not only historically accurate, but it has a ring to it. It sounds almost regal." James straightened his posture to add a comic accentuation to his comment.

It was not long before they were parking in Paul Murray's lot and stepping through his front door. The office was humming with activity unlike the last time they had been there. Paul was bent over one of the large design tables toward the back of the shop actively engaged in conversation with one of his draftsmen. The woman behind the counter greeted them with a smile. Paul looked up at the sound of the bell ringing from the opening of the door, as did everyone else. He made a motion with his head of acknowledgement and exchanged a few last words with his associate and came forward.

"Hello there, "Paul said excitedly. "I have something to show you." He opened the gate next to the counter and ushered them to another table in the office. There, he unfolded some blueprints.

"I got back to the office yesterday and just decided to see what I could do, design-wise with what we discussed yesterday," Paul said looking at Carol. "Now, realize that I will need to verify some of the measurements and see where the load bearing walls are situated, but I think we can pretty much plan on being able to make these changes."

He proceeded to review the design changes he had drawn floor by floor. Carol was ecstatic. James was impressed. James could see where the bedroom space lost on the second floor by expanding the master bedroom into a full suite could be more than made up for by adding a bedroom on the third floor. It would reduce the amount of storage area in the attic space, but Paul was pretty sure they would find unfinished space in the basement that could be used to replace it.

As Paul pulled out the blueprints he had drawn of the first floor, he showed Carol how he had redesigned the kitchen area. He had opened the wall of the butler's pantry into the main area of the kitchen. By doing so, he added twelve square feet of floor space to the end of the kitchen, and he could rearrange the appliances to accommodate a double refrigerator. The back stairs would now open directly into the kitchen instead of the small butler's pantry.

James noticed another page of blueprint set to one side. He picked it up and started looking at it.

"That's my plan for the garage," Paul commented, seeing James looking at the design. "As an alternative to using the third floor for office space, I think you could have the offices above the garages. It might make it a bit more of a business setting for you."

"I kind of like that idea," James said, "but, we haven't even been up there yet."

"If you decided not to put your offices there, we could make it into a sort of guest house or apartment for rental," Paul continued.

"It's something to consider," Carol said.

"Overall, what did you think of the house?" said James beginning to feel the pride of ownership.

"I think it's in great condition from what I saw," Paul Murray replied, "although… there was one curious thing I noticed." Paul furrowed his brow slightly and waved his finger in the air trying to remember exactly what it was. He reached into the drawer under the table and retrieved the digital photographs he had taken the day before. He spread them on the table.

"I suppose it's nothing, but I just happened to notice something that I thought was odd," he continues as he looked through the photographs and drew two together. He placed them side by side. Carol and James looked over Paul Murray's shoulders at the two pictures of two sides of the mansion. They saw nothing in the two pictures and looked at each other with a blank stare. Paul looked at the two of them and realized they had no understanding of what he saw.

"It's the window," Paul finally said. "There's a window missing. Well, I say it's missing. It may never have been there." Paul pointed to one of the pictures. "But, still, to an architect's eye, there should be a window right there, just like the one on the opposite side of the house. It would balance the wall. See? It's just me, but had I designed this house, I would have put a window there."

"Is that important?" Carol asked.

"No, not at all," Paul replied. "It just struck me as odd because Victorians are notorious for symmetry."

"Well, since we're going to be redesigning the attic, would there be a problem to put a window there?" James asked.

THIRTEEN

IT WAS STILL DARK WHEN JAMES WAS AWAKENED with a soft kiss on his ear. At first, he thought it was his imagination, but then he felt a warm breath on his ear, as well.

"Are you ready to get up, Sleepy," Carol whispered in his ear.

They had left Paul Murray's office late in the afternoon after reviewing all the blueprints and confirming with Paul that his cleaning crew would begin work on Friday. James and Carol had stopped at a liquor store after leaving the architect and purchased a bottle of Cristal. They could not decide whether to try to get to the Estate - their Estate - before the sun set to have a toast to their new home or wait for tomorrow morning and watch the sunrise from the front porch. When it became obvious the sun would set before they could reach the mansion, they laughed about it and laughed even harder talking about getting to the mansion before the sun rose. James had thought, at least, Carol had been joking.

"Come on, you," he heard Carol say, "the champagne has been in the fridge all night and we can still beat the sun. Don't you want to toast our new home with the sunrise?"

James suddenly realized that not only was Carol awake, but she was also already dressed! He threw off the covers and felt the chill morning air of the room attack his body. He raced into the bathroom and quickly shaved and brushed his teeth. He threw on jeans and a heavy flannel shirt and began to feel his body begin to warm. Carol was sitting in the one upholstered chair they had in the main room, waiting. She was dressed in boots and a heavy sweater with a high ruffed collar. In her arms she cradled the bottle of Cristal champagne. James quickly donned his coat and turned to Carol.

"As you commanded, my dear," he said in his best butler voice and motioned to the door.

The headlights outlined both sides of the lane leading to the estate. When they picked up the gate posts, James swung the car between them and slowly drove up the driveway – their driveway. It felt good.

The faintest glow was beginning in the eastern sky as James and Carol settled themselves at the top of the front steps. James sat on the porch with Carol seated on the step below between his spread knees. He opened the bottle of champagne and filled the two plastic cups they had brought with them. It wasn't elegant, but who really cared? Carol raised her cup and James gently touched his cup to it. Carol said, "Clink!" and they each took a sip.

The sparkling wine felt cool and refreshing as Carol leaned back against James's leg. She could feel the wine all the way to her stomach. The first discernible lightening of the eastern sky made everything around them barely visible in shades of gray, their outlines barely discernible. They watched the eastern sky change from those same colorless shades of gray to red and then into orange and yellow as the sun rose. They sat holding hands, saying little, and just enjoying the sounds and the sight. As the sky lit up, the color of the water beyond the lawn changed from slate gray through shades of blue to wintry green, the white caps setting off the crests of the waves.

Before they realized it, the time had flown by, and the sun was fully up. They had finished their bottle of champagne and were just enjoying each other's company in the growing warmth of the sun. As they were getting ready to leave, they both heard the faint sound of loose stones shifting under the weight of footfalls.

Ben Allen rounded the corner of the house and smiled at his new employers sitting on the steps of the staircase.

"Morning, folks," Ben said touching the brim of his baseball cap. "Beautiful morning, isn't it?"

"Yes, it is, Mr. Allen," Carol called back to him against the slight wind coming off the water.

"I wasn't expecting to see anyone here so early," Ben said snugging his cap on a little tighter against the freshening wind.

"We watched the sun come up," James said, "and we have a full day ahead of us."

Carol turned to James and said, "But, first …." She smiled and jangled the house keys in front of James.

She put her hand on the edge of the porch to help her stand and stepped up on the porch. She started examining the keys. "Which one do you think opens the front door, James?" she said puzzled.

James looked at the door and saw the lock was a Yale deadbolt. He took the keys from Carol and singled out the one Yale key on the ring. He slid it into the keyhole and easily threw back the bolt. He looked at Carol and gently pushed open the door with his arm. Carol just stood beside him in front of the door.

"Well?" she finally said.

"Well, what?" James looked at her uncomprehendingly.

"Aren't you going to carry me over the threshold?" Carol said as she placed her hands on her hips.

"Oh, oh… sorry," James said finally and, putting the ring of keys in his pocket, he put one arm around Carol's back and the other behind her knees and scooped her up in his arms in one complete motion. He carried her through the doorway and dropped her feet on the dust-laden floor of the hall. Carol had her arms around James's neck as he carried her, and she kissed him deeply on the lips when he let her legs down. She felt him return her kiss.

They stood embracing for a moment, happy to be together then they looked around. They could see where their footsteps had disturbed the layered dust on their previous visit. The air in the house was warmer than the air outside and still slightly stale.

"Shall we try the back door?" Carol said with quiet excitement to James. He nodded in agreement. Carol put her hand into James's coat pocket and retrieved the ring of keys.

She started to follow the footsteps that had already marred the even layer of dust from a few days before, trying to step only in the previous footsteps so no new tracks were evident. James just looked at what she was doing and realized how silly it was and, yet, it was what endeared her to him. Her attempt to make no new steps made her walk with a wiggle that James was enjoying watching, until Carol turned and saw him admiring her.

"You try it," she said to him.

"Why," he replied. "It's all getting cleaned starting tomorrow." James started walking toward the kitchen making fresh footsteps and without regard for the footsteps already marking the floor. He plucked the keys from Carol's fingers as he passed her. Carol gave up trying to follow the old shoe prints and followed James making a new set of tracks.

It took Carol two attempts to locate the right key for the back door in the kitchen. Unlike the front door, the hinges creaked slightly when she opened it. It led into a small entryway where a door led down to the cellar and a door led out toward the garage. One of the keys opened the cellar door; one opened the outer back door. As they walked around the first floor, they discovered another door leading to the basement under the front staircase. When they could find no more doors with locks in the house, they locked up the house and headed for the garage.

It was really the first time they had even thought about the garage. It was far more than just a place for automobiles. Its size alone nearly qualified it as a barn. Above the three double-door bays for cars were full sized windows, well-spaced and attractive; not the sort of windows you would find in a normal garage. As they walked down the path to the front of the structure, they approached the door to the left of the garage bays that led to the upper floor. Carol took the last two keys they had found no lock for and tried the first one. It didn't open the lock. She pushed the last key into the lock and turned it.

Carol and James were unprepared for the stairs that came into view behind the door. They were finished hardwood and wide. They looked far too elegant to be leading to the second floor of a garage. Carol and James climbed the flight of stairs to a small, enclosed porch at the top. It faced to the south and would have been warm even on the coldest fall day. They opened the door leading inside and were suddenly in a very large room. It was as wide as the building and half its depth. Against the far wall stood a fireplace of rounded native boulders with a wide mantel of wood with the same finish as the stairs. The hearth was raised with large andirons inside an oversized firebox.

The windows made the entire room bright. Unlike the furniture in the house, there were no covers to be seen on anything. The furniture was much more rustic, lodge-like in appearance. A large couch and three chairs were placed around a large coffee table in front of the fireplace. A small kitchen area was in one corner of the rear wall. Carol was taking in what she was seeing when it suddenly hit here. She turned to James.

"Where's the dust?" She said, looking at James. "Honey? There's no dust anywhere! Someone's been living in here."

She was standing across the room from James when a door in the middle of the back wall opened and Ben Allen stepped into the room. He stopped abruptly in mid-step when he saw first James and then Carol standing there.

"So, is this why you're always around?" James asked suddenly, realizing that he had never seen a vehicle of any kind when he had seen Ben.

"How long have you been living here?" Carol asked.

"Mr. Beckwith allowed me to stay here since my mother passed," Ben replied, removing his cap and looking more like the little boy caught doing something bad. "I'll move out if you want me to."

"It isn't that," James said. "You just didn't tell us."

"You never asked me," Ben said straightening his frame and squaring his shoulders.

"How long have you been living here, Ben?" Carol asked calmly.

"Almost twenty years, Mrs. Day," Ben answered quietly. "My mother died in 1990 at 83. I took care of her after she started having strokes and when the last one got her, I didn't really want to stay in her house anymore." Ben dropped his head on his chest and took a deep breath. "Mr. Beckwith took care of things for me and said I could clean up the garage and stay here."

Carol looked at James and saw the initial flash of anger he had displayed had disappeared. She liked Ben Allen, this man who had lived his entire life caring for a property that was not even his own. She could tell that his needs were few and his tastes simple based on the furnishings she saw. She caught James looking at her.

"Ben, since you're the caretaker now, officially, you can stay as long as you want," James said. "I think we'll need to spruce things up a bit for you, though," he continued with a little smile.

"Mr. Beckwith said that there were boxes of Mrs. Carlisle's personal things that had been brought up here when the house was closed up," Carol said, suddenly remembering about the boxes.

"They're here," Ben said reanimated by James's kind words. He walked over to a door leading into a closet and showed Carol six rows of boxes piled four and five high against the back wall of the closet. "No one's touched them since I put them here in 1971. I didn't pack them. I just put them here."

James looked at his watch. "Honey, we need to get going," he said tapping his watch as he showed it to Carol and Ben. "We need to get some keys made before we get to Stonington."

Carol looked at Ben. "I think it's time you have a key to the front door of your apartment," she said smiling at him. Ben smiled back.

"Yes Ma'am. I had one once."

Carol and James talked about their discovery of Ben's living arrangements on the way to Stonington. They felt that Stanley Beckwith should have divulged Ben's residency before the closing. James called Linda from the car and left a message for her when she did not answer. Although it was a surprise, Carol was really alright with Ben being there. It was probably what had kept the estate inviolate over the years. Vandalism is less likely to occur when a place is occupied.

James was more concerned about what the expense was to have Ben Allen living on the estate. When Linda returned his call, he needed to know if the power service to the property split the garage from the main house. He wanted to know from Linda if she had been aware of Attorney Beckwith's largesse. Even though Carol may have accepted Ben Allen's continuing to live over the garage, James was not completely in agreement – yet.

"I had no idea he had been living on the property," Linda said with surprise when she returned James's call a minute or two later. "I don't know about the electrical service, but I will certainly find out for you."

As they arrived in Stonington, James spotted a hardware store. He parked at the curb in the front of the store and jingled the ring of house keys at Carol. She understood he was going to have some keys made. Across the street was a Dunkin Donuts, the coffee Mecca of New England.

"I'll get us some coffee and meet you inside," Carol said, as she started walking around the front of the car to cross the street. As she passed James, he caught her in his arm and gave her a quick kiss that caught her off guard. He smiled at her as he pulled away, crossed the sidewalk, and entered the hardware store. She stared after him for a moment thinking how different he was when he was out of New York. Carol regained her equilibrium, checked for traffic, and crossed the street to the coffee shop.

It only took a few minutes to have three sets of keys made up and an extra front door, back door, and cellar key for Paul Murray. Carol had come into the hardware store halfway through the process. She had given James his coffee and was wandering around the store not really looking for anything.

This was not one of the large national chain stores that seemed to be everywhere today. This was an old-style country hardware store with wooden bins filled with hundreds of nails instead of little plastic packages containing only a few. Wooden bins, edges worn smooth from years of hands and arms running over them to remove what they contained, lined the walls. There were sets of tools out for display you could actually pick up and grip that were not zip-tied to a display board. The mingled smells of wood, leather, and something like lubricating oil and metal filled the store. You just didn't find that in the big, impersonal outlets.

James came up to Carol as she stood drinking in the odors of the store and held out a set of keys on a brand new ring with a brass disk on it. The disk read: My Home.

Carol smiled at James and put her arms around his shoulders and hugged him. James thanked the man who had made the keys as the two of them slipped out the door into the cool air of the street. He smiled broadly at the young couple.

They were only a few blocks from the library, and it was just past noon. James knew they needed to get a set of keys to Paul Murray in order for him to begin work Friday. It would be close, but he felt they could make the round trip to Pawcatuck and be back at the library by one. The couple crossed the street hand-in-hand and hopped into the car. Carol was exhilarated as they pulled out from the curb and headed for Murray Renovations. She could feel the man she had fallen in love with returning to her.

They were driving along sipping their coffees, talking about nothing of importance, and Carol was once again thumbing through Ellen Perry's *"Brief History."*

"James? James! Oh, my God! JAMES!!" Carol virtually screamed. James hit the brake pedal and stopped as quickly as he could on the shoulder of the road.

"What is it, Honey?" He said, thinking Carol was suddenly ill or something.

"The picture," Carol said pointing at the picture of Mr. and Mrs. Carlisle they had both looked at fifty times before.

What about it?" He said puzzled and a bit angered.

"Look!" Carol said pointing at the picture with her finger. James suddenly saw it. There, next to her finger, on the third floor of the mansion, was a window, right where Paul Murray had said it should have been.

"Are you sure that's the right side of the house," James said looking closely at the picture.

"I'm positive," Carol said. "I have to show this to Paul. Let's get going!"

James reset himself behind the wheel and looked in his side mirror for traffic.

When the Days walked into the library, Ellen Perry was nowhere in sight. The woman who had been sitting with her on Tuesday looked up from the same seat she had been in then and told the Carol and James that Ellen was waiting for them in the conference room. Carol thanked her and they walked toward the meeting room.

Carol looked through the glass panel in the door and recognized Ellen Perry, who was sitting with an elderly man and a woman who appeared to be nearly as old. In response to Carol's light rap on the door, Ellen turned to look at the door and motioned for her to enter. The retired librarian greeted James and Carol warmly and proceeded to introduce them to the two people in the room.

"Carol and James, I would like you to meet Mary Shields," Ellen began. "Her maiden name was McCann. Her mother was Cassie McCann."

"Cassie?" Carol perked up at the name. "Mrs. Carlisle's housekeeper, Cassie?"

Mary Shields nodded with a slight smile dancing over her lips. She had the map of Ireland on her face, as they say. Her hair was more silver than gray, and she wore it longer than most women of her age. She was dressed casually, and neatly as rural people do. Carol shook her hand warmly, followed by James.

"And this is John Grant," Ellen continued. "He worked at the *New London Times* in his younger days."

James almost fell over. There were so many questions he had for this elderly gentleman.

Unlike many his age, John Grant was still a wiry, energetic man. He was dressed like a man who might be in his fifties with tailored pants and pocketed button-down shirt and highly polished loafers. James knew that John Grant had to be at least in his eighties if he had worked on the *New London Times*. It was evident that he was in full command of his faculties and capable of matching wits with anyone.

"It's a pleasure to meet you," James said enthusiastically.

"Same here," John Grant replied, nodding to Carol.

"I also have another surprise for you, James, if I may be so familiar," Ellen continued. "I called the New London Public Library and spoke with my good friends there. They sent over microfilm of the *New London Times* for the month of August and September 1927," she said somewhat proudly.

"Microfilm?" Carol said a bit puzzled.

"Yes," Ellen replied. "It was what they used before the internet and computers to preserve documents and things. It's still very popular with libraries and the Government. We have a machine for viewing it in another room."

"What can you tell me about the murder that occurred at the Carlisle Mansion?" James asked John Grant.

"Well, to be honest with you, I don't recall much about the murders," said the elderly newspaperman in a strong and commanding voice. I was only about fourteen when the murders happened."

"You said murders, plural?" Carol interjected.

"Well, that was always conjectured, if you ask me." John Grant leaned back in his chair stretching his legs out. For a man in his nineties, he was in excellent shape. "I was only a news runner in the copy room in 1927. Kids started working young back then. I read what I carried to the editors as much as I could, but more important to me was what I heard being said. It was a big story that year, the biggest locally, anyway. There was a lot that never made it to the papers. I'm not saying the police didn't do their job. Investigative techniques back then were pretty rudimentary. There were only a few witnesses as to what actually happened, and they had their stories pretty set."

James and Carol sat listening quietly. Questions were rapidly coming into James's thoughts.

"I thought you wanted to know about the trial," John Grant suddenly continued. "I was sixteen, almost seventeen when they tried Mrs. Carlisle."

Two jaws dropped open. Carol and James were taken completely by surprise.

"Wait... wait a minute," James said after a moment of recovery, "Mrs. Carlisle was put on trial?" Carol was suddenly feeling very confused, as was James. "For what?" Carol and James said almost in unison.

"Why, for murder," John Grant replied.

FOURTEEN

THE THUNDEROUS CRACK OF THE GUNSHOT seemed to echo about the house. Edith Carlisle was seated at her dressing table just touching up the last of her makeup when the sound of the shot made her jump in her seat. She knew that sound from her childhood. Her father had hunted in the woods not far from their home. Her husband had enjoyed shooting skeet on the lawn of the mansion until the local ordinances were changed to prevent such activity. It was a sound that seemed incredibly out of place.

She quickly stepped into the hall only to see a slight wafting of grayish smoke floating toward the ceiling and to hear the horrific screams of young women emanating from the back bedroom. The unmistakable odor of gunpowder entered her nose as she ran into the bedroom.

The sight of utter confusion and the terrified screams of the women temporarily blocked Edith's view of her daughter lying on the floor. As she pushed the milling girls out of her way, she knelt beside her daughter. Her daughter's eyes held no sparkle; the pupils fixed. As Edith gaped helplessly at her daughter's motionless form, a burgundy-colored pool began spreading into the carpet surrounding her.

The bridesmaids were now huddled in a far corner of the room. They were holding each other, whimpering, and crying. Edith Carlisle stood slowly; the front of her dress where she had been kneeling coated with her daughter's blood.

"Who did this!" she screamed at the group.

"It was Mrs. Stanhope," one of them replied meekly. The others echoed her reply.

"Where did she go?" Edith demanded, not realizing that none of them could answer her question. All they could do was point at the door of the room as a fresh wave of grief overcame the group. Edith Carlisle turned and left the room.

As she entered the hall, George Allen was just clearing the final steps of the staircase. He had heard the shot while standing on the front porch and knew it had come from inside the house. Although it had only been moments, it had seemed like forever for George to identify the source of the screams and begin mounting the stairs to the second floor two at a time.

He saw his employer leaning against the door frame with blood staining her dress.

"What's happened?" he cried out as he approached her.

She did not answer; could not answer. He could see the shock registering in her face. He swung his head around the open doorway and saw the body of Elisabeth lying on the floor surrounded by a blood-soaked carpet, the bridesmaids huddling in a group in the far corner. He called to the girls and motioned for them to come to him. Slowly, reluctantly at first, they began skirting the still form on the floor and with increasing speed left the room. When the last one had left, they were standing in the hall just milling about. George took one of them by the arm and pointed to another room at the front of the house.

"Go in there and take them all with you," he said in a stern voice looking directly into the girl's eyes. She nodded her understanding and began moving the group toward the other end of the hall. George turned back to Edith Carlisle.

"Ma'am? Mrs. Carlisle?" George was holding her by the arms trying to gain her attention. She looked at him with a vague empty stare.

"I will go get help," he finally said, not sure that his message was understood. He turned and bounded down the stairs as quickly as his legs would carry him.

Edith heard what her trusted grounds man had said, but comprehension came as if through a dense fog. As she stood leaning against the door frame, her eye caught something lying against the wall in the corner. It was a gun. Without thinking, she reached down and picked it up. She slowly turned it in her hand, numbly looked at the polished steel sheen, the engraved barrel. The sulfurous smell of gunpowder was attacking her sense of smell.

Through the fog of her grief, Edith suddenly became aware of the sound of someone quietly sobbing. The sound was not coming from the direction of the room the bride's maids had gone into, but from the other end of the hall. It was coming from the nursery. Edith tightened her hand on the grip of the gun and laid the barrel gently against the fingers of her other hand. She quickly dropped her hand away. The barrel was still warm. She dropped her arm to her side and quietly approached the closed door of the nursery. As she did, the sound of the crying grew louder. She noticed that the door was closed, but not latched. Edith stood quietly, listening intently at the door for what seemed like minutes, but, in fact, was seconds. She placed her hand against the center of the door and slowly pushed open the door.

In a corner of the room nearest the crib, crumbled on the floor, her body trembling under the sounds of sobs lay Constance Stanhope. Edith took a step or two into the room looking directly at her adversary, the gun still at her side. She saw the spatters of her daughter's blood on the Sleeve of Mrs. Stanhope's blouse.

The muzzle flash snapped Edith out of her disorientation.

FIFTEEN

JOHN GRANT SEEMED SURPRISED BY THE REACTION his reply drew from Carol and James. It was obvious to him and the others in the room that they had known nothing about a trial, and they were totally at a loss to understand it.

"I didn't realize you didn't know about the trial," John said leaning toward the table they were all sitting around. "I thought that was what you wanted to know about."

"We had no idea," James said still trying to absorb this latest information. "Who was she accused of murdering?" he finally said.

"We had a real young State Assistant DA at the time, and he saw the Carlisle tragedy as his career maker. The case had really gone cold, if there was a case at all, but this young fireball thought there was really something there. He kept it simmering for about two years. There were all sorts of open statements the police had and questions that nobody was answering. There were a lot of unsubstantiated accusations."

"How could they charge Mrs. Carlisle in the death of her daughter? That's insane," James said in disgust.

"Oh, they knew who killed Becky Carlisle. No question about that.

The bridesmaids saw Mrs. Stanhope enter the room, pull the gun out and fire. And the reasons for it were pretty clear once Sophia Stanhope's body was discovered. The medical examiner determined that Sophia had been dead for some time before Becky was killed. Mrs. Stanhope must have been out of her mind," John replied with assurance. "No, it wasn't for her daughter's murder they indicted her. It was for Mrs. Stanhope's murder and the Baron's."

"You mean she was accused of TWO murders?" Carol said in total disbelief.

"But I thought Mrs. Stanhope threw herself off the rocks and the Baron, the groom, the fake, whatever you want to call him, I thought he just disappeared, and no one ever saw him again," James said thoroughly confused. "But, no one ever said they were murdered!"

"It seems the only person who made the definite claim about Mrs. Stanhope going off the rocks was Mrs. Carlisle. She and her handyman were the only ones to say they saw her go off the cliff. Although there were several people who had been on the front lawn who claimed to see someone, a woman they thought, walk past them in blood-spattered riding clothes. Some even thought they saw a gun in the woman's hand. No one else remembered seeing that for sure. You know how unreliable eyewitness accounts can be. But there were lots of people who heard the additional gunfire in the house, and no one ever claimed to have seen the Baron after that." John Grant was speaking as clearly as one who had witnessed the incidents he was relating.

"I sat through the entire trial testimony. From the day that Assistant District Attorney got the grand jury to issue a formal accusation against Mrs. Carlisle to the end of the trial, the whole thing was a farce," John Grant said shaking his head. "It was really suicide for that ADA to go ahead with his case. He might have had a motive on the part of Mrs. Carlisle, but he had no witnesses, no murder weapon, and, most importantly, no bodies. His real motive for pursuing the case was his personal ambition."

"How could they indict without any of that?" James asked incredulously.

"It was the ambition of this guy from the DA's office. Like I said, he saw this as the case that was going to make his career and put him in his boss's chair. Too bad the rest of the world spoiled his parade," John smiled wryly. "The stock market crash happened two days into the trial. Nobody cared about a murder case when the country was going bankrupt. The case was so weak; it had holes all through it. The trial took less than a week and Mrs. Carlisle was found not guilty."

"So, she was acquitted," Carol said.

"That's right," the newspaperman said smiling at Carol, "on all counts. It took the jury less than two hours to return a verdict. The whole case was built on circumstantial evidence and innuendo. There was not a shred of solid evidence to say Mrs. Carlisle did anything. But it broke her spirit."

"What do you mean?" asked Carol.

Ellen Perry broke in to answer the question.

"She may not have been convicted in a court of law, but, in the court of public opinion, and particularly in her circle of society, she wasn't so lucky. She had broken the cardinal rule of her social class: avoid scandal. Mary can tell you what I mean. Her mother was there."

Mary slowly shook her head in affirmation. It was clear from her demeanor that she was not comfortable speaking about the subject. When she finally spoke, it was in a low, barely audible whisper.

"My mother worked for Mrs. Carlisle for close to forty years," she said. "It was very hard on her losing her daughter that way, but it was the trial that made her a social outcast. Her so-called society friends ran from her like she had the plague. No more visitors, no more dinner parties, and the invitations just stopped coming.

"My mother went to work for Mrs. Carlisle shortly after the trial ended. Mrs. Carlisle trusted my mother completely and my mother owed much to her. Mother never spoke about what went on in the mansion except rarely. Once we kids were grown and my father passed away, my mother lived in the mansion with Mrs. Carlisle. She would visit us irregularly, but always had to be back at the mansion before dark. Mrs. Carlisle didn't like to be alone after dark."

"What did your mother tell you when she did talk about the Mansion," Carol asked softly, trying to draw more out of Mary Shields. Mary looked at Ellen Perry almost asking with her eyes for reassurance. Ellen answered with a warm smile and a nod.

"She said that Mrs. Carlisle never left the house except to go out on the porch and once or twice to her attorneys. My mother occupied a room across the hall from hers once she was living there so she was always available. Mrs. Carlisle said the servants' quarters on the third floor were too far away and if my mother were needed in the night, being across the hall was better.

"She said that Mrs. Carlisle would take her lunch in her bedroom every day in front of her window looking out on the water and that she never spoke about her daughter." Mary Shields was having a hard time keeping her composure. "My mother said there were times she heard crying in the house and, looking for its source, would quietly steal upstairs, and, occasionally, she would catch Mrs. Carlisle descending from the third floor when she thought she was not seen. My mother knew Mrs. Carlisle as a warm, but very lonely, person. The rest of the world saw her as a cold and austere old woman."

"Why the third floor?" asked Carol.

"That was where her daughter was dressing when she was killed, I was told," Mary answered looking wide eyed at Carol. "My mother said Mrs. Carlisle was once approached by her attorney to sell the property and she almost threw him out of the house. She was adamant about staying in her home. She told my mother the house had a spirit she had to watch over. It was the only place she felt safe. My mother felt it was the only place where Mrs. Carlisle could still remember her daughter. She once told my mother she knew people thought she was guilty of something, and she could be ostracized here as well as anywhere."

"Tell them what happened toward the end," Ellen Perry said looking at Mary sympathetically.

"One day, not long before she was taken away, my mother said, Mrs. Carlisle came out on the porch and told her that she was finally at peace and smiled for the first time in years. My mother thought Mrs. Carlisle had been slipping a little for some time by then and was becoming physically impaired. Of course, my mother had grown old as well and was not in good health herself. Here they were, these two old women, living in this big house, one totally relying on the other, who was no longer capable of caring for herself, let alone her charge.

"Shortly after that, my mother finally called the attorney – Bedworth or Beckwood, something like that – and told him he needed to think about making arrangements for better care for Mrs. Carlisle. When Mrs. Carlisle left the house, she saw to it my mother received a cash payment for all her years of service to her. It allowed my mother to live out her few remaining years with dignity.

"What do you think really happened, Mr. Grant?" James said looking into the old newspaperman's eyes.

"Son, I think it was a terrible tragedy," he replied, returning James's inquiring stare. "A woman of genteel social prominence lost her daughter under horrible circumstances and was accused of a heinous act of revenge by an overzealous hotshot with no evidence. As a result, she was forced to live through a ridiculous trial that found her innocent and still resulted in her becoming a recluse for the rest of her life. To my way of thinking, she would have been justified to have shot them both, Mrs. Stanhope and that fake Baron."

Carol sat quietly talking with Mary Shields and John Grant while Ellen Perry took James to the microfilm machine and showed him how to work it. James was emotionally drained by what he had heard from John and Mary. Before Ellen returned to the conference room, James asked her, "Why did you leave all of that out of your "brief history"?"

"Everyone who was directly connected to those events is long gone," she answered James. "History should not reopen old wounds just because it can; that serves no good purpose. I felt it was better to let that event continue to be left in the dark. Why should people, curious about the area, care about what happened so long ago? Mrs. Carlisle should be remembered as a lady of great wealth and quality who tried to bring society to Rock Cove and not as a crazy old woman living as a recluse and talking about ghosts and spirits."

James thought about what Ms. Perry said and decided he agreed with her. There really was no reason to open everything to re-inspection by dredging up old events. It would serve no purpose other than to interest the morbidly curious. In this case, it was better to leave the past forgotten or at least clouded in mist.

James began running through the microfilm. He had never run the machine before, but with a few instructions from Ellen, he found it easy to use and soon was zooming through the back issues of the *New London Times*. He found the original report of the homicide: a glaring headline followed by secondary headings of short phrases emphasizing the lurid details. He skimmed the text looking for anything that was a material departure from what he already had heard.

There seemed to be no question about who had killed Becky Carlisle and how, although the apparent murder weapon went missing. It had been seen and described in detail by three of the bridesmaids who were present and by Mrs. Carlisle and Ben Allen's father, referred to in the paper variously as the handyman, groundskeeper, and caretaker. However, when it came to the police collecting the evidence from the crime scene, the gun had somehow managed to disappear and, although thoroughly searched for, could not be found.

Contrary to what Mary Shields had related, the murder occurred in one of the bedrooms on the second floor, according to the paper. It was also reported that several of the guests remembered, or thought they remembered, seeing Mrs. Stanhope at some point on the lawn, but they couldn't be sure. It was obvious that the scene was total pandemonium once the shots were heard. By the time the police were notified and arrived on the scene, the shock of what had happened had settled on everyone.

The murder was front page news for about two weeks. It moved out of the headlines when Elisabeth Carlisle was laid to rest with great fanfare next to her father and the search for Mrs. Stanhope's body was abandoned. In those two weeks, reporters had constructed all sorts of scenarios, concocted all manner of gossip, into causes for and reasons why the murders had occurred. None held more truth than the story that Sophia Stanhope's fiancé had jilted her for no known reason other than to marry a younger (and, perhaps, wealthier) Becky Carlisle.

There were rumors of the Baron having changed his mind and run off and Becky shooting herself. Another had Sophia Stanhope, left by her lover after becoming pregnant, hanged herself because of it, and was found by her mother. Still another had Becky Carlisle being pregnant by the Baron. The combinations and permutations were endless and each one just as unfounded as the next. The reporters were having a field day making up whatever was sensational and even slightly possible and would sell the most papers. Those "unnamed sources" were in full voice about the society folks of Rock Cove. James could see what a minefield Ellen Perry could have opened by writing anything about the murder.

When James finished the last roll of microfilm, he sat back in his chair and just took time to mull over all he had heard and read. The whole concept of a small group of individuals designating themselves the sole arbiters of what was "society" was so foreign to his upbringing. How was it possible that this small group virtually controlled who was considered the social elite for nearly half a century? The answer seemed simple. The success of these families, achieved over three or more generations, had given these scions of the true founders of wealth a feeling if insularity. They saw themselves as the nobility of the American republic and they assumed their self-appointed mantle of responsibility with enthusiasm.

James had come to realize the one rule that had to be obeyed was to avoid scandal or even the breath of impropriety. Admission of such a failing reflected badly on the entire group. It impacted their ability to set the moral tone required of members of the elite. So, let the women have their dalliances. Let the men have their drunken parties and affairs. Just be sure these activities are assiduously kept from polite conversation. Articles addressing these activities and the private lives of the group in sections of the newspaper other than the society pages, were unacceptable. It wasn't so much that they did not exit. They did and in multiple instances. The shame attached to the public acknowledgement of these activities was what was to be avoided and the wealth of the group made covering up those indiscretions, in large part, possible.

When James had left the room with Ellen to view the microfilm, Carol had not really known what to say to Mary Shields or John Grant.

"Mary," she finally said, "when we were in the house the other day, I noticed a nursery upstairs. Did your mother ever mention there was a nursery in the house?"

Mary thought for a few minutes. "There was one time she mentioned something about a locked room on the second floor. She never said what it was exactly."

"There was no lock on the door when we were there," said Carol remembering the door had been open.

"Maybe I'm wrong," Mary said in reply. "It may have been she said it should have been locked. It was a long time ago and it is hard to remember."

Mrs. Day," John Grant broke in attempting to change to topic, "Ellen told me that you and your husband are moving here from New York City?"

"Yes, that's right," Carol replied taking the bait. "We're both originally from the Midwest, but we have been living in the city for the last few years building our businesses."

John Grant was an expert conversationalist. He continued to ask Carol questions about her background and James, drawing more and more information about them from her. He learned of her successful career and of James's reputation on Wall Street. She talked of New York and its nightlife and cultural opportunities, the restaurants, the museums, the mad pace of life in a world-class city. She spoke of how they had taken to urban life when they first arrived in Manhattan and how tired she had grown of it after a few years. She knew their success in business had given them the financial freedom to move out of New York and the maturing of the internet would allow them to continue to run their businesses from almost anywhere, virtually. Carol knew she was ready to move out of the urban lifestyle. She was not so sure that James was. She spoke of her desire to start a family and her feeling that New York was not where she wanted to raise her children. She had grown up with lots of space and she wanted her children to have the same along with something she had not had: the ocean.

When James rejoined the group, he thanked Mary and John for their time and information. He seemed somehow to have changed to Carol, but she said nothing. As the meeting broke up, James and Carol walked to the circulation desk with John and Mary. They again shook hands and turned to thank Ellen Perry.

"I hope you feel you have a better understanding of what happened," Ellen said inclining her head to one side and smiling at Carol. "Sometimes it's best if we let the past be forgotten and look to the future."

James looked at Ellen with a smile and said, "It will be a different place now that it's ours. What's past is past. We can look at making the future a lot better." James looked at Carol and she started to believe James now really did want this house and this life as much as she had grown to want it.

"We start tomorrow with a thorough cleaning."

SIXTEEN

GEORGE ALLEN RAN ACROSS THE MAIN HALL AND into the library. He snatched the newly installed candlestick phone off the desk. He removed the receiver and clicked the hang up bar several times before he realized the new phone required dialing to reach the operator. He stuck his finger in the dial and spun it. He heard the voice of the operator at the central switchboard asking, "Number, please?"

"We need the police and a doctor at the Carlisle Mansion!" he screamed excitedly into the phone. "Quick as you can! There has been a murder!"

As he spoke that final word, he heard the sharp crack of another shot. George dropped the phone on the desk and ran for the stairs. As he reached the hall, he saw the Baron standing on the first step of the staircase looking up the stairs hesitantly. He grabbed him by the sleeve of his jacket.

"Go! Get up there!" he said, urging him forward. "I will be right behind you!"

George turned and ran through the door into the butler's pantry. His only thought was to get something to stop any bleeding.

As the Baron mounted the stairs, he saw Edith Carlisle slowly backing out of the nursery. The room was filled with acrid smoke.

"What's happened?" he called to her. "Are you alright, Mrs. Carlisle?"

At the sound of his voice, Edith seemed to freeze. Slowly, she turned to face the Baron, the smoking gun still in her hand. He was standing at the top of the stairs with a look of confused concern on his face. She thought to herself she had never seen such an emotional display from him.

"Are you alright?" he repeated more calmly.

Edith turned her head, so her gaze fell upon the open door of the bedroom where her daughter lay dead. The Baron saw the movement of her eyes and cautiously crossed the hall and leaned into the room. He fell back against the open door with a gasp, repelled by the sight before him.

"My God!" he cried out. He looked at Edith. It was only then that he saw the gun in her hand, a small wisp of smoke drifting from the barrel.

"What did you do?" he exclaimed. He plastered his body against the wall of the hall in fear for himself and began inching away from her toward the back stairs. "My God, woman, what have you done?" he repeated loudly trying to stay calm.

Edith saw him moving away from her. She shook her head from side to side; her vision distorted by the tears flowing from them effortlessly. Her mind was not registering any emotion. She raised the gun and fired it in the direction of the baron.

SEVENTEEN

FRIDAY HAD DAWNED COLD AND GRAY WITH A nipping wind out of the northwest. James and Carol had rolled out of bed early to be at the house when Paul Murray's cleaning crew arrived. They stopped to pick up coffee and a bagel on their way to the estate; Carol commented that New York bagels were far superior. They were excited by the prospect of seeing each room as it was thoroughly cleaned for the first time in years. Who knew what furniture they would find? It was going to be an exciting exploration.

They arrived at the driveway still needing their headlights to help light their way. As they approached the house, they saw three box trucks pulled up around the back of the house. James drove behind the house and beyond the trucks to the front of the garage and parked. They saw a light burning on the second floor of the garage. A group of about a dozen people standing around the trucks were all dressed in identical white coveralls with hoods and face masks and matching booties on their shoes. One of them stepped forward and removed his white mask. It was Paul Murray.

"Looks like we beat you here," he said smiling broadly. "I've got a couple of extra suits you can wear if you'd like to join us."

"I'd love to," Carol said looking at James with a smile.

"Alright, alright," James said raising his hands playfully in surrender.

Paul laughed and led them to the back of one of the trucks and handed them each a set of white coveralls, masks, and booties. As they pulled on their outfits, Paul explained they were taking these protective measures because it was common for older homes to have asbestos in them, especially in the attics and basements. His plan of attack was to clean those areas first to reduce any exposure to harmful substances then work down from the second floor. He had divided his crew into two teams for the present.

Each group had two industrial vacuums, brushes, brooms, mops, bucket, rags, cleaners, detergents, and plastic trash bags for larger trash. After giving some final instructions to his crew, especially about the asbestos he expected to find, Paul got the set of keys James had given him the day before from his pocket and started toward the back door of the mansion. The teams, with Carol and James in tow, followed Paul as he unlocked and entered the back door, then unlocked the basement door, and led his crew down the staircase. The second team passed the doorway to the basement, entered the kitchen, and headed for the attic. James and Carol joined the crew headed to the basement. They realized they had never been in the basement. There might be surprises everywhere.

The stairs ended on a packed earth floor with a ceiling about seven feet high. Paul found a light switch on a wooden pole at the side of the stairs and turned it. A series of bare bulbs strung on twisted knob and tube wires sparked to life. The bulbs gave minimal light to areas of the basement. It was still dark, but it felt dry. There was no odor of must and fewer cobwebs than might have been expected, although the cobwebs that hung about were floor to ceiling and luxuriant. The basement ran the full base of the mansion. The outer walls were constructed of flat stone tightly fitted together and washed between with cement or concrete. There were numerous cracks and crevasses between the stones, but the walls were solid and appeared to have been impervious to ground water damage. There were massive, vaulted brick pillars to support the weight of the mansion above. Three massive wooden beams at least a foot square and thirty feet long ran across these pillars providing the primary support for the rooms on the main floor. The second set of stairs to the basement, descending from under the main staircase in the front hall, were visible on the far side of the basement. These stairs were much more finished than those the team had used to enter the cellar. As Paul worked his way through the draping of cobwebs toward these stairs, he noticed the dirt on the floor gave way to a poured cement floor and the ceiling was getting higher above his head. He turned to James and Carol and tried to tell them about it pointing at the floor, but with the noise made by the workers and the muffling of his mask, they could not hear him.

The basement was sectioned into small rooms on two of its walls. As members of the team showed their lights into these rooms, they called out what they found; most were empty, a few had some items stored in them. The first thing Paul was looking for was a heating system. He found it beside one of the small rooms built against the far wall. The furnace itself was a disaster, as any heating system that had not been run or serviced in thirty years would be. He began looking at the pipes of the system and saw what he expected: asbestos.

"Well, there's what I thought we would find," he said pointing his flashlight at the pipes radiating from the furnace. "We'll have to strip all that insulation off those pipes and replace it," he said to Carol and James, who were following the flashlight beam.

"Why is the furnace over here and not in the middle of the basement?" asked Carol.

"I suspect this was originally a coal fired furnace and this room next to us was built probably as a coal bin, and, if we look on the outside wall… Yep, see that door? That was the coal chute where they delivered the coal." Paul had walked to the opening of the little room as he spoke followed by James and Carol and had shown his light against the far wall where a small wooden chute met a metal door that was chained and padlocked.

"A lot of these old houses were built with coal furnaces. This one has been converted to oil, so there must be a tank buried outside, since I don't see one down here. We'll need to have that checked. I really think we were right to plan on installing a new furnace. I would bet this one is completely shot."

Paul's crew knew what to do without direction. They had found no electrical outlets in the basement and had run heavy duty power cords from a generator in one of the trucks outside. As they vacuumed, swept, wiped, and scrubbed, they had set up some work lights that illuminated everything. It also showed the amount of dust and particulate that was escaping into the air.

Paul called a couple of his crew over to the furnace and gave them some specific instructions as he pointed here and there. The noise level was beginning to rise. When the workers nodded to Paul, he motioned to Carol and James to follow him, and they climbed the stairs back to the kitchen. In the sunlight of the kitchen, they could see how dirty their overalls had become in just a short period of time.

"Let's see how the attic crew is doing," Paul said, his voice muffled by his mask. The three of them sprinted up the back stairs to the second floor following the electrical cords snaking along the stairs. As they started up the flight of stairs to the attic, they could hear the hum of the vacuums already in use. They reached the top of the stairs and were heading down the hall when James cautioned Paul about the hall narrowing.

"Hmmm," Paul said looking at the jog in the wall, "we'll take care of that with the renovations. Looks like somebody misjudged the studding for the wall. They probably didn't worry about it because it was on the way to the servants' rooms and the attic." He rapped the heel of his palm against the wood panel. "It's solid, at least."

"Tell me about it," James said with a smile. "I caught my shoulder on it twice."

They entered the main room and saw the flurry of activity of six people feverishly cleaning every nook and cranny. It was amazing what several layers of dust and grime over time did to the colors in a room.

"I'm recommending that you send all the rugs out to be professionally cleaned and remove all the drapes and curtains," Paul said to Carol in a muffled yell. She nodded in agreement. "I'm going to move the furniture downstairs to the main hall. It will be easier to take it out from there. I have another truck coming for it this afternoon."

As Carol nodded in agreement, pieces of furniture started leaving the room in the arms of three members of the cleaning crew. It was amazing how much bigger the room appeared without the furniture. She felt a tap on her arm and saw Paul holding a blueprint up to her and James. He proceeded to point at lines on the drawing and point at the walls of the servants' sitting room. It was too noisy for her to really hear him, but it was evident that James understood what he was saying. Then he turned and walked into the hall with James behind, followed by Carol.

He opened the door in the hall leading into the unfinished part of the attic. The noise of cleaning was diminished enough for them to hear each other there. He again unrolled the blueprint and, pulling his mask down on his chest, held it up for them to see.

"There is no reason why we shouldn't use this southeastern exposure as office space for one of you," Paul said pointing at the windows. "Those windows give you excellent morning sun and a beautiful view throughout the day, not to mention a view of the lights across the Sound in the evening. In the summer, you can open those windows and get the breeze off the water.

"We can make the same space on the southwest side, with the same advantages, and you two can fight over who gets which space for their office," Paul said smiling broadly. "I just build rooms, folks, I don't get into who gets them." He laughed at his joke, as did James and Carol.

"I was looking at that silly little hall out there and I don't see any need for it," he said returning to his blueprint. "I think we can have the staircase just open into a larger sitting room with your offices running toward the front of the house." He nodded to himself as if confirming his thoughts. "Maybe even make that staircase wider."

Paul began talking with James about updating wiring and adding circuitry for phones and the internet, things that Carol had no immediate interest in. She walked out of the unfinished area of the attic across the dust laden floor and pulled down some hanging cobwebs with her gloved hand to look out the front window at the water beyond the lawn.

It was so unharmonious. She knew that the waves were making a sound she could not hear, as were the seagulls she could see gliding on the air currents, as was the wind as it swept across the open lawn. Yet, here, in the noise of the finished attic, behind the thick pane of glass that let her observe it all, she could hear only the sounds of brooms sweeping, vacuums whirring, and people working. She was lost in her thoughts when she realized that James was saying her name.

"Carol?" he was saying, "Are you alright?"

"Mmhhmm," she replied coming back into what was going on around her.

"We're going to check on the progress in the basement, alright?" James said, looking at her with mild concern.

"Okay," Carol said, "I'm coming.

EIGHTEEN

THEY WORKED AT CATCHING UP ON THEIR BUSInesses on Saturday, having full confidence in Paul's cleaning crew. It had taken most of the day to answer the most important of their emails, catching up on correspondence, and reading reports sent to them. But, before the sun set, they knew they wanted to drive to the mansion and walk through it. Their curiosity was getting the better of them.

Paul's telephoned report on Saturday afternoon on his progress was optimistic except that the basement was taking longer than expected. As the crew was cleaning, they discovered that the dirt floor was a layer of dirt nearly eight inches thick. Beneath it was rough concrete flooring. The removal of the dirt took nearly half the day but, as a result, the ceiling height was now almost eight feet throughout the cellar. Even with the unexpected delay, only one corner of the basement was left to be cleaned. That corner had several pieces of furniture piled in it. Once it was emptied and cleaned, both crews would combine their efforts on the second floor. James and Carol were unsure what they were going to do with that furniture but assumed it would be moved out with the rest.

They arrived to find the mansion dark. Their headlights reflected against the garage as they pulled up in front of it. James looked up to the windows above as he got out of the car and saw Ben standing in the window. He waved at Ben, who waved back, and retreated from the window. James turned and followed Carol to the back door of the mansion. She inserted the key and unlocked the door. She flipped on the light switch on the inside wall.

The cleaning crew had laid down runners so anyone going to the third floor would not track dirt back upstairs. The rustling of the paper runners was the only sound the Days made on their way to the third floor. The sound echoed through the empty house. In the second-floor hall, James turned on one of the work lamps brought down from the third floor by the cleaning crew. Its bright light illuminated the entire space, and it had an eerie effect on the hall, seeming to increase its dimensions. Carol looked at the shadows she and James cast against the walls. They were strangely distorted, being thrown on the ceiling and walls. As James moved the work light, the shadows shifted on the doorways going off the hall. Carol thought to herself, if someone were prone to seeing ghosts and spirits, this would be the conditions under which one would see them. After a few minutes, they climbed the stairs to the third floor.

The view from the windows on the third floor was incredibly beautiful. The lights from the eastern-most tips of Long Island and the lights from Mystic and New London to the west gave the sky a rosy glow. Carol and James tried to imagine how the attic would look once the changes were made. It would really be a dramatic difference.

Standing side by side looking out across the darkening expanse of water to the lights far away, Carol could tell she was winning James back. She had sensed a change in him that encouraged her, and, even though they had spent the day working on business, he had not once said he needed to be in his office or New York.

As Carol and James looked at the servants' rooms on Saturday, it was hard to remember how dingy and grimy they had looked such a short time before. The finished rooms and attic were completely cleaned. They were surprised to discover the floors of the finished rooms were made from fine hardwood and the windows were of the same exceptional quality as those on the lower floors. The furniture had all been inventoried and moved to the downstairs hall by Friday night and loaded into trucks to be taken for cleaning, and the rugs had been rolled up and moved out as well. The cleaning crews had worked a small miracle so far and Carol and James were excited by the prospects of having the entire house clean. The Carlisle Mansion was being transformed by a thorough top to bottom cleaning.

NINETEEN

THE CLEANING CREW ARRIVED EARLY MONDAY morning, as usual. Ben Allen was watching them preparing for another long day when the Days drove up the driveway. He was not going to be caught again by early arrivals. He walked over to the car as Carol and James got out.

"I was wondering if and when they were going to be working on the garage apartment," Ben asked James. He touched the bill of his cap to acknowledge Carol.

"They were supposed to when they started," James replied, "but, that was before we knew you were living there, Ben."

"Jim, it could do with a good cleaning," Ben said a little sheepishly. "I'd be willing to go out for a day or two if they could clean it. I have a place I can stay if that's alright."

"Sure, Ben," James said. "I'll let you know when they will do it. I would guess it would be the end of the week after they're done with the main house."

Ben thanked him and started walking into the garage. There had been little for him to do the last few days and he had tried to busy himself as far from the house as he could. He was not sure he liked so many people going in and out of the house. He still could not bring himself to enter it.

Carol and James were greeted by Paul with an update. He did not know that they had walked through the house on Saturday night. Paul expected to be done in the basement by midday and be finished with the majority of the second floor by the end of the day. He was going to have much of his crew starting upstairs right away. Another truck was due to pick up the furniture from the second floor that afternoon.

The members of each crew began picking up the last of the equipment and heading into the house. By now, the front hall and the front stairs had been cleaned to facilitate carrying the furniture down from the upper floors. A group of three workers headed for the basement to finish cleaning the remaining corner. After a couple of hours work, Carol and James were standing in the front hall discussing the blueprints with Paul and talking about the next step after they finished cleaning.

BANG! The explosion sounded like it came from directly beneath their feet. It seemed incredibly loud. The three of them froze.

"Boss! Boss! Mr. Murray!" called a voice from the basement. Paul dropped the blueprints and ran to the cellar stairway under the front staircase. As he descended the stairs followed closely by James and Carol, they saw one of the workers writhing in pain on the floor. A red stain was quickly spreading over the left leg of his white overall.

"What happened?" Paul Murray said kneeling beside his employee.

"I don't know," one of the others said. "We were just moving the furniture and there was an explosion and Manny fell over and started screaming."

James walked over to the corner where the furniture had been shifted. A portable work light illuminated the area brightly. As he looked at the tangle of furniture, something near the wall under the pile near a back leg of a table caught his eye.

"Jesus Christ," James heard Paul say. "You've been shot, Manny!"

"Over here, Paul," James called above the moans of pain. By this time, the rest of the cleaning crew was flooding into the basement having heard the gunshot.

Paul Murray came over to where James was standing and saw the shape James was pointing to on the floor. It was a revolver. The pungent smell of black powder started filling the air.

James had dialed 911 for medical assistance after the gunshot and the discovery of the weapon. Because it involved a shooting, the resident State Trooper had responded along with an ambulance and paramedics. Before the State Police had arrived, the injured man had been carried upstairs to the kitchen where he had been placed on the table and attempts were made to stop the bleeding. While the paramedics began treating the gunshot victim, the State Trooper had secured the crime scene with yellow tape. The gun was left where it had been discovered. Everyone had been ushered out of the basement and out of the house. Paul had stopped work and had all the members of the crew outside by the trucks.

Trooper Anderson had been busy obtaining a statement from each of them and was now about to take the statements of the Days and Paul. The sound of the siren as the ambulance left the estate broke the sullen silence of the scene.

All three were standing in the kitchen, the shock of what had just happened setting in. James was leaning against the counter, his arm around Carol offering some support. Paul was standing by the window watching the ambulance as it disappeared down the drive.

"That's a nasty little weapon you found," Trooper Nathan Anderson said as he made notes in his report pad. He was standing in the kitchen with Paul Murray and the Days. His athletic profile was only enhanced by the cut of his uniform. He looked to be about James's age and his demeanor displayed cool confidence in his ability to perform his job. His face showed little emotion; it was chiseled and composed. His deep-set eyes were shadowed by his trooper's hat and, when he removed it, the short buzz-cut hair style completed the image of a dedicated Officer of the Law. The police officer was following procedure. He had called his sergeant after his initial assessment of the scene.

"It's fortunate the injury was not worse," Trooper Anderson stated. "The three of you were standing where when you heard the shot?"

"In the front hall," James replied flatly. "We were reviewing plans for the house." The officer made a note in his pad.

"Who was first to reach the scene?"

"That was me," Paul said. "I was first down the stairs."

"Tell me what you saw," the Trooper was firm, but businesslike.

"My worker, actually my foreman, was on the ground holding his leg screaming in pain," Paul related. "My other two guys were standing around him not really knowing what had happened. I knelt and saw the blood on his leg. I pulled up his overall and saw the hole through his calf." Paul was shaking his head and his complexion had paled noticeably. "Never seen anything like that in my life in a man."

"You knew right away it was a gunshot wound?" Trooper Anderson asked as he made notes in his pad.

"I used to hunt deer," he said looking at the Officer.

"Who found the weapon?"

"I did, Officer," James said straightening his slumped posture slightly. "When the guys said they were just moving the furniture, I walked over in that direction and saw it lying on the floor."

"Who moved the injured man upstairs?"

"We all did," said Paul. "The guys and I got him up and they carried him up here and put him on the table. Mrs. Day found a compress in the first aid kit in the truck, and we applied pressure to the wound until the rescue arrived. They got here maybe five minutes before you."

"I got everyone who had come running from upstairs out of the basement," James chimed in. "No one has been down there since we came upstairs."

"Folks, I want you all to stay as calm as possible. I've called my supervisor, and he should be here any minute." The Trooper spoke with the confidence of one who had seen this a hundred times, knowing full well that he had not. "When he arrives, he will want to talk with you, just as I have, after he reviews the crime scene and my preliminary report.

"Crime scene," James exclaimed! "What crime? It was an accident!"

"Mr. Day, I can understand your concern, but right now, we don't really know that," Trooper Anderson said calmly. "It appears to be accidental. However, we need to identify the weapon and find out if it has been used in any other crimes, determine who it belongs to, and ascertain it was the weapon that fired and caused the wound. Now, that may take a little time and it may require we involve some other people. That will be determined by my supervisor."

"Well, Paul," James said, "I guess we won't be getting any more work done today."

"I guess I should tell the crew," Paul said with disappointment.

"I'm sorry, Sir," Trooper Anderson said, "no one leaves until my supervisor says they can go."

"But these guys are on the clock," Paul said pleadingly.

"Sorry. They stay until they are released." The Trooper spoke the words knowing the reaction of resignation they would invoke.

They were just beginning to talk about how long the delay might be when a Connecticut State Police cruiser pulled up in the driveway outside the kitchen windows. The Trooper behind the wheel had the same rugged looks of Trooper Anderson and his hair was cut in a similar fashion except it was considerably grayer. He entered the kitchen after gathering some papers from the trunk of his vehicle and introduced himself as Sergeant Bennett, Trooper Anderson's supervisor from the Montvale Barracks of the Connecticut State Police. He advised everyone in the kitchen that he was now conducting the investigation. He requested their complete cooperation. He then requested they remain in the kitchen while he spoke with his trooper. The two police officers stepped out to the supervisor's cruiser and began to converse.

James looked at Paul Murray and sarcastically said, "I guess we've been told what for, huh?"

"He's just doing his job," Carol said feeling very drained.

The two State Troopers could be seen comparing notes and sharing information. After about ten minutes, the supervising Officer pulled a cell phone out of his pocket and made a call. The Troopers came in the back door of the house and were heard to descend into the basement where the shooting had occurred. Suddenly, Paul, James and Carol heard Trooper Anderson's voice loud and clear.

"Sir! Stay where you are! You have entered a crime scene! Do NOT move!"

Paul looked out the window and saw all his crew milling around the trucks in the driveway. He shook his head at James. James and Paul bolted for the cellar stairs. As James ducked his head below the ceiling as he was coming down the stairs, he saw Ben Allen on the floor. Trooper Anderson was placing manacles on Ben's wrists.

"Do you know this man?" Sergeant Bennett asked, turning around. He was replacing his sidearm in its holster.

"Ben?" James questioned. "What are you doing down here?"

"I'm sorry, Mr. Day," Ben said quietly as he was brought to his feet by Trooper Anderson. "I just wanted to see if it was the one."

"He works for us," James said to the supervisor. "He's the caretaker. He's been here for years." He turned back to Ben. "How did you get down here? We were in the kitchen."

"I came down the stairs in the hall," Ben said averting his eyes, so he did not have to see the look of surprise on James's face.

Carol could see Ben sitting disconsolately in the back seat of Trooper Anderson's police cruiser through the kitchen window. He had been led out of the basement in handcuffs and placed in the car despite James's protests. She could also see her husband and Paul Murray talking with the members of the cleaning crew by the trucks in the driveway. Trooper Anderson was busy stringing more yellow "crime scene" tape she had seen him take from the trunk of his vehicle. She was sitting at the kitchen table with Sergeant Bennett answering his inquiries.

"Mrs. Day, what did Mr. Allen mean by 'the one'? Do you know?"

Carol began to shake her head to say no when she suddenly stopped. The Sergeant saw her expression change.

"I think he might have meant the gun that was used to kill Becky Carlisle," she said, somewhat surprised that the thought had come to her.

"Who is Becky Carlisle, Mrs. Day?" Sergeant Bennett began making more notes on the pad in front of him.

"She was the daughter of the family that owned this house before we bought it."

"And, when did you buy the house?"

"We just bought it," Carol replied. "We haven't even moved in yet."

"Mrs. Day, I'm a little confused. If there had been a murder in my area, I would know about it."

"Sergeant Bennett, how long have you been a police officer here?" Carol asked him kindly.

I have been assigned to Montvale Barracks as the Supervising Sergeant for twelve years, Ma'am," Sergeant Bennett responded with obvious pride.

"This happened in 1927," Carol told him bluntly.

"1927?" The officer murmured in disbelief. There was a visible deflation in the posture of the police officer accompanied by a blank stare of incomprehension.

"It's very confusing," Carol continued. "There was a murder here in the house in 1927. The daughter of the owner was shot by a neighbor. The gun disappeared after and was never found."

"What connection could Mr. Allen have to that incident that he would risk compromising a crime scene?" Sergeant Bennett asked. "He isn't old enough to have even been alive in 1927."

"His father was caretaker of the estate before him. He would have been on the estate when the murder happened."

The Officer sat for a moment tapping his pencil on the pad. "If his father was the one who would have seen the weapon used in the 1927 murder, how would the son have had any knowledge about it being 'the right one'?"

With a puzzled look on his face, Sergeant Bennet made a couple of additional notes on the pad before him.

"Thank you for your cooperation, Mrs. Day," she heard Sergeant Bennett say. "Would you mind asking your husband to join me?"

TWENTY

CAROL DAY WALKED OUT THE BACK DOOR OF THE house still repeating the question Sergeant Bennett had posed to himself just before telling her she could leave. How would Ben Allen know if it were the gun used by Mrs. Stanhope to murder Becky Carlisle? She walked up to James and absent-mindedly told him that the police sergeant wanted to speak with him next. James asked her if she was alright, and she nodded and answered yes. She stood with her hands grasping her arms as James entered the house.

Sergeant Bennett had been joined by Trooper Anderson in the kitchen. The supervisor was just finishing saying something to the trooper when James entered the kitchen. The Trooper acknowledged his understanding and went out the back door.

"Thank you for joining me," Sergeant Bennett said engagingly to James.

"I guess I didn't have much choice," James replied.

"Mr. Day, I'm not trying to give anyone a hard time here," the officer replied. "I'm just trying to find out what happened."

"Sergeant, it was an accident, plain and simple," James said spreading his hands in front of him on the table. "They were moving some furniture and it fell from somewhere and discharged. That's all it was. Paul's worker just happened to be in the wrong place."

"I hope you're right, Mr. Day," the Sergeant replied. "But we still need to determine who owns the weapon and if it has been used in any other crimes."

"How far back do your records go?" James asked sarcastically.

"Sir, if you'll allow me to ask the questions, we can get through this much faster," Sergeant Bennett said with more authority in his voice. "Do you know what Mr. Allen meant when he said he wanted to see if it was 'the one'?"

"I didn't when he said it, but I've had time to think about it and I think I know," James replied showing a bit less sarcasm. "But I assume you're going to ask him, so why ask me?"

"Mr. Day, I'm asking you because I want to know what you think." The Sergeant leaned forward on the table. "It's my job to find out what happened. What I have so far doesn't sit too well with me. I have a gunshot victim, shot by a gun nobody knows anything about, that came out of nowhere and looks like it should be in a museum. I have someone who wasn't there when the shot occurred attempting to compromise my crime scene trying to see if the weapon is a weapon, he shouldn't be able to identify. Do you think I should be happy, Mr. Day?"

"Mrs. Day said you had just purchased the house," Sergeant Bennett continued.

"Yes," James replied calmly. "We haven't even moved in yet. The house is being cleaned and we have some renovating to do."

"Your wife said something about a murder taking place here in 1927?" Sergeant Bennett's question was left hanging in the air.

"Sergeant, I don't believe that has any connection to what happened here today," James replied in dismay. Ellen Perry's words came back to James. "That was a long time ago. Sometimes it's best to let the past be forgotten."

The Trooper made a few notes on his pad. He thanked James for his cooperation and asked him to send Paul Murray to him. James stood up from the kitchen table and started to walk past the officer who was still seated.

He suddenly turned and said to the officer, "Sergeant, I apologize for my attitude. I can understand you want to find out about the gun. That I can understand. But, as far as what went on here, I really think this is a little overkill, don't you?"

"Mr. Day, I don't believe this was anything but an accident. But, this weapon… this is a deadly weapon. It had to come from somewhere and I don't mean a museum. How did it get here?" Sergeant Bennett was more puzzled than angry. "I'm more interested to know why Mr. Allen, out there in the car, wanted to get to it."

Paul Murray sat at the kitchen table shaking his head.

"Officer, I don't know anything. I was hired to clean the house and remove the furniture for cleaning. This gun thing is totally nuts."

"What is your impression of the Days, Mr. Murray?" the Sergeant asked.

"I'm not sure what you mean, but, if you're asking me if I think they had the gun, the answer's no," Paul replied. "They were up here in the hall with me when we heard the shot."

"What do you know about this Ben Allen?"

"I just met him when we started the job." Paul answered with a puzzled look on his face. "He lives over the garage and has been a caretaker here for his whole life. His father was caretake here before him. That is my understanding."

I think that about covers it, Mr. Murray." The officer looked at Paul and smiled. "If there is anything further, we'll be in touch."

"When can we get back to work?" Paul asked hurriedly.

"I think we'll be done here in an hour or so, but by tomorrow I would think," Sergeant Bennett answered.

The Officer stood to his full six foot-five-inch height and walked over to the window. Trooper Anderson was standing by his cruiser and saw his supervisor appear at the window. Sergeant Bennett motioned to his trooper to bring Ben Allen to him.

"Thank you, Mr. Murray." The officer motioned for Paul to leave.

As Paul passed into the back hall, he had to flatten against the wall to allow Trooper Anderson to pass guiding Ben ahead of him. Paul joined the Days by the trucks and told them he would probably be able to resume work the next day.

Trooper Anderson sat Ben Allen in a chair at the kitchen table. His hands were still manacled behind him. The supervisor was sitting at the table reviewing his notes on the pad in front of him saying nothing to Ben. Trooper Anderson left the kitchen and returned carrying an evidence bag with the revolver in it. He placed it on the table in front of his supervisor.

"Mr. Allen, you know you're in serious trouble, don't you," Sergeant Bennett said finally looking up at Ben. "You attempted to compromise a crime scene."

"I'm sorry, Sergeant," Ben said not looking at the police officer, but looking at the weapon. The supervisor saw Ben's eyes looking at the weapon.

"It's quite the gun," Sergeant Bennett remarked turning the evidence bag for Ben to see. "It's a Colt single action revolver. Textured grip, short barrel makes it what was called an 'Artillery' model. Serial number 192020, which makes it manufactured after 1900. It fires a .45 caliber cartridge at about a thousand feet per second. The victim was lucky, it was only a flesh wound. Funny characteristic about single action revolvers: they can fire when they're dropped if a live round is left under the hammer, especially if the ammunition is old and unstable. Now, everyone has said there was just one shot fired. Yet, we seem to have five spent cartridges in the cylinder. Any idea why that is, Mr. Allen?"

Ben was straining to look at the revolver. He could see that a fine powder had been applied and there was a fingerprint clear as day on the barrel.

"Mr. Allen, you crossed a yellow-taped crime scene area to try get to this gun and I want to know why!" The supervisor had stood so rapidly his chair had clattered across the tile floor. He was now leaning across the table right in Ben's face, looking for all the world as if he intended to do harm to Ben.

"I... I, uh... I just wanted to see it," Ben stammered out as he drew back awkwardly in his chair because of the handcuffs.

"No. No, it was more than that," the Supervisor stayed right in Ben's face. "You knew something. What was it you wanted to do? Did you want to hide it? Like it was hidden before? Where was it hidden?"

"I don't know. No, I don't know. I swear I don't know where it came from." Ben was clearly feeling the pressure of Sergeant Bennett's questions.

"What were you going to do? Did you want to touch it?" The police officer noticed Ben suddenly shift in his seat and avert his eyes even more. "That's it, isn't it? You wanted to touch it. No, you didn't want to touch it. You wanted to wipe it off!" Sergeant Bennett knew he had guessed correctly because Ben turned to face him. "What are you afraid we're going to find? A fingerprint? Someone's fingerprint? That print right there?" He pointed at the fingerprint on the barrel. "Your fingerprints?"

"No! No, I swear. It won't be mine!" Ben said, ignoring the beads of perspiration that were standing out on his forehead. "I've never touched that thing, I swear it! But... I'm afraid... It... It could be my father's," Ben said with resignation. "I don't know that it's his, but it could be."

Sergeant Bennett stepped back from the table knowing he had broken Ben Allen's will. He retrieved his chair and sat down at the table. He looked at Trooper Anderson, who had been standing in the corner behind Ben, and gave him a gesture to remove the handcuffs.

"Ben, talk to me," the Supervisor said calmly, consolingly. "Tell me why you think it could be your father's. What are you afraid we'll find out?"

" Oh, what's the use," Ben said rubbing his wrists where the handcuffs had chafed his skin. "You're going to find out anyway."

"You mean about the murder?"

Ben looked at Sergeant Bennett completely dumbfounded. "You already know about that?" He turned around to look at Trooper Anderson just to confirm what his supervisor had said. The trooper's face was expressionless.

"Okay... okay. I don't know whose print that is going to be," Ben said regaining some of his composure. "My father was a good man, and I didn't want him to be implicated in that mess. I was afraid that would happen if his fingerprints were on that gun."

"Why would you think we might find his prints on the weapon?" Sergeant Bennett could see Ben Allen was no longer trying to be deceptive.

"My father was working for Mrs. Carlisle back in 1927 when her daughter was murdered. He told me he didn't see the actual murder, but he saw the gun lying on the floor after the police arrived. He told me it disappeared after that."

"You think his prints might be on it?"

"I just know that he was devoted to Mrs. Carlisle and if she had wanted him to get rid of it, he would have. I don't think Mrs. Carlisle would have hidden it down here. She was a great lady. My father would have done it; the hiding, I mean. I just didn't want him labeled a murderer because he didn't do it. I just know he couldn't have." Ben was almost pleading his father's innocence.

"Ben, I'm not going to arrest you, although I could," Sergeant Bennett said. "I understand your concern and I will note it in my report."

"What's going to happen to the gun now?" Ben asked.

"It will go to the Major Crime Squad Lab for testing and analysis and storage as evidence," replied the supervisor. He thanked Ben for his cooperation and put his hand on his shoulder. "I don't think your father had anything to do with what happened here today." He smiled at Ben.

Ben appeared at the back door of the house rubbing his wrists and looking ashamed somewhat over his actions. He walked over to where James and Carol were standing, talking with Paul Murray. Carol was the first to see him approaching. She noticed immediately Ben was not manacled.

"Are you alright, Ben?" Carol asked with concern. He nodded his reply.

"You were in there a long time," James said turning to him. "What were you thinking, Ben, to go anywhere near it?"

"I wasn't thinking," Ben replied still trying not to look at James's face.

"It had to have been really important to you, Ben," Carol said. "You went into the house."

The four of them noticed the two State Police officers coming out of the house carrying their notebooks and the revolver in a sealed evidence bag. The Trooper went to his car; the Sergeant walked toward the group.

"I think we're done here. We've photographed the scene and conducted our initial investigation. I'm satisfied that it was an accidental shooting, Mr. Day," Sergeant Bennett said.

"Oh, by the way, Mr. Murray, the injured man was taken to Lawrence and Memorial Hospital in New London. We're on our way there to interview him. I somehow think he's not going to be able to tell us a great deal more," he continued. The Sergeant turned and addressed the Days.

"We'll be turning our reports into headquarters, and you may be contacted by one of the members of our Detective Squad. Thank you for your assistance and good day to you." Sergeant Bennett placed two fingers of his right hand against the rim of his wide-brimmed hat in salute, turned and walked toward his cruiser. The Sergeant leaned against the passenger door of Trooper Anderson's cruiser to exchange a few words and then the two police cars drove out of sight down the loose stone driveway.

The group left standing by the white box trucks in the driveway began stripping off their overalls. There was very little conversation, and the mood was somber. Paul looked at the Days and said, "Well, we'll see you tomorrow morning and we'll try it again. I need to get to New London and see how Manny is doing."

"Please tell him how badly we feel about this," Carol said.

It was not long before the trucks had departed, and the Days were left alone on the driveway of the estate. Ben had excused himself and gone into the garage. It had been quite a day. Carol and James were solemn as they locked up the mansion. Now they had their own tragedy with which to deal. Granted it was not of the magnitude of murder, but it was violent and more immediate and frightening because it was more real to them than something they had read about and been told about that had happened over eighty years ago.

They walked around to the porch to lock the front door after locking the cellar and back doors. They stood on the porch for a few minutes, an arm around each other and saying nothing, looking out toward the water beyond the lawn. Carol turned her head to look at the house she had come to desire to be hers. Every time she started to feel the house was becoming hers, something happened to make it feel more distant. It seemed like the past still wanted to control the present.

TWENTY-ONE

IN THE NEXT TWO DAYS, PAUL'S CREW MADE A VALiant effort to make up for the lost day of work. The work in the basement was quickly finished the day after the accident. The pile of furniture there turned out to be terribly beaten up and broken and it was decided to discard it. Temporarily, it was put in one of the bays of the garage. In a few days, when Paul was scheduled to begin renovations on the Victorian, a roll-off dumpster would be delivered and the furniture in the garage would be the first thing contributed to it.

The cleaning of the second-floor rooms went rapidly. The remaining furniture was brought down to the front hall, inventoried, and left to await pickup. The carpet in the upstairs hall and the area rugs in the bedrooms were all rolled and piled in the downstairs hall. They, too, would be cleaned off premises. The drapes were heavily faded where they had been facing the sun for all those years. It became very evident when they were taken down that they would need to be the first item replaced. Once the furniture and drapes were gone, the cleaning went quickly. The room that took the most time to clean was the nursery and that was because Carol insisted that every item be saved and cleaned.

James and Carol had been there both days. They had tried to pitch in to make up for the crew being short one person. There was another reason that James wanted to get the cleaning done before the end of the week that he had not shared with Carol. He needed to spend a few days in New York the next week and he wanted to leave Carol free to finish renovation plans with Paul. Although Carol was having no trouble running her business through her surrogate managers in Manhattan, James was finding his business, and the regulatory requirements surrounding it, more difficult to conduct by internet alone. He needed to spend two or, more likely, three days in New York.

As the crew moved to the main floor of the mansion to begin cleaning, Paul asked James and Carol to meet him in the kitchen. The Days came into the kitchen through the butler's pantry from the dining room. Paul was standing with his blueprints spread on the table where the police interrogations had taken place.

"Hi, guys," Paul said as they entered. He seemed preoccupied with his drawings. "Have you two noticed anything odd about what we are finding as we uncover the furniture in these rooms?"

"What do you mean, Paul?" Carol said looking puzzled.

"Most houses have pictures or paintings on the walls and framed photographs on end tables or on mantels. There are none in this house, anywhere."

Carol smiled. "We were told by the attorney that all of those kinds of things were packed up when Mrs. Carlisle was moved into a nursing home and Ben showed us the boxes. They're in a closet in the rooms over the garage. Oh! That reminds me. Is it possible we could send a couple of people to clean the apartment over the garage? I think Ben's place could use a good cleaning."

"Of course we can," Paul replied. "Do you want me to remove the boxes when we clean?"

"Could you move them into storage until we have a chance to go through them?" Carol asked. "I would love the opportunity to look at them, but I would feel uncomfortable doing that in Ben's rooms."

"I'll go one better for you, Mrs. Day," Paul said. "I have a small amount of onsite storage at the shop. I could put them there and you could come to the shop when you have time and look through them."

"That would be wonderful, Paul," said Carol at the suggestion. It was funny that, even though James and Carol had started addressing Paul by his first name, he could not do the same for them and continued to address them as Mr. and Mrs. Day.

"And, as long as we are talking about that, it's time to look at the final plans now that I've had a chance to revise my drafts," Paul said, changing the topic of conversation and returning to his blueprints. "I think we'll be finished with the cleaning tomorrow. This floor seems to be moving along pretty well. I've ordered a dumpster for delivery this weekend and I've told Ben to expect it and where I want it. Since you want us to clean Ben's rooms, if we don't get to it tomorrow, we have Saturday to finish that."

Paul was on a roll looking at his blueprints.

"Okay, now, here is what I propose we start with." Paul pulled one drawing out and placed it atop the others. "These are the plans for the third floor. What I propose to do is ...." And Paul was off, explaining his proposed changes to the uppermost floor of the mansion.

He wanted to eliminate the hallway at the top of the stairs; it made the top of the stairs unnecessarily tight, as James already could attest to, and was just plain annoying. He had studied the staircase and felt he could steal two feet from the large room next to the stairs on the second floor and widen the stairs so they would accommodate the office furniture that would be required once the two offices were configured at the front of the house. His most exciting feature he could not wait to explain to the Days.

"You see this space that is created in front of this area when I steal the footage from this room?" Paul asked Carol, as he explained his plan. Carol nodded in understanding. "That," Paul said triumphantly, "that is your elevator!"

James and Carol were thrilled and smiled in satisfaction at Paul's idea.

"We can run a shaft all the way to the basement. It will come up to the first floor opening into the butler's pantry, and the second floor right next to the back staircase, and, finally, into the big room next to the stairs on the third floor. Once I knew there was concrete flooring in the basement, it was feasible to look at doing this. And, here's the best part; we're still under budget."

Paul walked James and Carol to the location the elevator would have on each of the floors. He showed them how, by using the floor space on the third floor, they were taking maximum advantage of the beautiful views of the water and breezes to be enjoyed. Storage space they might lose by finishing the space could be more than made up for by utilizing the basement and the garage area. In fact, Paul had not even told them of his plans for that structure.

"I need to work on the plans for the second floor," Paul was saying as they descended the front staircase to the front hall. "I have an idea of what you want for the master suite, but I need to know about the other rooms. And, for down here, let me show you what cleaning can do."

Paul guided Carol and James through the pocket doors at the bottom of the stairs that had mysteriously been closed. When he pulled the doors back, Carol and James were amazed at what they saw. The room gleamed from the beautiful hardwood floors to the intricately carved cornices. The cleaned crystals of the chandelier sparkled and danced with the light of new bulbs. Natural light streamed through the spotless windows to augment the brightness of the room. It was the first time Carol and James could see how bright their new home could really be.

By late Saturday afternoon, the entire mansion was completely cleaned. Ben's rooms over the garage had been scrubbed and polished and all the boxes stored there had been moved to Paul's shop. Renovations were due to begin on Monday. Paul had subcontracted work for the electrical and the plumbing systems. Everything appeared to be right on schedule, including James's needing to be in New York come Monday morning.

He had avoided saying anything to Carol, hoping that he might be able to resolve issues over the internet, but he now knew that was not going to happen. He would have to be in New York on Monday. He would miss the start of the renovations.

They were on their way back to their rented apartment to wash off the morning's grime when James broke his silence about New York. Carol was angry that he had not told her right away when he knew he would need to go. James thought, initially, Carol would want to go with him, but he knew she needed to be here at the house and not in New York. He had never been so wrong.

"I don't understand why you have to go now," Carol had told him heatedly. "This is where you need to be. I need you here with me. This is where I want to be and where I want you to want to be."

"I promise I'll be back before Wednesday night. You'll have two whole days to work with Paul on plans for the second floor and the basement," James was saying as they pulled into the parking spot at the apartment.

"I'm just saying you should have told me," Carol said pouting slightly.

"You're right. You're absolutely right," James admitted. "But, now that I can't get out of going, let's make the best of it and talk about what is going to happen at the house come Monday."

They unloaded the two bags of groceries that would supplement the larder they had been building slowly over the last week or so. As they entered their apartment, James took the bag of groceries Carol was carrying and, with his own, put them in the small kitchen while Carol headed for the shower. It was amazing how the grit from cleaning seemed to get into everything.

James quickly put away the few perishables and decided to check his email account while Carol was in the shower. James had asked Paul for a set of blueprints, and he had offered to upload them onto the internet for him. James found the site and began examining the plan for the third floor. He could see the stairs now opening into a large sitting room. A full bathroom replaced the small one that was presently off the small servants' room. Two identical offices across the front of the house were reached by arched doorways off the main room. As James was studying the drawing, Carol came out of the bathroom toweling her hair.

"What are you looking at?" she asked James.

"I'm just looking at the plans Paul sent over," James said continuing to study the blueprints. "And I think I found a mistake."

He looked up from his computer screen triumphantly.

"Oh?" Carol said with surprise.

"He forgot your window," James said smiling broadly.

"Show me," Carol said. She came up behind James and leaned over his shoulder to see the screen. James traced the line of the wall that showed two windows and then traced the line of the opposite wall where only one window was shown.

"Paul forgot to put the window back in." James sat back crossing his arms on his chest, smiling at how clever he was. "You better remind him." Carol could see the mistake and made a mental note to be sure to tell Paul first thing Monday morning.

Carol was excited about the work beginning on the house. She was disappointed that James was putting business ahead of their plans. It would finally make the house theirs with changes that were of their making. She and James reviewed all the changes that would be starting on Monday. They looked at the second-floor blueprint and started planning the kinds of changes Paul had visualized. The master suite alone would be almost the size of their New York apartment. It was fun allowing their thoughts to envision what might become reality.

James and Carol spent the remainder of Saturday quietly enjoying an early winter day. The weather was turning cold, and the sky was very gray. The forecast was for rain, sleet, and snow showers, and it looked like it was going to be accurate. If the weather were going to turn nasty, James would have to leave earlier on Sunday than he had originally planned. He did not feel like doing any preparation work for his trip to New York. He did not want to even look at his computer. He just wanted to spend the evening with his beautiful wife, warm and dry in their apartment in Rock Cove. If he needed to prepare anything so that New York would require less time, he could work on it Sunday morning.

With the freezing rain pelting against the windows, James and Carol retired for the night, still discussing the wonderful changes they would make in the mansion transforming it into a home of the twenty-first century. Carol was still angry, feeling that New York and business continued to hold a position of higher priority than she did in her husband's life.

TWENTY-TWO

MONDAY MORNING DAWNED GRAY AND COLD. Carol awoke alone in the apartment. James had left for New York on Sunday afternoon as large flakes of snow were falling. It had taken him nearly an hour longer to drive into the city than usual because of the weather and Carol had been relieved when he finally called her to say he was in the apartment.

She had eaten a solitary dinner and looked at the blueprints for the house again before getting ready for bed and calling James to say goodnight. He was also getting to bed in order to be at his office early. He wanted to get done what was required of him so he could get back to Connecticut, the house, and his wife. It was one of a handful of nights they had spent apart since they had been married.

Carol forced herself to get out of her nice warm bed and into the shower. She knew today would be an important one. It would be the beginning of the transformation of the old Victorian mansion into the new Victorian mansion that belonged to them. Her excitement was tempered by knowing that the changes would begin without James. The warmth of the shower felt good against her skin, and she hated to have to leave it for the coolness of the bathroom. She knew she needed to get moving because Paul and his workers would be at the house early to get in a full day of work. She dried her hair and applied the minimal amount of makeup she usually wore, tossed on her bulky sweater, blue jeans, and boots, and picked up the ring of house keys and dropped them into her pocket. She looked outside one more time and saw a few flakes of snow falling, so she decided to wear her heavier coat. She jumped in her car and drove out of the driveway in the direction of Dunkin Donuts. A morning without coffee was an unthinkable burden.

Paul's truck and utility van were already in the driveway when Carol arrived in her Lexus. She passed the dumpster that was on the far side of the house near the garage and parked in front of the garage. Carol could see in her rear view mirror a group of people standing around Paul as he pointed at his blueprints. She felt the blast of chill air as she got out of her car and walked toward the group.

"Morning," Paul said smiling in a way that showed he, too, felt the cold wind, "James not joining us today?"

"He had to go into New York last night," Carol replied trying to be cheery.

"Ready to start tearing things down?" Paul continued with a smile.

Carol smiled at Paul. "I can't wait to see what it's going to look like."

"Most of the heavy equipment is already upstairs, so, let's see how far they've gotten." Paul rolled up his blueprint and started walking with Carol into the house. When they passed through the kitchen, Carol saw other pages of Paul's plans rolled up on the table. They started up the back stairs to the second floor. The house echoed now that the furniture, the carpets, and drapes were all removed. The sound of their work boots was lost as they climbed up the stairs to the third floor where there was an amazing amount of noise.

Paul was talking to Carol almost in a shout so he could be heard over the cacophony of demolition noise funneling out of the room into the hall at the top of the stairs. Paul was so intent in his conversation with Carol he was not really watching where he was going. Before he realized where he was, his right arm smacked into the same narrowing section of paneling that had gotten James twice before.

"That's the last time that's going to happen," Paul said rubbing his upper arm.

As they stepped into what had been the old servants' sitting room, Carol could not believe what she saw. Two walls were already dismantled. The studding that had supported the walls stood like bare skeletons bathed in halogen work lights. Beyond them, Carol could see the larger area of unfinished attic space with its dark, aged, raw roofing trusses and the spaces between them lacking insulation. It was astonishing to see how small the space taken up by the finished room really had been in relation to the entire attic. The lathe and plaster from the dismantled walls raised new clouds of dust as the workers made pieces small enough to be stuffed into plastic bags and taken out to the dumpster.

As the frames of the dismantled walls were being removed, Paul began laying out the dimensions of the new rooms. He tapped one of the workers and had him hold the tape measure as he marked the floor to identify where the new wall framing would be built. Carol was standing in what was left of the old room. One of the walls forming the hall at the top of the stairs suddenly came apart. The workers had gone behind it into the unfinished attic and used demolition saws to cut the lathe and plaster from the studding. The noise was deafening.

When the wall was completely down, it was amazing to see how leaving the staircase open would enhance the new rooms. The work lights showed the expansive space that would be seen when ascending the stairs. They also showed that the wall on the right of the staircase was built in a very different manner than all the other walls. Where the other walls were of lathe and plaster construction, this wall was constructed of unfinished tongue and groove solid oak planks. The section of wall inside the servants' quarters that continued from the right side of the hall doorway resisted the sledgehammers and saws of the wreckers. The workers soon discovered that the plaster and lathe finished wall lay directly over the same solid oak planking.

Progress stopped as the workers studied this newly discovered puzzle that enclosed a corner of the attic. Paul Murray stopped his measuring and approached the oddly constructed wall. The planks were at least twelve feet long and close to an inch thick. He asked one of his workers for a crowbar. He walked up to the wall at the point where the planking appeared to overlap, where he and James had both caught their shoulders. He inserted the crowbar and attempted to lever the board away from the wall. It did not budge.

Two of the workers came forward carrying circular saws. Paul stepped back as they started making two cuts, one high and one lower, across three or four vertical planks. The worker Paul had taken the crowbar from grabbed it back out of Paul's hand and began prying the planks between the cuts. With muscles straining, the boards began to part and come off the wall.

To everyone's amazement, behind the boards was another set of planks of the same material running horizontally. The workers were scratching their heads. No one had ever seen anything like this.

"What is it, Paul?" Carol asked. She had been watching with the same interest as everyone else as to what was going on.

"I don't know," Paul said rubbing his chin. "I've never seen this kind of construction before." Paul thought for a long moment and then turned to his crew and said, "Take the first layer of planking off and let's see what we've got."

The circular saws came alive, and the sawdust began to fly as the remaining part of the extended section of planking was assaulted. The distance from where the planking overlapped to what had been the doorway into the servants' room was about six feet. It took half a dozen burly workmen twenty minutes of hard work to peel back the boards. With the removal of the vertical planks, the horizontal planks were now visible. In the center of the section that had been cleared, a door was cut into the horizontal planks. The edges of the door were set flush to the planking. The large hinges were recessed into the remaining layer of planking. Set in the door was a lock. Beside the door was a light switch also recessed into the planking.

When Carol saw the door and the lock she reached into her pocket and felt the ring of house keys. She stepped between the sweating workers and up to the door. She pulled the keys from her pocket and found the one that she had found no lock for previously. She inserted it into the lock. The key easily slid into the track. She turned it. She felt the bolt slide back. No one spoke. Carol looked at the faces around her; everyone was watching intently. She gently pushed on the door.

The meetings had been long and boring. James had gotten to the office early to complete the required regulatory updates. After taking the rest of the morning to clear his desk of pending business, he joined three of the other partners for a business lunch. They wanted to discuss his proposed new work arrangement. James felt confident in his ability to answer their concerns if they had any.

Lunch began on a light enough note. His partners asked about the house in Rock Cove and his plans for changing it. James talked about the changes but did not disclose the history of the house. About the time the second round of cocktails arrived, James began to sense a change in the tone of the conversation. It was evident that they had concerns about one of their number not working from the office. James began to look more closely at these three highly successful partners.

George Cummings was a fifty-one-year-old who had been a legend in the investment business for two decades on Wall Street. Along with that success had come two broken marriages and a third that was quickly going on the rocks.

Across the table from James sat Herb Porter. He had been largely responsible for James being made a partner so quickly. Herb was a dynamo of energy that could put in thirty-six hours straight to complete a deal. James had seen him do it on more than one occasion. At fifty-four, he had already had two stints in a very private, very expensive rehabilitation clinic for an undisclosed addiction.

Richard Warner was the youngest of the trio at forty-eight. His sharp intellect and clean-cut manner had brought many large accounts to the firm. It was fortunate that these same accounts did not know about his frequent trips to Atlantic City and Las Vegas with certain members of the secretarial pool.

As James sat there fielding questions from these three highly successful businessmen with impeccable reputations in business about his desire to change his lifestyle, it suddenly hit him. Were these three icons of the business, his business, successful, happy men? Perhaps they had made their mark in the world of business, but at what expense? Was this what being successful in his business required? Was success in terms of business attainable only at the cost of one's personal life? Were they mutually exclusive? If they were, which would James choose? As the two-hour luncheon ended, James had many questions running through his mind. He spent the rest of the afternoon looking at the other partners of the firm. To a man, every one of their private lives was a shambles. James was beginning to question the validity of what his driving force for almost half his life had been.

It was late afternoon when James finally had a chance to answer the five messages he had received since noon from Carol. Most of the people had already left the office for the day when James sat back in his chair and brought up the first text message. It was Carol's usual "I love you. Missing U." The second message said, "Xiting discovery – CALL." The next message was a voicemail. James entered his code, and he could hear the excitement in Carol's voice.

"Honey! Remember the key we couldn't find a lock for? I found it!! We have a secret room in the attic. CALL ME!!"

James did not bother with the other messages. He dialed Carol's number.

"Hi there," Carol said answering the phone.

"What's this about a room in the attic?" James asked excitedly.

"You remember the top of the stairs, the part that narrowed? Well, we started to take that wall down and found there was a door behind it! And that key we had, Honey, it fit the lock." Carol sounded almost conspiratorial.

"So, what was in the room?" James asked.

"We looked inside, but we didn't go in. There was plenty of other work to do and I thought you should be here before we went in," Carol said being upbeat. "Are you coming home tonight?"

"What kind of room was it?" James was asking questions faster they could be answered. "How big was it? Why was the door boarded over? What did Paul think?"

"Hold on!" Carol shouted into the phone. "It was good sized, maybe ten feet by twelve. Paul said he had never seen that kind of construction, but he thought it looked like an attempt to soundproof the room. The walls were triple thickness, and the floor was doubled."

James continued to ask questions that Carol could not answer. She kept telling him he needed to get there. James replied that he needed at least a half day more before he could leave New York. He didn't tell her he had made the decision to leave New York for good. Carol was disappointed but understood that James could either take care of everything he needed to now or have to go back into New York again the next week if he left early. She assured him that Paul had said there was plenty of other work that could be done before the room needed to be dismantled. If James required another day before he could be back, Paul would begin the rewiring and plumbing.

By eleven o'clock the next morning, James was crossing the Harlem River out of Manhattan to reach I-95 heading to Connecticut. He had left what amounted to an ultimatum on his desk addressed to his partners. He had realized they needed him more than he needed them and had said as much in his letter. He doubted they would have any problem accepting his proposal of working from home. He pulled his phone out of his pocket and held it low against his stomach. New York had made it illegal to talk on a cell phone without hands-free service. He dialed Carol's number and put the speaker on. Carol answered after the second ring and James told her he would meet her at the house in a little over two hours. He settled back into his seat and watched his speed.

Carol had answered James's call sitting at the kitchen table in the mansion. Workmen were busy snaking electrical wires from the basement to the third floor. She had sought refuge in the kitchen to look at Paul's plans and wait for James to call. She was staying out of the way. First thing that morning, the workers had started to enlarge the staircase. Access to the third floor was restricted for most of the morning until they dismantled the old staircase and hung the stringers for the new stairs. They had broken through the wall of the bedroom behind the original staircase and built the supporting braces for the new risers. The new staircase would be nearly five feet wide, and each step would be a full twelve inches wide.

The new wall in the second-floor bedroom left the space for the elevator shaft next to the new stairs. It was then that Carol realized the location of the elevator would have its entrance on the third floor inside the hidden room. Carol began to wonder about the room. It had been hard not to enter the room, but Paul had suggested waiting until James was there. She had turned the light switch, but nothing had happened. All they could see peering into the room was the illumination provided by a small skylight cut in the high ceiling. Because the day was cloudy, the light coming through the skylight was minimal and there was very little in the room that could be made out. Carol slowly closed the door and locked it. Tomorrow would be soon enough to explore it, she thought. And now, James was on his way.

Work on the stairs to the third floor stopped promptly at noon as the workmen took their lunches. Most of them stayed inside because the weather had turned nasty. Some had camped out in the front hall; a couple had stepped onto the porch to have a cigarette. The rest had stayed on the third floor. They were curious about the manner in which the room was constructed. Each of them had a theory about it. One thought it was a safe room which was roundly laughed at by the others. It was obvious the room had been built long before the concept of a safe room had existed. How could it be a safe room with a lock on the outside? Another thought it might have hidden illegal drugs or prohibition liquor. It was an amusing topic of conversation while they consumed their lunches and rested for a bit.

At one o'clock sharp, they went back to work and within forty-five minutes, James brought his rental car to a stop in front of the garage next to Carol's Lexus. He left his tie and suit jacket in the car, took his heavier winter jacket out of the trunk, and trotted across the driveway and into the house. Carol was in the kitchen. When she saw James, she got up from the table, ran across the kitchen, and threw her arms around him. He hugged her back.

Let's see this room," James said looking at his pretty wife. Carol showed James she had the key by bringing it up in front of her. They smiled at each other and started up the stairs.

James was surprised by the length and width of the new stairs. When he reached the top, the openness of the floor made him stare in stunned silence. The workmen were already building the studding for the new walls. He then turned his attention to the wall of oak planks. With the wall opposite removed, the light flooding through the windows at the front of the house made it possible to see how expertly the planks had been fitted together and the door cut so tightly into it. Carol handed him the key. Paul had been making measurements across the open attic space and saw James looking at the oak-planked wall. He came from across the attic space with a portable work light in his hand. He nodded to James welcoming him back.

"Ready when you are," Paul said with a smile.

James placed the key in the lock and turned it. The levels of noise from construction ceased as the workers stopped their work and were drawing near the wall. Everyone was curious as to what was in the room. He gently pushed the door open, and the room was illuminated by the high intensity work light.

TWENTY-THREE

IN THE BRIGHT GLOW OF THE WORK LIGHT, THE layers of dust and the accumulated cobwebs that had covered the interior of the house before it had been cleaned were evident in the hidden room. The room was small by the standards of the rest of the house, perhaps ten feet by twelve feet. There were no windows other than a small skylight cut into the sixteen-foot-high ceiling. Beneath the skylight opening was a mesh of what looked like quarter-inch metal screening. The internal walls were of the same oak planking as on the outside. The planks were running vertically just as they were on the outside of the wall. The thickness of the door jamb indicated that the wall was made of three layers of oak planking. The outermost layer had been removed to access the door.

    Paul was admiring the construction of the wall as James and Carol stepped across the threshold sweeping the hanging webs away from their faces and making the first imprints in the pristine dust on the floor. The bright work light lit up the interior of the room. A bed was against the wall to the right. It was of simple construction, an unadorned headboard and footboard. A small table stood against the opposite wall. Beyond the table, against the same wall, stood an old-style bench, the kind with a storage box under the seat. On the far wall, a small wash basin with a tap and a commode were installed against the outside wall.

Paul noticed a bare bulb hanging from the ceiling on a bare cord. He turned to one of the workers, all of whom were staring through the doorway, and asked him to get a step ladder. His voice resounded strangely in the room, almost deadened. Paul took the ladder from the worker and placed it under the hanging bulb. From his pocket, he pulled a new bulb. He unscrewed the burned-out bulb and screwed in the new one and the room was thrown into light from a new source.

The newly installed light bulb and the work light removed almost all the shadows from the room. The room was extremely quiet. It was eerie, how there was no echo, no noise from outside. When anyone spoke within the room, their voice seemed dampened by the thick walls.

Carol was looking at the spread that covered the bed. It had a simple pattern to it beneath the layer of dust. She noticed the seat of the bench had a slender cushion on it that was of the same pattern. Other than the cushion and the spread on the bed, the room was barren of any soft touches. It was then James noticed that the bed, the table, and the bench were all bolted to the floor.

"What was this room for?" Carol said softly to Paul. Paul just stood shaking his head. He had folded the ladder and was just looking around the room.

"I don't think I have ever seen anything like this," he said in an amazed tone. "If the house was older, I might have said it was possibly a stop on the Underground Railroad. You know, slaves gaining freedom? But, in any event, I guess we need to clean it and then tear it down."

James was looking at each item in the room. The bed, the table, the toilet, the sink; nothing seemed to make sense. He looked at the walls, but all he saw were the neat tongue and groove joints of the planks. He looked up at the skylight and saw the wire screening below it. There was no purpose he could see to the existence of this room.

Carol walked over to the bench. The layer of dust was gritty under her fingers as she ran them over the top of the backrest brushing aside the cobwebs draped there. She reached down and placed her fingertips under the edge of the seat that formed the lid of the storage chest. As she lifted the seat, she froze.

"James," Carol said softly, her voice shaking. "James," her voice getting edgier, "Please. Get over here."

James crossed the room and looked over Carol's shoulder. In the shadowed interior of the box, their gaze fell upon the empty eye sockets and toothy grin of a skull staring up at them.

"Jesus Christ!" James exclaimed before he could stop himself. Carol released her grip on the lid and recoiled in horror, but James grabbed it before it could slam shut. She turned and buried her face in James's chest. He pushed the lid gently back open, by which time Paul had crossed to the bench and was able to see inside.

"What the....," escaped Paul's lips in a quiet whisper. "Don't touch it, Jim!" It seemed odd that Paul would choose this moment to suddenly address James by his first name, but no one appeared to even notice. "Let's just get out of here and call the authorities."

James was strangely fascinated by what he saw. For a few moments, his gaze was fixed on the grizzly sight. He noted the leathery remains of dried skin that covered the face of the skull; the mop of hair still attached to it. He heard what Paul was saying, but he had no desire to touch anything. It was just the sight of it that entranced him. He had never seen, let alone been near, anything like it.

The three of them left the room immediately. James had gently closed the lid of the box and straightened the cushion seat. He lifted Carol gently and guided her through the doorway pushing through the group of curious workmen. Paul had followed with his cell phone in his hand. Three of the workers found a place for Carol to sit on a pile of building materials. The shock of what she had seen was beginning to wear off. Paul was on the phone dialing 911 to summon the authorities to the house for the second time in a week. James looked into the room one last time as he grasped the jamb to close the door. He saw the starkness of the room and the dust that had covered the floor marred by their footsteps and the cobwebs, now hanging wrecked to some extent. He pulled the door closed, flipped the light switch off, and turned the key, leaving it in the lock.

Trooper Anderson reached for his radio. The dispatcher repeated the call: discovery of a body. The trooper acknowledged the call and asked for a repeat of the address. The address was all too familiar. He was only a few miles away when he received the call and he knew that Sergeant Bennett would be on his way as well. He thought to himself, "first a weapon and now a body."

He turned on the police cruiser's lights and made a U-turn at the next intersection and headed for the Carlisle Estate. It only took a matter of ten minutes to reach the gateposts, but it was long enough for Trooper Anderson to review in his mind his last visit to the estate. Less than a week ago it had been the accidental discharge of a lethal weapon resulting in an accidental wound. Now, it was the discovery of a body. Wryly, he wondered what the next week would bring.

As he approached the house, the construction vehicles of the workers were parked to one side of the driveway. The Trooper pulled his cruiser up to the back of the house and called in his location to the dispatcher. He was advised that his supervisor was in route. He gathered his report pad and went to the trunk to retrieve a roll of yellow tape. As he closed the trunk, Ben Allen appeared out of the garage. At least the trooper knew he was not the body that had been discovered.

"Mr. Allen," the Trooper said touching the brim of his hat. "Hadn't planned on seeing you again quite so soon," he continued. "Do you know where the body is?"

Ben Allen stopped in his tracks. "Body?" He responded. From the look on his face, Trooper Anderson realized that Ben had no idea what he was talking about.

"Do you know where everyone is?" the Trooper asked.

"I think they were starting on the third floor today. What body?" Ben questioned again.

"Would you show me the way, please?" the officer asked Ben without acknowledging his question.

"Sorry, I don't go in the house," Ben replied. "Was inside for the first time in thirty-eight years the other day and I damn near got arrested! If you go in the kitchen and up the stairs there, you can find your way."

Trooper Anderson thanked him and headed inside, leaving Ben to scratch his head and continuing to wonder what body? He passed the cellar door and entered the kitchen where the interrogations had taken place the previous week. He followed the stairs to the second floor and saw the construction on the stairs leading to the third floor. As he mounted the last steps, he saw the workers and James, Carol, and Paul quietly sitting about.

"Officer Anderson," James said rising.

"Mr. Day, is it not?" Trooper Anderson replied. "Where is the body?"

James pointed to the planked wall. He walked to the door and turned the key in the lock. Trooper Anderson followed James in the direction of the door. James pointed to the chest under the bench.

"If you will just stand back, Sir," Trooper Anderson spoke with authority. He glanced into the room and then turned to address the people assembled in the work area. "If all of you will vacate the premises until further notice, it would be appreciated."

"Can we stay in the house?" Carol asked.

"For the present, you may stay in the kitchen until advised further," the Trooper replied.

The workers started to gather up their tools when the officer requested they leave everything just as it was. They grumbled under their breaths about their tools being their livelihoods but did as requested and trooped down the stairway. Paul followed them along with Carol and James.

They had not been in the kitchen for long when James saw another

State Police car through the window coming up the drive. It was Sergeant Bennett. No sooner did he leave his car than another vehicle came up the driveway followed by a black SUV. On its door it read State Medical Examiner. Two people exited the unmarked car and two more appeared out of the M.E.'s car. The Sergeant was approached by one man from each of the other vehicles. The three men met outside and shook hands all round. They spoke for several minutes and then entered the mansion through the kitchen followed by a person carrying a large silver case and another carrying a small black case.

Sergeant Bennett shook hands with James, Carol, and Paul for the second time in a week. He introduced the others: Doctor Edward McDonough of the Medical Examiner's Office and Lieutenant Martin Chambers of the Major Crimes Squad. Assisting Lieutenant Martin was Frank Koslick, CSI. Lieutenant Chambers would be in charge of the investigation.

"Where is the body?" Dr. McDonough asked politely.

"It's on the third floor," James replied. "Trooper Anderson is up there with it."

Dr. McDonough motioned to his assistant with the black case and the two of them with Lieutenant Chamber's assistant, Frank Koslick, mounted the stairs and disappeared. Lieutenant Chambers turned to the group assembled in front of him.

"I understand from Sergeant Bennett that a weapon was discharged here less than week ago," he said. "And, because that occurred in the basement, I'm going to ask that you all leave the premises until we can clear the body and gather any evidence we can."

"There are some rooms over the garage," Carol piped up. "Can we go there?"

"That would be fine, Mrs. Day," Lieutenant Chambers replied pleasantly. "I will want to speak with those who discovered the body, but, first, I need to speak with the M.E."

Sergeant Bennett and Dr. McDonough appeared at the top of the stairs on the third floor. Trooper Anderson was standing watching Frank Koslick of the Major Crimes Squad carefully brushing fine powder on the key, the lock, the light switch, and the face of the door. He saluted the Sergeant.

"What have we got, Nate?" the Sergeant said.

"Body's in the room, Sarge. No one has been in since I got here."

Sergeant Bennett looked around at the construction going on around him. He then looked at the doctor.

"They just opened this place after it had been closed for thirty-something years," Sergeant Bennet said to the M.E. "Now they've started renovating. I don't know how much in the way of evidence you'll find after all the cleaning they've done," he said to Dr, McDonough.

"My concern is the body right now," Dr. McDonough replied.

"So, these fingerprints are probably from the people assembled downstairs?" Frank Koslick asked as he lifted a print from the side of the key.

"Afraid so, Koz," Sergeant Bennett replied.

"Are you done with the door?" Lieutenant Chambers asked from the top of the stairs where he had stopped. Koz, as the crime technician was known, nodded he was done.

The Sergeant motioned to Trooper Anderson to open the room. As Koz backed away from the door, the Officer turned around, turned the key, and stepped out of the way. Dr. McDonough donned a pair of latex gloves and was about to push the door open when he heard a snap behind him. Lieutenant Chambers had snapped the cuff of the latex gloves he had slipped on. The Doctor smiled at the Lieutenant, swung the door open, and flipped on the light switch.

Immediately, Koz started taking pictures of the interior of the room. The documentation of the scene would be critical to their examination. The tracks of footprints would verify the stories of what James, Carol, and Paul had done while they were in the room. Koz and Lieutenant Chambers eased into the room, their shoes covered in booties so their footprints could later be identified. Koz continued to take pictures. For those standing outside the room, it was an odd sight to sporadically see light from the flash of the digital camera blasting from the doorway of the room.

Lieutenant Martin Chambers had been in the Major Case Squad for twelve years. It was Connecticut's version of a crime scene investigation unit. It was their responsibility to document crime scenes, collect evidence and forward it for analysis to the Forensics Laboratory. Martin Chambers looked all of his forty-four years. He was born and bred in New York but had lived in Connecticut most of his adult life. His accent had faded after all this time. He was fit and his frame was trim. He was fair-haired with a complexion that showed his Irish heritage. And his eyes could dance with light when so inclined, but they had a keenness that served him well in his work. He and Frank Koslick had worked as a team for nearly five years. Frank was noted for his attention to detail and his powers of observation. His round face and short stature were a compliment to Frank Chambers' lean height. "Koz" was relaxed and meticulous in his approach to work. The two of them could be counted on to do a thorough investigation..

As Koz made his way around the room photographing, he reached the bench and noted the staining on the floor around the base of the chest. As he continued to photograph, Lieutenant Chambers began examining the table surface. It was a rough finished surface that was coated by a thick layer of dust. It was well made, and the legs were bolted with angle irons to the flooring. There appeared to be no impressions on the surface and no marks on any of the legs.

Koz had set his camera aside and had begun examining the bench. There seemed to be nothing remarkable about it. The heavy layer of gritty dust obscured every flat surface and had long since destroyed any chance of recovering any meaningful fingerprints. Koz slowly raised the seat of the bench and picked up his camera. He ran off a half dozen photographs of the remains that were revealed to him.

"You better have a look at this, Marty" he said to his Lieutenant.

Marty Chambers approached the bench and peered into the box beneath the seat with his high intensity pen light. What he saw was not what he was expecting. The partially mummified remains appeared to be articulated and untouched from the time they had been placed in the box.

"Is it okay for us now?" Dr. McDonough called from the doorway.

Martin looked at Koz and he nodded his assent.

"Come on in. It's all yours. Take your time. There's no hurry. This one has been here a long time," Marty Chambers replied.

TWENTY-FOUR

DR. MCDONOUGH ENTERED THE ROOM AND WAS immediately struck by the quieting effect the walls had on sound. He and his assistant knelt in front of the bench and began to analyze what they saw. Lieutenant Chambers stood by watching the two examiners work.

Marty Chambers had worked with Ed McDonough many times over the years. He watched the doctor carefully examine every aspect of the box containing the human remains. The doctor had been in the M.E.'s office for eight years and loved what he did. His hazel eyes showed intensity in his oval face when he performed his examinations. His reports were pithy and direct and, most importantly, always complete.

"Well, this is a rather unusual find," Ed McDonough said. "Note the staining of the flooring around the bottom of the box."

"Yeah, I noticed that," Marty Chambers answered, even though no response was really expected. The M.E. turned enough to see the detective's inquiring face and smiled at his interest.

"It's under the layer of dust, see," Ed continued, pointing to the outline of the stain. "It's probably from the time of death, the initial liquefaction that occurred; definitely not recent. My guess is that death occurred either just before winter or in the winter in order to get this level of mummification along with the desiccation.

"How do you figure that, Doc," Marty Chambers asked.

"See those brown casings in the bottom of the box," Ed showed his flashlight into a corner of the box, "those are pupae casings. If death had occurred in the warming weather of spring or summer, there would be much greater stripping of the skin, less mummification, and a lot more of those casings. Since the colder, drier weather of late fall or early winter would give the corpse a chance to desiccate before being consumed. By spring there would have been less fresh flesh for the pupae to be attracted to and consume; ergo, fewer casings and greater mummification."

"You're amazing Ed," Marty said admiringly. "See anything that suggests a homicide?"

The Medical Examiner looked with his flashlight as best he could at the collapsed body in the box. The arms were folded across the body and the legs were drawn up against them. The entire body leaned slightly to one side. The skin was the color and consistency of beef jerky. It was shrunk against the bones and had split as it dried, exposing portions of the underlying bones.

"I don't see anything right away, but once we get it to the lab…" The Doctor continued looking but saying nothing.

Dr. McDonough motioned for his assistant to lay out the zippered bag he had brought from the car. Being very careful not to cause any injury, the two of them lifted the partially mummified remains from the box and placed them carefully in the bag. Although the remains were not heavy, they were awkward to move. Still, Marty was impressed by the care taken by the assistant M.E.

"We'll let you know what we find," the Doctor said straightening up. "As for the bench, I'd like that looked at very carefully. In fact, we should probably take it for examination in the lab. And I think you can be pretty assured that none of those people in the garage had anything to do with whatever happened here. I'll be able, hopefully, to tell you how and what happened, but you're going to have to figure out who and why."

"Thanks, Ed." Marty Chambers said. "Maybe they can tell me something."

Carol, James, and Paul were all sitting in the main room over the garage where they could see the back door of the mansion. Ben had made himself scarce. There was very little conversation passing between them. Carol had never seen a corpse, let alone one in that state, and it had shaken her. She could not get beyond the sight of that skull with its sunken eye sockets and leathery, brown skin pulled back to expose those teeth in a hideous, macabre smile.

James was trying to analyze the identity of the mummified remains. He ticked through the information he had about the mansion and its tragic past. James was positive that the body had to be the result of the events from 1927. He felt there was only one possible identity for the remains: the Baron. His disappearance was unsolved. He was known to have been in the house at the time of the murder. It had been reported that there had been additional shots fired after Becky Carlisle had been murdered. The Baron would have been a logical target for Mrs. Stanhope's fury - or Mrs. Carlisle's (?).

Paul was sitting quietly lost in his own thoughts about the room, the job, the delay. He was a businessman and delays meant additional cost and, this time of year, delays meant flirting with inclement weather. Even though it was an inside renovation, winter presented problems that warmer weather did not.

As each of the three was being intently quiet, James suddenly noticed the back door of the mansion open. He alerted the others to the activity. Trooper Anderson held the door as the two medical men carried something out in a zippered black bag and carried it to the back of their vehicle. They were followed by Lieutenant Chambers and Frank Koslick carrying several sealed plastic bags with broad red bands imprinted "EVIDENCE" plainly visible. Sergeant Bennett was the last person to come through the door. He stood just outside the door as Trooper Anderson locked it and sealed it with yellow tape.

As the State Trooper and his Sergeant started to walk toward their cruisers, Lieutenant Chambers and Koz began walking toward them having placed their evidence bags into their vehicle. They spoke for a few minutes and then the Lieutenant and the CSI started walking toward the garage with Sergeant Bennett in tow.

"It looks like they're coming to talk to us," James said tentatively. All three of them were now standing looking out the windows in the direction of the house.

"Let me go first," Paul said. "I don't know anything, and I need to get my people out of here." It was true. All of Paul's workmen had been sheltering in a garage bay beneath them talking with Ben Allen. Paul did not know that the detective and the Sergeant would quickly question all the workmen before arriving in the upstairs apartment. The only thing any of the workers had seen was from the doorway of the room and none of them had seen the body. None of them had entered the room so there was no need to take any shoeprints or fingerprints to exclude them.

A knock on the door from the stairs that led to the garage introduced Sergeant Bennett, the CSI, and Lieutenant Chambers and Paul's temporary foreman into the rooms on the second floor of the garage. The foreman only wanted to know from Paul when the workmen should return to work. Paul looked to the investigators for an answer.

"We'll be done here today," Lieutenant Chambers answered.

Paul looked at the foreman and said, "Tell the men we'll start again, day after tomorrow."

The foreman left and the six people remaining made themselves comfortable.

"Folks, I am going to ask all of you to submit shoeprints and fingerprints so we can exclude you from the crime scene," Lieutenant Chambers began. "Koz is going to help me."

"So, it is a crime scene?" James asked.

"Mr. Day, we really don't know at this point. The Medical Examiner will need to do his examination and make his report. Until we know the cause of death, if it can be determined, we'll treat it as a homicide. The thing I can assure all of you is that none of you are under any suspicion.' Marty Chambers smiled at his small joke.

"Who do you think it is?" Carol asked anxiously.

"At this point, I have no idea, Mrs. Day," the detective replied. "I was hoping you folks would be able to give me some clues."

"Lieutenant," Paul Murray said, "If I may, I know very little about the history of the house. The Days hired my firm to clean the house and we were just starting renovations when we discovered the room and then the body." Paul was obviously anxious when he spoke. "Between the accident last week and now this...."

"What accident?" the detective asked.

"We had a call here last week, Lieutenant," Sergeant Bennett interjected. "We had an accidental discharge of a firearm in the basement that resulted in an injury to one of the workmen."

"Who has the weapon now?" Marty Chambers asked the Officer.

"It was transported to the Ballistics Lab and delivered to Lieutenant Vance," Sergeant Bennett replied checking back in his notepad.

"So, Sergeant, this is your second time here in a week?" the detective mused.

Frank Koslick had finished taking prints from Paul and had moved on to Carol. Paul was cleaning the print ink from his hands when he asked if he might be excused. Martin Chambers thanked him for his cooperation and released him. Paul shook hands with James and Carol and assured them he would be available in the morning and quickly left.

"Tell me what you know about the house," the detective said to James and Carol. He set a tape recorder on the coffee table.

James began to tell Martin Chambers all they knew about the history of the house. Carol interjected comments here and there. They related the history of the Carlisle – Stanhope rivalry and the murder of Becky Carlisle on her wedding day in 1927. They related what they knew of the trial of Mrs. Carlisle some two years later. They explained how they had investigated the history of the house and spoken with Ellen Perry and John Grant. The detective was making extensive notes. James explained how they had gone about purchasing the property and the circumstances surrounding the trust; how the house had been maintained externally and when they had first entered the house, it was evident no one had been inside in years. James suddenly realized the extensive cleaning of the house had probably impacted the chances of recovering any evidence that might have existed. They related the connections of Ben Allen and Stanley Beckwith to the property. Detective Chambers continued taking voluminous notes, asking for clarification on certain points.

James presented Detective Chambers with his own theory about the body. He was sure that the remains they had discovered would prove to be those of the fortune-hunting Baron. He theorized that the Baron, too, had been killed by Mrs. Stanhope while on her bloody murder spree. The fact he was known to be in the house at the time of Becky's murder and was never seen afterward was now explainable.

After almost two hours of questioning, Marty Chambers felt he had some clues to pursue. Koz had gathered fingerprints from everyone and had been listening intently to James and Carol discussing their home. At one point, when discussion centered around the gun that had been found the week before, the Sergeant admitted he had not looked for, nor recovered, the bullet. With that, Detective Chambers asked Koz and the Sergeant to see if they could find it. They had been gone not more than twenty minutes when they returned, Koz holding up a plastic evidence bag with a deformed slug in it to the approval of his associate.

The sun was beginning to set behind the garage. The investigating team began packing up their notepads, recorders, and satchels. Lieutenant Chambers and Frank Koslick thanked the Days for their cooperation, as did Sergeant Bennett. Lieutenant Chambers replied to James's inquiry regarding how long it would take for them to know anything by saying he would be in touch as soon as they knew something. It did not satisfy James, but he accepted the answer. He was tired; it had been a long day. The Days stood with arms around each other looking at the cars winding down the driveway in the fading light. In the half-light of dusk, flurries began to fall.

TWENTY-FIVE

BEN ALLEN HAD WATCHED THE CARS DISAPPEAR down the drive from inside the garage. When he saw they were safely out of sight, he quietly climbed the stairs to his rooms above. As he opened the door, he saw Carol and James standing silhouetted against the windows facing the drive. He gently cleared his throat to announce his presence. James turned to see Ben reaching for the light switch.

"Sorry, Ben, we didn't mean to take over your place today," James said.

"It's alright, Jim," Ben replied with a wave of his hand. "I don't really know what all went on today, just pieces here and there. Would you mind telling me what happened?"

James and Carol sat on the couch and related to Ben everything they could remember from the day. They described the room, its construction and location, the furniture within it, and the remains that had been found in the bench. They included James's theory about the identity of the body. Ben listened intently, especially when it came to the theoretical identity.

"If the room was built the way you describe it, it might certainly contain the smell of something rotting," Ben said. "I'm just not sure I agree with you that it has to be the Baron."

"Who else could it be?" James questioned.

Carol and James hopped into their car in a real snowstorm. They had spent perhaps another forty-five minutes talking with Ben about their plans for the mansion. Carol had expressed again her feelings that every time she began to feel like the house was really hers, something had happened to push the house back into its past.

James finally had a chance to ask Ben why he had entered the house the week before when the revolver had been found. Ben related the same story he had given the police. But, when James pressed Ben further, he said much more than he had told the police.

"My father always said the gun never left the house," Ben had said. "I have always suspected he hid the gun to protect Mrs. Carlisle. I think my father suspected she had used the gun after Mrs. Stanhope dropped it and that her fingerprints were on it. I didn't want his memory spoiled by any findings on the gun. All that happened a long, long time ago and it should stay buried. At least I know that my father didn't build that room you found. He was a handyman, an outdoors type. From what you said about how that room was constructed; I don't think he was capable of that level of quality work – as good as he might have been."

It was obvious that Ben had a deep respect for his father, and he was willing to do almost anything to protect his father's memory. In the same way, he felt a responsibility for the memory of someone he considered a great lady, even though he had only known her for a short time during his life. Recent events were beginning to raise questions in him about those he had always believed were above reproach.

"Do you think there is an answer somewhere in the boxes that were here?" Carol asked Ben.

"Mrs. Day, if the answer is there, I have no idea where. When they moved Mrs. Carlisle to the nursing home, Mr. Beckwith had someone come in and just go from room-by-room boxing up everything that was of a personal nature."

"Were the boxes marked in any way?" Carol asked.

"It seems to me they were," Ben said, trying to remember the writing he thought he remembered on those boxes that he had passed by so many times over the years and given so little regard. "I'm not sure how they were marked, I have to be honest," he said.

"James, I want to start looking through those boxes," Carol said looking at James. "There may be an answer to all this somewhere in them."

The snow was falling heavily as James negotiated the unplowed roads back to their rented apartment. The headlights made the falling snow seem to float as the car sped through them. There were no other cars on the road, and everything felt so quiet and peaceful. Carol was feeling the first few moments of relaxation she had felt all day. She was emotionally drained from the events of the day. All she wanted to do was take a hot shower, change her clothes, and have a nice hot cup of tea.

James was strangely quiet on the short ride to the apartment. He was becoming frustrated with the history attached to his new home. It really did not feel like his home. No, it was strangely separated from him because of the events of the past week. Maybe Carol was right in saying the past was not ready yet to let the present have sway. The past still needed to be settled before that could happen. He had hoped to be celebrating Christmas in his newly renovated home, but it did not look like that was going to happen. Here they were nearly at Thanksgiving, and they were weeks behind on their renovations. And now the weather had turned against them, as well.

By the time Carol had emerged from their bedroom after a nice shower, James had brewed a pot of tea for the two of them. The spotlight that lit the parking area outside their apartment showed the snow falling even more heavily than when they had been driving. There were already four or five inches of snow on the ground. The forecast was for a foot or more. James was disgusted that work would not continue tomorrow because he had not made any arrangements for the estate to be plowed out. He had forgotten that Ben Allen would be prepared for the snow.

What James and Carol could not tell looking out on the quietly falling snow while they were sitting in their warm, cozy apartment was how steeply the temperature had dropped. By morning, the falling snow would be replaced by gusting winds and blowing snow and temperatures in the single digits. With the heating and electrical systems under repair, work on the mansion would have to be delayed until the weather moderated. Workmen did not mind working under inclement conditions, but there was a limit.

In the morning, James would receive a call from Paul Murray suggesting that the weather would have caused most of his workers not to show up to the job anyway. He would suggest a couple of days' break in the work schedule to allow things to calm down a bit. Some of his men had been a bit "spooked" by the events of the previous day. Carol would ask Paul if she could begin looking through the boxes that had been removed from the garage since she would not have to be at the mansion for a few days. He would assure her that she was more than welcome to spend as much time as she wished looking through them. His storage area at the shop had a separate entrance and he could provide her with a key.

But all of that would be tomorrow. For tonight, Carol just wanted to cuddle under a blanket, sipping her warm tea next to James on the sofa in their temporary residence and watch the snow falling quietly outside. It seemed like they had had very little real quiet time for themselves since they had started this project. Carol felt she handled the stress of business extremely well and always had. But this was a different kind of stress. Stress from business was stress to perform, to meet deadlines, to complete projects. The stress she was experiencing now was emotional stress. It was brought on by unpredictable events that played on one's thoughts and feelings. Those events had been mysterious, horrifying, and unresolved. It was draining. And for some reason she was not handling it well.

The fact was she had not felt well for several weeks. She had attributed it at first to the excitement of looking at houses. The travel had disrupted her normal schedule, and she was a woman who had grown accustomed to having order in her life. Her Midwestern upbringing had taught her that schedules got things done; they defended against disorder and whim. Unfortunately, deciding on where one wanted to live and finding a house there did not conform to any set schedule. After that had been decided, she attributed her continuing fatigue, her short-tempered frustration, her gastric upsets to the excitement of learning the history of the house she had determined to make hers. She just did not feel herself.

James was quietly mulling things over in his mind. He was wondering how long it would be before he would hear from any of the authorities regarding the body and the cause of death. He wondered if they would ever be able to identify who it was. He had never been involved in anything like this and he had no idea how long it took to make identification or if one was even possible. The only thing he was absolutely sure about was that no one who had entered the house in recent time could possibly have had anything to do with the death of the person whose remains they had found or with the construction of the room in which it was found. He could swear on a bible to that.

He was upset at the delay the investigation would cause in the plans Carol had for the house. If the weather continued to be uncooperative, it could easily postpone activity at the mansion for a few more days. There were so many factors that seemed to be impeding progress on the mansion. He was beginning to wonder if maybe they had made a mistake in buying the old place.

TWENTY-SIX

MORNING BROUGHT THE PREDICTED CALL FROM Paul Murray, along with the subfreezing temperatures and blowing snow. Carol was excited by the prospect of beginning to look through the boxes of personal affects that were at Paul's shop. But, the weather looked miserable and the towns in the area had issued parking bans. The high winds and snow were raising havoc with power lines. It was really a day to stay home.

Carol and James had just decided it was a day for using the internet to catch up on work that had gone unattended for too long when James's cell phone rang. It was a very agitated Ben Allen calling to let James know that the mansion had again been invaded early that morning by a group of uniformed and plain clothed people who were at that very moment removing things from the house. James asked if Ben recognized any of the people there.

"Yes, Sir," Ben said without thinking. "That Lieutenant is here. You know the one who questioned you and Mrs. Day? He cornered me this morning and was asking all sorts of questions."

"Where is he now?" James asked.

"He left me about half an hour ago and went to the house," Ben replied. "I tried to see what was going on, but, when I tried to leave, there was a police officer posted at the bottom of the stairs."

Ben, I can't get over there," James said feeling a bit of panic. "The roads are terrible. Can you see what they are taking out of the house?"

"The only thing I've seen them putting in the cars that I could identify were long planks of wood. Oh! And a bench with a solid bottom."

James was furious when he ended the call. Who did Lieutenant Martin Chambers think he was? Explaining to Carol what Ben had just told him made him even angrier. James was debating whether to call his attorney or some agency of the State to complain about the detective's high-handed actions when a knock came at the door. James opened the door to see Lieutenant Chambers braced against the blustery wind.

"Mind if I come in?" he said with a smile.

"Just the person I wanted to see," James said with a slight sneer in his voice. It was not lost on the detective. "What the hell were you doing at my house this morning?'

"The Medical Examiner and the forensics people wanted some additional evidence collected," the Lieutenant said calmly removing his overcoat. "I have a receipt for you right here that details what we removed for examination." Carol took the detective's coat and hung it on one of hooks by the door.

"Why didn't you tell us you would be back?" James's anger had not subsided. He snatched the receipt offered by the detective and tossed it on the coffee table.

"Mr. Day, may I remind you that the Carlisle Mansion is still a crime scene until we release it and we have not done so at present." Marty Chambers was beginning to feel the need to be the hard-as-nails cop he hated being. If James Day wanted a cop, he was going to get one. Carol motioned to the detective to take a seat.

"I took the opportunity to interview your caretaker, Mr. Allen," The detective said regaining the smooth exterior he preferred to try to employ in his work. "You didn't mention that his father had a connection to the incident in 1927."

"We were not hiding anything," James said caught off his guard. "It just never came up."

"Just like the subject of the boxes you had removed from the premises recently never came up?" Marty Chambers had learned of their existence from his interview with Ben. Although he did not intend it so, his statement came out with a sinister turn to it.

"Those contained the personal property of Mrs. Carlisle and were packed away when she left the house almost forty years ago," Carol said defensively. "Mr. Beckwith told us they were part of the sale, specifically. We were not trying to hide anything. We haven't even looked at them."

"Mrs. Day, I did not mean to intimate you were trying to hide anything. It just seems there are a lot of open questions." Marty Chambers did not want to alienate James and Carol. "Folks, I need your help. None of you are under any suspicion regarding the remains we recovered. They had evidently been there for a long, long time. All I want is to find out who we found, determine how they got there, and find out if there was any foul play. I want to be able to close this case."

"Isn't that the job of your Medical Examiner and Forensics Lab?" James asked, still warm over what he considered an invasion of his property.

"Yes, it is for the most part." Marty said bristling slightly. "But, since you have already done so much research into the history of the house and the events in its past, I was hoping you could help speed up our investigation."

"But we've already told you everything we know," Carol said.

"Yes, I believe you have, Mrs. Day," Marty replied with a slight smile. "I've already got a couple of our interns researching some of the leads we've developed. I have members of the squad holding interviews with Mr. Beckwith and Ellen Perry. I am hoping to have the M.E.'s report in a day or two and we'll have a cause of death. It will take us longer to identify the body, I'm afraid."

"So, what more can we do to help?" James asked.

"I would like to have a look at those boxes that you had removed," the detective said looking at Carol. "Of course, I don't have enough evidence to force them to be turned over to us, but I would like to sit down and go through them with you, if you are willing." Marty waited for a reaction from Carol.

"If it could help, I will be happy to allow it," Carol said. "I am curious myself as to what may be there." Marty smiled at Carol a genuine smile that defused the tension that had been in the room.

"Can we meet tomorrow morning at Mr. Murray's shop?" Marty said to Carol as he rose from his seat. "Is nine o'clock alright? Would you like me to pick the two of you up?"

"That's alright," James said. "We'll meet you there at nine. We had already planned on starting to look through them since work has stopped at the house for a couple of days."

Carol stood and retrieved the detective's coat. Lieutenant Chambers donned his overcoat and bundled it around him. He headed out into the wind and blowing snow to his unmarked police car. Except for the searchlight mounted by the driver's door, it would have looked like any other Crown Victoria on the road. James and Carol watched as the car slowly pulled out of their drive and disappeared into the blowing snow.

TWENTY-SEVEN

AFTER DETECTIVE CHAMBER'S VISIT, JAMES AND Carol attempted to concentrate on getting through as much backlogged work as they could. They still had jobs and responsibilities that did not revolve around solving the mystery that was developing around their newly purchased house. It was no easy task to concentrate on affairs pertaining to business after having a discussion with a person who was only concerned with that mystery. Carol was having an internet conference with her general manager in the bedroom while James was attempting to reply to inquiries from his clients. Neither of them felt very accommodating about anything. It was a relief when the late afternoon sun allowed them to call it a day and think about dinner.

They decided to brave the weather and go to the Dogwatch Café for a quiet dinner. They were fairly sure there would not be many who would be joining them because of the weather, and they were right. The parking lot at the restaurant was virtually empty, but the lights inside looked warm and inviting. James and Carol ordered a bottle of Merlot to enjoy with their dinner and sat back in the empty dining room to enjoy the view of the marina covered in snow.

Conversation between them was stilted. They were, each of them, trying to find a topic that could sustain a conversation. James was concerned about his business interests and being out of the loop of daily attention that his business required. Carol was thinking of the boxes that would be opened starting in the morning, boxes that had been sealed for over thirty-five years. She did not need to be concerned about her business because she had a staff that she could rely on to continue business as usual. James's business required his personal involvement every day. That was the difference between a business of creation like Carol's and one that required personal analysis and insight to formulate forecasts. They finally settled their conversation on the subject of tomorrow's activity: the boxes.

"What do you think we're going to find?" James asked calmly.

"I don't really know, Honey," Carol replied. "Mr. Beckwith said they were items of a personal nature. That could be anything from photographs to papers, to nick-knacks, I suppose."

"Yeah, it could be toothbrushes and deodorant too," said James with feigned levity. "I suppose there could be something significant in those boxes, although I have no idea what."

"If there are photographs, I am wondering if we will be able to identify who the people are in them." Carol said warming to the topic. "Mr. Beckwith said the boxes contained 'things of a personal nature;' those were his exact words."

"My guess is that someone just went from room to room and emptied contents of drawers and took down pictures and boxed them up without even looking at what they were," James said as he refilled their wine glasses. "I remember my mother doing that when her father went into a home when I was a kid. I would bet my mother still hasn't looked at those boxes."

"We never had to do that," Carol said lifting her glass. "My grandparents never had enough to fill a box."

Their dinners arrived with a smile from the waitress who remembered their generous gratuities from earlier visits. They lapsed into silence as they ate and watched the few boats still in the marina, their hulls closely held by a skim of ice. Along the shore, a jumble of broken blocks of ice lay piled by the changing tide on the pebbled sand. The food was delicious, and the wine was warming. It was one of those nights that became a memory.

Martin Chambers of the Major Crime Squad was leaning over a set of blueprints speaking intently with Paul when Carol and James came through the shop door. The day had dawned with bright sunshine and frigid temps. The wind was still gusting out of the northwest and the thought of sitting in a nice warm storage area going through boxes making discoveries was a lot more attractive to Carol than being in the cold attic at the top of an old mansion. As they approached the table, Carol and James realized Paul and Marty were looking at the blueprint plans of the mansion.

Carol noticed that the detective was neatly dressed in jeans and a green mock turtleneck shirt. It was the first time they had seen him in anything other than a suit and tie. Marty noticed Carol looking at him as she approached.

"I hope you don't mind," he said to Carol. "I figured I could dress down for today."

Carol caught the humor in his voice and smiled at it.

Paul changed the subject by saying to James, "The Lieutenant was asking about the plan of the mansion and the location of the secret room."

"I don't know if it is significant," Marty said to James motioning him to look closer at the blueprint.

"But you see here? That room sits directly over the nursery on the second floor." Marty looked up from the blueprints with a smile of triumph on his face. "Since that room was unoccupied, there was little likelihood that anything that went on overhead would have been heard."

"What do you mean?" Carol said a bit puzzled.

"The forensics guys tell me, the way that room was built, you could fire off a shotgun and it would not have been heard in the rest of the house. It also would have prevented any odor of decomposition from leaving the room. Does the date December 10, 1969, mean anything to either of you?"

"That's seven years before I was even born," James said. "Why are you asking?"

"It's not important right now," the detective replied nonchalantly. "Let's get started on those boxes."

Paul reached into his pocket and handed Carol a key on a small key ring. It was the duplicate key to his storage area in the back of his office space.

"If the office is open, you can come through this way if you want to, but the key will give you access through the outside door on the back of the building," Paul told her. "Hope you find what you're looking for."

"What exactly ARE we looking for, Lieutenant?" James asked Marty.

"I wish I knew for certain," Martin replied. "I think we will know when we find it."

The three of them followed Paul to the back of the office where he showed them the inside door to the storage area. He opened the door and hit the light switch inside the door. The area was part of the old millworks that had not been modernized. The floor was made of wide planks worn by years of machinery being moved on it and work boots walking over it. It reeked of the oil and varnish that had permeated them over the decades. The windows in the bare brick walls had all been boarded over and rough wooden shelves had been built in the center of the room and along the walls. Paul walked them over to a section of shelving against one wall where the boxes from the garage were all neatly stacked.

"I wish you luck," Paul said. "There is a table and some chairs down at the end and you are welcome to them." He turned and left the room, closing the door to the offices behind him.

James looked at Marty and Carol. He took a box off the top shelf and handed it to the detective. He took the box behind the first and slid it off the shelf into Carol's waiting hands. He then reached farther back onto the shelf and slid the last box in the row off the shelf. Having hefted all three boxes, James felt they were all about the same weight. He walked to the end of the row of shelves built in the center of the room and joined the others at a fairly long plain wooden table with two droplights strung above it. Each of them took a seat and placed their box in front of them. They all looked at each other. If nothing else, they were about to be drawn into a much more intimate relationship with the past.

Carol looked at the label on her box that was yellowed by age. It read, "Living Room." James looked at his label: Dining Room. Marty's label, though blurred, read, "Dining Room 2". James reached into his pocket and pulled out the pocketknife he had carried every day since he was sixteen. He opened the blade and slit the tape on the top of the box in front of Carol. He then slit the packing tape on Marty's box and, finally, his own.

Carol bent the flaps back to open her box. As she did, a face in a frame came into view. It was that of a woman who looked to be in her twenties. The tresses of her abundant hair were swept up and gathered high on her head. Her skin appeared flawless as she seemed to be gazing at something beyond the scope of the camera with captivating eyes. Her cheeks were high and round, and her lips were full and slightly parted, her chin perfectly shaped. The soft focus of the picture added to her beauty. She was dressed in a high-necked, long-sleeved lace gown with a heavily embroidered bodice and seated in a leather armchair. A long single strand of large pearls adorned her neck. Her posture indicated someone of breeding and culture.

"This has to be Mrs. Carlisle." Carol said softly as she lifted the picture carefully out of the box. The gilded frame still glittered in her hands. It was a masterful portrait of a beautiful woman captured in the shades of black and white photography.

Carol began pulling framed photographs from her box. As she

did, James and Marty tried to identify who the people might be. They decided the older gentleman in one picture was Mr. Carlisle. Carol saw a distinguished looking man staring back at her in a business suit with a high white collar typical of the early turn-of-the-century attire with wavy white hair and matching moustache. Carol could see in his eyes the confidence of a successful businessman and tenderness of a loving family man.

There was a portrait of a beautiful little girl of fourteen or fifteen seated on the front steps of the mansion. Carol was sure it was Becky Carlisle. She wore a large, brimmed hat to shield her from the sun. Her smiling face held many of the same features as the first picture they had viewed.

Carol reached for the last picture frame in the box. It was upside down in the bottom of the box and felt thicker than the others. When she turned it over, she was startled to find, not a picture, but a glass cover over black velvet with a small shadow box insert. In the shadow box was a lock of pure white hair. A small plaque of polished brass affixed below the box was inscribed:

Edward T. Carlisle
April 14, 1912
RMS Titanic

"This is sort of unusual," Carol said handing the framed remembrance to Marty.

"Not really," he said reaching out to take the frame from Carol. "It was fairly common in the Victorian Era to preserve hair from loved ones who had passed. I've seen some pretty elaborate things made of hair."

"That's it for this box," Carol said looking in the box. "Just a couple of pieces of newspaper left in the bottom."

"Can you pull those out," the detective asked quickly.

Carol looked a bit surprised by the request but did as asked. They were two pages of the *Hartford Courant* dated June 12, 1970.

"Okay," Marty said, noting Carol's look of surprise. "It's the detective in me. I just needed to know that the date was right."

"You are kidding, aren't you?" James said.

"Hey, that's the kind of stupid mistake someone might make if they had gone through these boxes anytime since 1970," Marty replied. "Remember, we are looking for something, anything here, to help us resolve this case. If someone else knew anything of an incriminating nature was in here, don't you think they would have looked for it at some point in the last thirty some-odd years?"

"Okay, my turn," said James. "Let's see what goodies came out of the dining room."

James opened the flaps of his cardboard box and began removing linen napkins discolored by age and compressed along their fold lines. In the corner of each one was an ornately embroidered "C." Beneath about two dozen of these oversized dinner napkins, they uncovered a beautiful matching tablecloth. It, too, showed the effects of over thirty-five years of undisturbed storage. When the tablecloth was taken out of the box a layer of velvet pouches came into view. James removed one from the box and handed it to Carol.

The pouch was about eighteen inches long and heavily weighted on one end. The flap of the pouch was folded over and neatly tied about halfway down its length with an attached cord. Carol placed it on the table in front of her and carefully untied the bows formed so many years ago by unknown fingers. She pulled back the flap and reached inside the pouch to reveal a beautiful silver candlestick only slightly tarnished from the passage of time. She let out an uncontrollable gasp.

"Oh, my God, it's beautiful!"

"And it's yours," Marty Chambers said in wonder.

"There are about six more of those pouches here, Honey," James said softly.

Carol sat transfixed by the beautiful workmanship of the candlestick. She barely heard James's voice. She rewrapped the object almost reverently and retied the closure. She handed it back to James. He repacked the box and marked the top of the box with his pen and set it on the floor.

"Well, that was certainly a surprise," James said. "Let's see what's in your box, Lieutenant."

Marty had almost forgotten about the box sitting at his feet. He lifted it onto the table and reread the label.

"Dining Room 2," he stated in a clear voice. "Let's see what we find in here." He bent back the flaps of the box and found newspaper. Everything in the box was wrapped individually in newspaper. Carol reached into the box and removed a lump of compressed newspaper. She carefully began to peel back the crinkled, discolored print page to reveal a pair of cut crystal salt and pepper shakers. She displayed them still partially wrapped to James and the detective. James and Marty each took a similar package from the box and began to carefully pull back the old newspaper wrapping. James revealed a beautiful cut crystal candy dish. Marty's newspaper concealed a small porcelain creamer.

"I think we can safely assume what the rest of this box contains," he said smiling at Carol and James. "Let's check some of the other boxes. Carol and James nodded their agreement.

The second round of boxes yielded little of significance to Marty Chamber's investigation, but much of interest about Mrs. Edith Carlisle. There were mementos and photographs, books, and trinkets. One box looked like the contents of a drawer had just been dumped into it. There was a deck of playing cards held together with a rubber band that disintegrated when touched, its elasticity lost long ago. This set of boxes was quickly set aside in favor of another round of boxes from off the shelf.

The trio had been at it for nearly four hours. James suggested they break for lunch. As they were getting on their coats, Carol casually looked at the label on her next box. It read, "Library Desk."

They had appreciated the warmth of the sun as they had walked up the block from Paul's shop to a small lunch place recommended by one of Paul's employees. Lunch had been accompanied by pleasant conversation with Marty sharing some of his background and James and Carol doing the same with him. They talked about the boxes and what it was like delving through the remnants of someone's life left packed in boxes so many years ago. Carol felt sad about what they found. She could not imagine that this woman, any woman, would have wanted people she did not know, and would never know, going through boxes that represented what had survived, what had endured, from her life.

They ate quickly, realizing that it had taken four hours to get through six boxes. There were three shelves of boxes which quickly translated into several days' work at the rate they were progressing. The wind was directly in their faces as they walked back to Paul's shop at a quick pace. They were happy to be back inside and settled down to work. James slit the tape on a new set of boxes with his pocketknife and Carol started in.

She flipped back the cardboard flaps of the box and removed a bound over-sized book that she thought, at first, was an old photograph album. She opened the front cover and realized it was a scrapbook. Attached to the first page were clippings from two newspapers. The one from *The New York Times* dated September 15, 1901, announcing the attendance of Miss Edith Master at the New York Cotillion as she was presented to New York society. Above the clipping was a picture of the woman Carol had admired from the first box, younger and dressed in the style of the 1890's. The second clipping was from the *Hartford Courant* and was nearly identical in content. She turned the page.

There were clippings about trips and weddings and social gatherings; anything and everything Edith Masters had attended, been part of, done, or even visited. It was her life laid out in newspaper print. It amazed Carol that someone could have taken the time and gone through the effort to have so conscientiously maintained such a record of their life over the years. Was it pretentious of someone to think their life so important that they needed to record every mention of themselves?

Or was it a desire to create a legacy to be handed down through family as a personal record of an ancestor?

After a half dozen pages of clippings from different papers detailing the life of an up-and-coming socialite, Carol turned another page and saw the same photo as in the frame she had held earlier in the day. The clipping from *The New York Times* announcing the engagement of Miss Edith Masters to Mr. Edward T Carlisle, February 18, 1905, was still firmly pasted to the page. It was a full two columns six inches in length. Surrounding *The New York Times* centerpiece were similar clippings from several other well-known papers. It was an event that obviously rated major coverage in the society columns. Carol was instantly entranced by the delineation of the pedigrees of the bride and groom. James had to poke her on the arm to get her to turn the page.

Almost predictably, the next two pages celebrated her wedding to Edward T. Carlisle. A copy of the formal wedding invitation was affixed to the left page, followed by a copy of the wedding program printed in an ornate font on vellum. This was followed by a sample of one of the place cards from the reception. On the right-hand page were the wedding announcements from all the large east coast papers. On the lower half of the page was a formal portrait of the bride holding her bouquet of long-stemmed roses and looking radiant. Carol felt tears welling up in her eyes as she looked at this woman who was so beautiful on her wedding day.

She turned the next page and saw the same young woman who was now a mother. The birth announcements from the same newspapers were pasted across the top of the page. Elisabeth Caroline Margaret Carlisle was born July 21, 1906, a fair-haired infant of six pounds four ounces delivered at home and named for her maternal grandmother. A photograph of a cherub-faced infant in a bassinet was pasted to the bottom of the page. This was the innocent whose murder would mar the history of Carlisle Estate. Here she was at an age when no hint of future tragedy could be known or even suspected. The beautiful infant sleeping in her bassinet forever preserved in this book of remembrance. Carol could feel the tears on her cheeks.

James was looking at the page over Carol's shoulder and saw the tear leave her eye and begin to stain her cheek. He took his index finger and gently wiped the tear from her cheek, then put his arm around her so she could turn her face into his chest. After a minute or two, she began to regain control.

"Are you alright, Mrs. Day?" Marty asked with great kindness in his voice.

"Yes, it's just," Carol felt a catch in her voice, "life seemed to hold so much promise for her. How could her mother have survived her loss?"

TWENTY-EIGHT

TURNING THE PAGE CHANGED THE ENTIRE TENOR of the album. On the next page was the announcement of Mrs. Carlisle taking residence in Rock Cove and her introduction to the society circles of Newport, Watch Hill, and Rock Cove. The newspaper article covered a reception held for her by Mrs. Constance Stanhope at the Ocean House in Watch Hill.

"This must have been the honeymoon period before they became rivals," James said as he read the article himself.

"In any event," Carol said, "it says here that Mrs. Carlisle was pregnant, and that Mrs. Stanhope was looking forward to the Newport horse exhibition in the spring where her daughter Sophia, would be presenting the awards."

As Carol continued turning pages, it was clear that this record of what had initially been a celebration of a debutante's fairy tale life was changing into a record of her jousts with her rival for preeminence in society. There were pages detailing the growth of her daughter both in age and in social standing. Each birthday was carefully detailed with photographs and newspaper clippings and details of parties held and guests   invited. And soon, there started to appear newspaper articles detailing the birthday celebrations of Sophia Stanhope. Between pages commemorating personal accomplishments and celebrations were pages with articles clipped from various sources detailing not only the social triumphs of the Carlisle women, but those of their rivals for local social supremacy, the Stanhope women. For every mention of Mrs. Carlisle or her daughter attending some social event or other, there was a notation or an article detailing the activities of Constance Stanhope or Sophia. If Edith Carlisle were updating her parlor with the latest European designs, it was a sure bet that Mrs. Stanhope would be upgrading and adding to her stable of Arabians in short order. If Sophia Stanhope was spending a vacation on the Maine coast, Becky Carlisle was attending the opera in New York City. Mrs. Carlisle's scrapbook of her life, her daughter's life, and their triumphs in society had become, even more, a record of her bitter rival's activities.

"These gals were serious about this rivalry thing," Marty said as he read a few of the articles.

"I guess it doesn't make much sense to us today," James said shaking his head. "But this was serious business a hundred years ago."

As each page was turned, the years went by. There were mentions of flower shows, horse shows, society gatherings and trips. There were notations of every birthday for Elisabeth. And then Carol turned a page and they saw the headline from the *New York Times* of April 15, 1912, screaming of the loss of the RMS *Titanic*. Set below the headline and centered on the page was a lone obituary notice.

Before long, Carol turned another page that was completely devoted to a single subject. It was the social presenting, the coming out celebration, of Sophia Stanhope. There was a photograph of her dressed in virginal white being presented at the New York Debutante Cotillion of 1919. Her pose made her features seem incredibly sultry framed in her jet black hair. Her poise and figure radiated confidence and maturity. She was no longer a little girl. This was the formal announcement to high society and the world that Mrs. Stanhope's daughter was on the marriage market and looking for a man. But, not just any man; he would need to have a pedigree and, most importantly, a title. The last line in the article was notification that Mrs. Stanhope and her eligible daughter would be sailing for Europe by the end of the month. On the facing page, was a newspaper article reporting Elisabeth Carlisle's celebration of her thirteenth birthday.

It was here that the focus of the scrapbook definitely changed. There seemed to be more articles pertaining to society events and activities and fewer and fewer pages celebrating individual events like birthdays. There started to appear clippings of events where both daughters were in attendance. One clipping had a picture showing both Sophia Stanhope and Becky Carlisle. It was the first time Carol and James had seen the two of them together. The contrast was striking: Sophia, the older, with beautiful black hair and faultless face and Becky so fair and blond. The former, a woman in every sense, in the full bloom of femininity: the latter still displaying the youthful innocence of a child.

As Carol continued turning pages and scanning the newspaper clippings, photographs, and other memorabilia affixed to them, she began to realize how powerful the need for social recognition was to these women. It was like a drug for them. They needed it and felt it was theirs by right. It had become their fixation. They sought every opportunity to be seen, to be talked or written about. They were addicted to status and obsessed with how to keep it. These were rich and powerful women who manipulated people and situations to gain a level of recognition and notoriety among a select group of individuals they considered to be America's royalty and their peers. Nothing and no one else mattered. Their daughters were nothing more than pawns to enhance their own status. The pages before her showed just how important this drug of social standing was to them. It also showed how shallow those who sought such recognition were and how frightened they were about how quickly it could be lost or taken away by scandal.

With every entry to the scrapbook, Edith Carlisle had demonstrated her fear of losing her social position to someone else, most notably her nearest rival, Constance Stanhope. As their daughters came of age, it became evident that the enmity of the mothers had been instilled in their daughters. Carol wondered if this was a natural consequence of two wealthy society widows raising daughters. These girls, who might have been great friends, instead turning into bitter rivals like their mothers before them. Did the arena of the socially prominent require this of its young? Was this a way to attract greater social notice? Being foes was certainly more fodder for the gossip mills of the elite than being great friends. Carol found it hard to identify with such thinking.

Even during the years of the First World War when the entire world was experiencing the horror of reports from the battlefields, the newspaper clippings in the scrapbook detailed the activities of Sophia Stanhope and Becky Carlisle. They were wrapping bandages for the doughboys, volunteering with the Red Cross and organizations sponsoring relief to the displaced civilian population in Europe. These young women of privilege were putting forth their best effort and making sure it was duly reported to everyone.

The pages continued to reveal the activities of the wealthy few as the 1920s began. Many of the elite had supported the campaign for women's suffrage; some had been outspoken in their opposition. America's prosperity after World War I was certainly influencing their circle of the elite. New wealth was attempting to storm the gates of society. As much as the flapper might become a part of the socially elite scene, the "nouveau rich" would never be considered for membership in what was considered the "old money." The fact that alcohol had been banned by prohibition never seemed to slow the pace of parties in Newport or Watch Hill or any place else for that matter. It was the best of times for those still young enough to enjoy them. It was scandalous to the older generation.

At the height of the decade, Elisabeth Carlisle came of age. The scrapbook showed the young, blond girl of earlier pages suddenly transformed into a stunning young woman with a figure made for the flapper dress. Her bobbed blond locks fell freely about her face. Her eyes sparkled and her lips were full and slightly parted. She was every man's dream, and she was now marriageable. Here presentation at the New York City Cotillion of 1924 was duly reported in *The New York Times* society section. A professionally taken photograph accompanied the report. Her departure for a Caribbean adventure following the festivities was also noted.

On the facing page was a newspaper clipping that caught Carol's eye because it seemed out of place. The headline and secondary headings read:

Sophia Stanhope Home from Europe
Returns Early to Nurse Mother
Injuries Serious But Not Life Threatening

"Listen to this," Carol said, beginning to read the article to James and Marty. "Sophia Stanhope of Rock Cove, Connecticut, arrived in New York from London by fast steamer today, cutting short her annual tour of the Continent two weeks earlier than expected, having been wired of her mother's injuries incurred at the Newport Horse Show. Constance Stanhope, the nationally renowned equestrian, was thrown from her Arabian, Saladin, during the jumping portion of the competition. She suffered multiple injuries including a broken collarbone and wrist and several ribs. Although the injuries are not considered life threatening, it was felt best by those concerned that Mrs. Stanhope's daughter be notified at once."

"I guess they kept track of each other's social mishaps, as well," James said wryly.

"What's the date on that report?" the detective asked.

"There isn't one. Carol said. "But, from where it is in the book, my guess would be 1924."

Marty made a note on his pad. He had actually been making a number of notes about various things he had seen and read. He was hoping to find something important; he just did not know what it would be. His years of being a detective had taught him that sometimes the smallest fact could resolve a case.

Carol had nearly reached the end of the scrapbook. In the few pages remaining, there were newspaper reports similar to what had gone before: reports on garden parties, flower shows, society gatherings, etc. Again, there was the juxtaposition of the activities of the Carlisle's and the Stanhope's. Their war was continuing, and the competition was intensifying.

Carol turned the last page and read the engagement announcement of Elisabeth Carlisle to Baron Richard Albert Nevis, Lord Alethar. On the same page was a clipping from the same society column relating the termination of the engagement of Sophia Stanhope to the self-same Baron Nevis.

"That's it," Carol said, "unless there is another volume in one of these boxes."

"It's getting late," Marty Chambers said stretching in his chair. It was true. James looked at his watch and could not believe the hour.

"I think we could all use a drink," James said. "Lieutenant, would you join us?"

"I would love to, but I'm afraid I need to check in with some people," Marty said with a smile. "I'll take you up on that offer another time. Shall we pick up again tomorrow?"

"Sure," James said. "Same time?"

"I'll bring the coffee," Marty shot back with a smile.

TWENTY-NINE

THE END OF THE COLD SNAP WAS A WELCOME relief to James and Carol. It was wonderful to step out into the sun in the morning and actually feel some warmth from it. The icicles on the eaves of the apartment were beginning to drip and the ice on the drive was turning to slush.

Carol and James had spent half the night talking about the story that had unfolded in the scrapbook they had found. They had gotten on the internet and read about Victorian ideals and attitudes in an attempt to understand the actions of these two women. They discovered that the late 1800s in America brought about a new social class of the super wealthy. Membership in this group was dependent on the whim of a few women who decided who belonged and who did not. Becoming a part of that group was difficult enough, but keeping that membership was dependent on being seen as above reproach – at least publicly. One of the fastest ways to be shunned by the group was to have any involvement in scandal. The entire situation was so foreign to anything Carol or James had ever experienced, it seemed surreal to them. James was hoping they would find a second volume to the scrapbook. Carol suspected strongly they would not.

"What would have been the point of continuing after her child's death?" Carol had said. "There was no one else to whom the record would mean as much. Besides, I think her desire to be socially prominent died with her daughter. And, if not then, I'm sure the trial was the final straw."

They had both awakened early, excited by the prospects of what might lie hidden in the remaining boxes. They arrived at Paul's shop half an hour before the time they had agreed upon with Marty Chambers. Paul was in his shop. He smiled at them as they came through the door.

"How did it go yesterday?" he asked with interest.

"It was very interesting," Carol replied smiling sweetly. "We found a scrapbook Mrs. Carlisle had kept."

"Really?" Paul said with interest. "Did she tell you where she buried all her money?" He was smiling broadly at his cleverness. Carol laughed brightly, as did James.

"Actually, I'm glad I saw you this morning," Paul said after the laughter subsided. "I am going out to the house today to meet the electrician I've contracted to do the rewiring and to check on the work being done on the heating system. They started work in the basement yesterday. In any event, I don't think we can resume the renovations for another couple of days."

"And Thanksgiving is coming, too," James said with a touch of resignation.

"Well, if we can get the heating system up and running and the electrical updated to code, we can work through the winter. When you see Lieutenant Chambers today, will you just ask him if we are clear to resume work on the third floor?"

James nodded. He could tell that Paul was getting frustrated by the delays the investigation had brought to the job. They both knew that the delay was unavoidable. That did not mean they had to like it. Paul started to explain to Carol and James some of the changes that needed to be made in order to bring the electrical wiring in the mansion up to code. They were extensive because the wiring was so old. As he was explaining the concept of knob and tube wiring, Marty Chambers came in carrying a tray with three steaming cups of coffee. Everyone looked toward the front door at the sound of the bell.

"Good morning, all," Marty said smiling. "It's a beautiful day!" His casual dress of yesterday had been replaced by his normal work attire of white dress shirt, dark slacks, dark sport coat, and tie. On his belt were his badge and his sidearm.

Carol and James both agreed with Marty's assessment of the day and Paul excused himself and headed out the door with his blueprints tucked under his arm. Marty handed a coffee to each of the Days, and they headed for the storage room at the back of the shop. James remembered Paul's question and said to Marty, "Paul wanted to know if your people were finished with the house so we could start working again."

"I think we are," Marty said, "but I can check to be sure today. I can only be here for this morning. I am meeting with a couple of our interns that have been doing research for me on this case and I will have the M.E.'s report this afternoon."

"Does that mean we'll know who we found and how they were killed?" James responded.

"Well, we'll know some things about who we found, and we may know the cause of death," Marty said. "We may never be able to establish a definite identity or cause of death."

The three of them shucked off their coats and settled into the boxes left from the day before. As James slit the brown packing tape on the top of his box, he noticed that the label identified it as from the nursery. He stopped for a moment and wondered if this box could have any significance to their search. What he was really thinking was what effect the contents of this box might have on Carol. Anything to do with that room had seemed to send her into a tailspin. He tapped Marty on the arm.

"I don't think this one is worth going through right away. What do you think?"

Marty looked at the label. "I would agree. Why don't you get another one?"

Carol was curious at the exchange and quickly looked at the label as James set the box aside.

"Don't put that too far away," she said. "I'd like to go through it."

James closed the flaps and set the box next to the table. He handed Marty his pocketknife and headed for the shelves where a good two dozen boxes remained. Marty was about to cut the packing tape on the box in front of him when he looked at the label. It read "Library." He felt his level of anticipation rise. He slit the packing tape closure and folded back the flaps.

"This is one from the library," he said quietly to Carol. James returned carrying a box for himself and a second box for Carol. He had heard Marty's words. Marty turned the box in Carol's direction. "I think you should go through this," he said. Carol smiled.

When the flaps were bent back, the contents revealed did not promise any great discoveries. The top layer of contents held items from the top of the desk and probably the middle drawer. An old crystal inkwell, several nib pens, an old style blotter, an ornate letter opener, a fountain pen, all made their appearance. Carol carefully removed these items and more that held no immediate special interest.

Once these things had been removed from the box, the first item of interest Carol removed was an annual calendar for 1969-1970 bound in a green leather portfolio. She handed it to Marty, who quickly riffled through the pages and noticed entries through the first few months.

"There are entries here. It looks like they end about midyear. Would you mind if I borrowed this?" he asked Carol.

"Of course not," she replied as she began delving into the remaining contents of the box. There were several envelopes from foundations and charities containing requests for donations. The cover letters were not the normal, mass-produced requests. These letters were each personally written by a member of the Board or the Director of the charity.

"I guess these people didn't know she was running out of money," Marty commented.

"Actually," James said, "she was still a very wealthy woman in 1970. The attorney, Beckwith, told us that her funds paid the property taxes and upkeep on the estate and her nursing home care for nearly a decade and then continued to pay the property taxes on the estate and the upkeep of the house until now. That took a lot of money."

Carol placed the desk items back into the box and removed the box from the table. James replaced it with another box and Marty took the pocketknife and slit open the top of it. This one proved to hold nothing of any interest or importance. It was labeled "Bedroom" and it seemed to be the contents of a nightstand or bed table. The one curious item in the box was the discovery of a Bible, its pages dog-eared from use.

And so, it continued box after box, hour after hour, each box looked through and set aside. They seemed to number in the hundreds rather than a few dozen. Each box brought its own surprises. Some were interesting; most were not. The three of them continued opening boxes and evaluating what they held until Marty suddenly looked at his watch and announced he needed to go. He told Carol and James to keep at it and, if they came across anything that they felt lent any information about the remains that had been recovered from the attic room or looked of interest in any way, to please set it aside for him to see. He assured them that he would be in touch as soon as he had any concrete information.

James and Carol decided to take a break from the boxes and have some lunch. They put their coats on as they strolled past the unopened dozen or so boxes that were left on the shelf. They were tired and sore after nearly two days of digging through boxes. They just wanted to get through the rest of the boxes and start to work on the mansion again. With only that number of boxes left, they were pretty sure they would finish today.

Carol and James were feeling pretty good when they returned to Paul's shop. They were beginning to be seen as regulars at the diner down the block. It was something that they had never really felt in their time in New York. There were so many restaurants and diverse cuisines present in Manhattan it seemed they were always eating in different places.

They settled into the remaining boxes tenaciously. They were tearing through boxes marked kitchen, first floor study, butler's pantry, guest room, finding things of interest, but nothing they could see in any way assisting the police investigation. But, they kept at it until only a couple of boxes remained to be opened.

Suddenly, Carol's cell phone rang. It was Lieutenant Chambers. They talked for a few minutes and then Carol looked up at James who was listening intently to her half of the conversation.

"Yes," she was saying. "Yes, I am sure it is here. Hold on." She moved the phone away from her lips.

"Honey, Marty is asking about the scrapbook," she said to James. "Where did we put it?"

James reached behind him and picked it up off the shelf. Carol motioned for him to give it to her. She turned the phone back to her mouth.

"Yes, I have it," she said. "Alright, we can do that. Okay, I will bring it. See you there." Carol ended the call and looked at James. "Marty wants us to meet him at the estate at seven tonight, at Ben Allen's rooms. He wants us to call Ben and be sure he will be there too."

"Did he say anything else?" James asked as he pulled his phone out of his pocket and punched the speed dial for Ben's number.

"Just to be sure we brought the scrapbook with us," she answered.

The phone was ringing in James's ear as he and Carol talked. He was afraid his call was going to go to voicemail when Ben finally answered.

"Hello," he said in a voice that was groggy from sleep.

"Ben? It's Jim Day," he said in a voice that probably indicated more excitement than it should have. "Carol and I are meeting Lieutenant Chambers at your place at seven. He wants you to join us."

"Do you know why?" Ben asked, his voice showing him fully awake from James's statement.

"He didn't say anything except to be sure you were there, as well," James said firmly.

"Alright, I will be here," Ben replied.

Ben Allen was slow to close his cell phone. He was sitting on the edge of his couch having been awakened from a heavy nap by the ring of his phone. He had heard what James had said, but his sleep-addled mind needed a minute to comprehend it and, by then, the call was ended. It was just now registering that people would be arriving in a few hours at his rooms. He looked around and saw the clutter of a bachelor's rooms. He ran his fingers through his hair and decided he had better collect the dirty dishes and glasses from the coffee table in front of him and pick up the clothes scattered about the room.

It had been a busy day on the estate. For the second day in a row, the electrical contractor and the heating company had been there for most of the day. But, like all good rural contractors, most of the day meant arriving early and quitting early. That was a full day of work for them. The electrician and his assistant were snaking wires throughout the house. It was a rough, time-consuming job. The heating company had delivered the new furnace midmorning and had spent the rest of the day connecting it to a temporary source of fuel. It would do for the winter, but once spring arrived and the weather improved, a new tank would need to be buried in the lawn and the old one removed. This temporary tank stood outside the house next to the foundation on a small cradle. Ben had just laid down for a nap when his phone rang.

It had taken Ben forty-five minutes to pick his place up and make it look presentable. The clothes were stashed in a closet in the bag he used for laundry. The dishes were heavily rinsed if not thoroughly clean and sitting in the drainer. He took a beer from the refrigerator, twisted off the top, and sat down heavily on the couch. As he took a swallow, he started trying to figure out why the detective wanted him there for a meeting. He did not think he was in any trouble. If he were, he doubted the police would call and "request" him to be present, especially if there was time for him to be long gone. Did he know something he did not know he knew? Was there something they wanted to tell him? He could think of nothing that he had left to hide and nothing more that he could tell them. He looked at the clock on the wall: five-thirty. He had an hour and a half to change his clothes, throw something in the microwave for dinner, and turn on the outside lights for his visitors. He took another swallow of his beer and picked up the remote for his television.

All of the boxes, save three, had been opened and looked through and were neatly stacked back on the shelving in the storage room. The three remaining boxes were placed in front of the others: two that had not been opened at all and the one that James had set aside from the nursery. Carol and James had spent the entire afternoon sorting through boxes and finding nothing that seemed of interest. But, their mood was buoyed by the prospect of their imminent meeting with Lieutenant Chambers. They spoke to each other excitedly about what the police might have discovered and what significance the scrapbook had in all of it.

Carol cradled the book in her arms protectively as they closed the outside door of the storage room securely and headed to their car. The winter sun had set, and the lights of Pawcatuck showed brightly in the crisp winter air. What had melted in the warmth of the day was now beginning to freeze. Carol held the scrapbook as they drove out of town and their conversation turned to dinner. They only had a little more than an hour to eat and get to the estate.

THIRTY

THE MOON WAS SHINING IN A CRISP COLD SKY FOR the first time in several nights. Its light illuminated the snow on the ground beneath the barren trees. Carol and James had eaten quickly at their apartment and were on the road to the estate ahead of schedule. Carol held the scrapbook in her lap. When they arrived at the entrance to the driveway, the gateposts were lit, and the driveway was plowed. James turned in and drove up to the mansion. As they rounded a bend in the driveway where the house and great lawn came into view, the moonlight on the snow-covered lawn was brilliantly unblemished. James pulled behind the mansion and followed the driveway to the garage. The lights were on in front of the doors and lights were showing through the windows upstairs. They could see Ben's silhouette in one of the windows. They were ten minutes early.

Carol and James quickly left the car and mounted the side stairs to Ben's rooms. As Carol reached for the doorknob at the top of the stairs, Ben opened the door from the inside.

"I saw you coming," Ben said holding the door open.

"Sorry we're a little early, Ben," Carol said as she rushed past him into the warmth of the room. James was right behind her. Ben quickly closed the door.

"The Lieutenant's not here yet," Ben said seemingly unconcerned. Of course, Carol and James knew Marty was not there because his car was not there. "Do you have any idea why he wanted me here?" Ben said betraying his concern.

"He didn't tell us, Ben," James said. "You have nothing to hide, do you Ben?"

"I told them everything I know," Ben said emphatically.

"Then maybe they have something to tell you!" Carol said with excitement.

James was standing by the window casually listening to Ben and Carol when he saw headlights coming down the driveway.

"Here come the people who, hopefully, have some answers to our questions," he said only half in jest.

James was joined by Carol at the window and Ben started toward the door. They saw Marty get out of his unmarked police car and enter the stairway. Under his arm was a briefcase. They could hear his footsteps mount the stairs and Ben opened the door just as Marty reached the top step.

"Hey, everyone," Marty said as he entered. "Thanks, Mr. Allen. I appreciate your being here." Ben silently nodded assent. Marty quickly shed his coat and started walking toward the table that sat against the wall by the kitchen.

"I think it would be better if we could use this table," he said not really to anyone, but looking toward Ben. The table was quickly cleared of some papers and the group gathered about the table. The tension was building in the room.

"I have some information to share with you," Marty began. "Some of it is conclusive. Some of it is ninety-percent conclusive. All are based on the facts we have established from the evidence and the work of our research assistants. That's what we refer to our interns as."

Carol was sitting across from Marty with the scrapbook squarely in front of her on the table. James was to her right and Ben to her left. Her right hand had reached out and found James's and was now holding it firmly. Ben sat nervously nibbling his lower lip on the side away from the detective.

"Shall we begin?" Marty said smiling. Carol was nodding excitedly. James was looking at Carol's barely controlled exhilaration and felt his own interest rising. Ben still looked worried.

"First of all, no one here is connected with the findings of our investigation from the standpoint of involvement," Marty said. "I am not here to arrest anyone." Ben visibly relaxed.

"Mr. Allen has a direct connection to the events we have been investigating, which is why I asked you to be here, Ben. I have copies of the ballistics reports, forensics analysis, and the Medical Examiner's report, the findings from which I want to share with you.

"I will tell you this is the strangest case I have ever investigated." Marty sat for a moment shaking his head indicating his disbelief. "We think we know what happened, but the why, and how? We just don't know for sure."

"I think we all can agree that the events that occurred here in 1927 with the murder of Elisabeth Carlisle are connected to our recent findings. Unfortunately, that crime was considered closed years ago and all the evidence folders from the investigation were purged from the records. So, there were no ballistics reports available to compare against the weapon that surfaced recently and no direct reports of the events from a police perspective."

"However," Marty continued, "the investigation file of the death of Sophia Stanhope is still in the records, oddly enough. In conducting that investigation, a notation regarding the library in the Stanhope house was made. According to the report, an array of arms was prominently displayed on a wall of the library. One of the spaces on the display was empty. In addition, a box of cartridges was found spilled on the floor in front of the display. The caliber of the ammunition? Forty-five caliber. The scene had the appearance of someone attempting to load a weapon rapidly and carelessly dropping some of the cartridges."

"You mean there are no fingerprint records from the 1927 crime to compare?" James asked.

"Not a one. So, even if we could get a print from our human remains or from the weapon, we would have nothing to compare it to on file." Marty seemed unconcerned about his revelation. "Mr. Allen did not need to fear we might find his father's fingerprints on the weapon. We do not have his father's prints on file to use for comparison." Ben put his elbows on the table and placed his head in his hands. His relief was complete. Carol put a comforting arm across Ben's shoulders.

"Let's begin with the weapon. We have not been able to determine completely that this Colt revolver is the one Mrs. Stanhope used in her actions in 1927," Marty said as he opened one of the folders he had placed on the table.

"The ballistics people were able to determine the description given in the newspaper reports at the time are compatible with the weapon we recovered. Forensics determined that a clear print was found on the weapon, but with nothing to compare it to, it was impossible to determine to whom it belonged. However, the size of the print and smoothness of the ridges would indicate the print was most likely that of a female."

"That means it was either Mrs. Stanhope or Mrs. Carlisle who hid it?" Ben said lifting his face from his hands. "My father was innocent."

"When it comes to the weapon and its disappearance, yes, we believe he had no involvement," Marty said reassuringly to Ben. Carol reached out her left hand to gently touch Ben's arm.

"Let's review a little of what we have been able to confirm," Marty said shifting in his chair. "We believe from the sources we have checked that there is little doubt that Mrs. Stanhope murdered Elisabeth Carlisle in cold blood. We believe her motive was the jilting of her daughter by this Baron fellow and his subsequent plans to marry Ms. Carlisle. When she found her daughter had hanged herself the morning of the murder, we think Mrs. Stanhope just completely lost it. People have been known to lose it for a lot less." Marty looked at the people around the table and could see he had their full attention. "We feel we are dealing here with what happened after the murder of Ms. Carlisle."

"What about the body, Marty?" James said, "and the room? What about the room?"

"Interesting subject that room," Marty said looking through another folder as he spoke. "That room was constructed of solid oak planking: walls, floors, ceiling. It was built three planks thick. That's three solid inches separating it from the outside. There is no record of that room even existing. Neither is there any record of who built it or when. However, based on other evidence from the construction, we think it was built right around the time of the murder."

"Why was it built?" James asked.

"I'm getting to that, Jim," Marty said. "We believe the room was built specifically to hide something. At first, we thought it was the body."

"What about the body," Ben said suddenly interested.

"It was the Baron, wasn't it?" James said with self-assurance.

"You mean Edward Lowe?" Marty said with a smile. All three of his audience collectively exclaimed, "Who?"

"Edward Lowe," Marty repeated. "He was our mysterious Baron Nevis." Marty pulled a paper with a copy of a picture on it out of his file and tossed it out on the table. As it spun to a stop, it faced Carol. It showed the face of a man perhaps twenty-four or five with incredibly chiseled good looks dressed in a dark suit with a full ascot tie and vest. A top hat was neatly held in the crook of his arm and his hair was neatly cut and jet black. This was a catch for a husband if there ever was one.

"How did you ever find him?" Carol said as she looked at the picture.

"Are you sure this is him?" James said.

"That's our man," Marty said. "Thanks to the sharp eyes of one of our researchers, we found this photograph from a horse show held in Newport in 1926. Once we had a picture, we could run it through our systems. Most of our records are computerized now and digitized. We produced an arrest record from 1945 in Philadelphia. For some reason, he went back to using an old alias." Marty pulled another sheet from his folder and tossed it into the middle of the table. Here was the face of the same man, several years older with graying hair, but still distinguished looking and still very attractive, standing before a height measure and holding a placard in front of him imprinted "PPD" with a number and his name, Edward Lowe.

"He was arrested on five counts of larceny," Marty continued. "He was still hustling women for their money. He died in prison at age 51."

"Okay, so the body we found wasn't the Baron," James said in resignation. "But who was it then?"

Marty reached into his stack of folders and pulled out a different folder labeled "Medical Report". He opened it and began to read.

"The remains recovered from the premises are those of a human. By examining bone structure and examination of the pelvic structure, they appear to be the remains of a female."

"Mrs. Stanhope," Carol said quietly.

"According to all the reports our researchers were able to find from the newspapers and from the court records from Mrs. Carlisle's trial, there were only two people who said they witnessed Mrs. Stanhope going off the rocks into the water. No one else said they actually saw her," Marty said looking at the people around the table.

"Is Carol right?" James asked. "Is it Mrs. Stanhope? Is there a DNA match or something?"

"DNA requires having a reference sample to compare against. Unless we disinter Sophia Stanhope's body to obtain a sample or invade the Gildersleeve family plot for a sample from her parents, we have nothing to compare a DNA analysis to," Marty explained.

"So, does that mean we will never know for sure whose body we found?" Ben asked.

"Not exactly," Marty said with a slight knowing smile. "Carol, you looked at something in that scrapbook we found. Can you find that article about Mrs. Stanhope's mishap at the horseshow?"

"Yes, I remember it," she said with a start. Carol had been leaning on the scrapbook that was in front of her on the table. She opened it and started to quickly turn the pages scanning for the article. "Here it is," she said after a few minutes.

" Can you read it for me?" Marty said. Carol nodded and began reading.

"Sophia Stanhope of Rock Cove, Connecticut arrived in New York from London by fast steamer today, cutting short her annual tour of the Continent two weeks earlier than expected...."

"Can you read the section where they talk about her injuries?" Marty broke in.

"Uh... yes, here it is... She suffered multiple injuries including a broken collarbone and wrist and several ribs." Carol looked up at Marty.

The Detective picked up the paper from the folder in front of him.

"Let me continue with the M.E.'s report. Upon examination," he read, "the subject showed evidence of spinal compression fractures and injuries to her coccyx bones. In addition, prior injuries to her left side including a broken collarbone, broken wrist, and two left thoracic ribs were noted. The compression injuries would be consistent with someone who rode horses as would the other injuries resulting from a fall. These injuries were sustained sometime prior to death having fully healed." Marty looked up from his form. "It may not be conclusive, but how many other people do we know involved in this case would have the exact same injuries?

"Mrs. Carlisle killed Mrs. Stanhope, hid the body in that room, and concocted that story about her jumping off the rocks into the Sound to cover everything up," James said shaking his head.

"Not exactly," Marty said. "Someone else was involved in the cover up." The Detective looked at Ben.

"Your father, Ben, was the other person it was said who saw Mrs. Stanhope throw herself off the rocks."

Ben sat bolt upright. He could feel his heart pounding in his chest. His mind was racing. The man he had admired all his life, who had taught him right from wrong, had outright lied. In this one moment that seemed to last forever, his father began to transform from the good man of simple tastes to a conspirator in a heinous act that he took part in and lied about afterward. He looked at Marty unable to respond.

"Of course," Marty said, "We could not find a single source that actually quoted your father directly. It was always said by others that he saw it, notably Mrs. Carlisle. He was never called as a witness at Mrs. Carlisle's trial, and he never was directly asked to swear to what other's said he saw." He could see the hurt in Ben's expression. Marty looked at Ben with an understanding smile. "Ben, you need to know that your father never lied. Every source we found always referred to him as having seen it, but he was never quoted directly as having said it and he was never put under oath about it."

"What about the room?" James said changing the subject slightly. "Someone had to have built it."

"Yes, that is true. However, there is nothing to indicate who built it. A woman like Mrs. Carlisle, with her wealth, could have contracted anyone to build it and paid enough to be sure it was never talked about. There is nothing to implicate Ben's father or anyone else in the construction of that room," Marty concluded.

"How did she die?" Carol said softly. "Mrs. Stanhope. Was Mrs. Stanhope shot?" Carol asked quietly. The three of them sitting at the table with Marty all wanted to ask the same question. Marty picked up the Medical Examiners report again.

"Due to the state of preservation of the remains, death from traumatic injury to the soft tissues cannot be completely ruled out. However, no signs of traumatic injury that could be considered fatal were found. Other changes to the body were noted."

"What does that mean?" James said with some concern. "How did she die, then?"

"Folks, I don't think you understand," Marty said leaning forward putting his elbows on the table and continuing to read from the ME's report.

"Based on the presence of moderate to severe osteoporosis, the level to which arthritis is present in the phalanges, and the wear of dentition, the remains are those of a female whose age at death was between eighty and ninety years of age."

THIRTY-ONE

THE ROOM WAS ENVELOPED IN A STUNNED SILENCE. It took a few minutes for the significance of the finding of the Medical Examiner's report to be comprehended.

"Oh my God," Carol was finally able to whisper. "She was an old woman... All those years......"

"Do you remember my asking you and James if the date December 10, 1969, had any significance to either of you?" Marty asked.

"Yes, I remember," Carol replied still finding the realization that Mrs. Stanhope had been kept prisoner all those years difficult to understand.

"The Forensics Lab discovered that date written in pencil on a planking of the door," the Detective explained. "Does that date mean anything to you, Ben?"

Ben slowly shook his head in response. "The date is right around the time my dad decided to retire and I took over most of the work on the estate," he said.

"What is the significance of that date?" James asked.

"We think that is when Mrs. Stanhope died of natural causes from what we can tell and the door to the room was boarded over. We think whoever boarded it over put the date of their work underneath. If our records are correct, Mrs. Stanhope would have been well into her eighties by then," Marty said with resignation.

"All those years," Carol said, again, almost to herself, "living in that room."

"More like being held a prisoner in that room, the way I see it," the Detective said sitting back in his chair.

"So, Mrs. Carlisle wasn't just losing it when she used to talk about having to take care of the spirit of the house," Ben said staring blankly at the table.

"I guess not," Marty said. "Mrs. Carlisle and your father, Ben, were the only two who might have known there was someone else in the house..."

"And the housekeeper," James said suddenly becoming animated and pointing at Marty. "We met the daughter of Mrs. Carlisle's last housekeeper. She said her mother had told her Mrs. Carlisle often took meals in her room and that she had seen Mrs. Carlisle coming down from the third floor."

"She said her mother was not permitted to use the servants' quarters on the third floor," Carol chimed in. "She had told her daughter Mrs. Carlisle wanted her across the hall from her."

"That also would have kept her from discovering the room on the third floor," Marty said thoughtfully. "Although, our guys felt that unless you had been looking for it, somebody could have walked right by it and never noticed it."

"She said Mrs. Carlisle gave her mother $50,000," James added.

"That could buy a lot of silence, too," Marty said.

"Ben, I think your father and Mrs. Carlisle were protecting you in a way," James said looking at Ben, "by not letting you go into the house. You really could not have known about any of this."

"I feel like I have been safeguarding a secret until everyone involved was beyond the reach of justice once it became known," Ben said softly.

"I think Mrs. Carlisle knew what she had done would become known someday," Marty said. "I think she paid her own price for her actions."

Murder in Rock Cove

As the four of them sat at the table in Ben's rooms over the garage letting the answers to so many questions sink into their consciousness, almost simultaneously, they became aware of a noise, a kind of roar, like a wind. Marty was facing the windows across the front of the apartment when he noticed a kind of glow flickering off the outside frames of the windows.

"What the...," he started to say. By now, Ben and James had turned their attention to the noise and light beyond the windows.

"It's the Mansion," James screamed, "it's on fire!!"

The four of them sprang up from the table, Ben knocking his chair almost across the room. They tumbled down the stairs with Ben in the lead. They ran out into the cold night air to see flames leaping sixty to seventy feet into the dark night sky. Windows on the second floor were bursting from the heat and the smoke rose gray black into the night sky. The entire front of the building was fully involved. Smoke was pouring from every window and flames began to shoot through the roof.

Marty pulled out his phone and began dialing "911". Carol gripped James's arm as the two of them looked at their recent purchase burning before them. James had never felt so helpless. Ben had run back to the garage and came running by them with a hose he had quickly connected to a water supply in the garage. The puny stream of water coming from his hose turned instantly to steam as he attempted to quench the flames. Then Carol suddenly turned to Marty, took her hand, and pulled the cell phone away from his face. She looked at James in the light of the inferno.

"Let it burn," she said to her husband. "Please, let it burn."

James looked at her face. She was calm and collected and knew what she was asking. James's own anxiety over the situation suddenly stilled. He understood.

James turned to Marty who was standing with his cell phone in his hand watching the two of them with their arms around each other.

"Put it away," James said to Marty over the roar of the flames, pointing at the phone.

"But we need the fire trucks," Marty replied excitedly.

James leaned closer to Marty and said in his ear over the crackle and roar of the flames, "We own it, don't we?" Marty nodded. "Then we can let it burn."

Martin Chambers began to understand. As he stood back from the heat of the flames, he watched this couple he had come to know over the past few days stand with their arms around each other silhouetted against the growing conflagration.

Ben Allen was finally forced back by the heat and the realization of the futility of his effort to save the mansion. He saw the Days standing in the driveway beside the barren branches of the lilac bushes in the chill winter night. It was obvious they were making no effort to save what had been the centerpiece of his life. At first, he was angry; then he began to understand. The mansion was the last connection to the events of so long ago.

There were reports that the night the Carlisle Mansion burned, the flames reached one hundred feet into the night sky. Other reports said the fire was visible on Fishers Island and as far away as Montauk Point. A freighter coming into Long Island Sound reported it, as did several airliners passing overhead. Residents of Rock Cove had started arriving at the estate having seen the flames leaping into the sky and smelling the billowing acrid smoke. By the time the fire department was called, the mansion was a total loss. All they could do was contain it. As the sun was rising, one lone fire engine remained in the driveway with its crew wetting down the few hot spots that still existed.

James and Carol sat together at the front windows in Ben's apartment, a cup of good, strong coffee in hand, looking at the smoldering ruins. Carol was at peace with her decision. James felt he understood, too. Marty Chambers left once the fire engines arrived and the fire chief assured him they could contain the fire. He had said nothing about the delay in reporting the fire. He had shaken hands with Ben and James and accepted a hug from Carol.

Ben Allen had taken the loss of the mansion hard. He had finally fallen asleep on the couch and was quietly sleeping. James had assured Ben that his services would still be needed when he and Carol built their home. Ben would still have his lodgings.

Carol turned her head and looked at James smiling. "Are you upset with me?" she asked. James took his empty hand and reached for Carol's.

"We can build our own place now and make our own history," he said.

It had been several days since the fire. Carol had been physically unwell but had felt emotionally relieved with the loss of the mansion. James had been busy conferring with Paul about the removal of the charred remains of the house and both she and James had decided that they would design their new home with Paul.

She had been working on the internet at the rental apartment when her cell phone rang. Carol was surprised to hear Stanley Beckwith's voice in her ear.

"Mrs. Day," he said, "I was very sorry to learn of the fire and saddened to see the loss of such a beautiful old house." Carol thanked him for his words.

"You may remember when you were last in my office, we had begun the task of putting all our records on computer," Attorney Beckwith was saying. "In the course of our doing that, I came across something that I think must be given to you and Mr. Day. Could you and James stop by the office one of these days?"

Carol assured him she would let James know and ended the call with the same inattentive detachment with which she had conducted the entire call. When James returned from another day at the estate, Carol remembered the call from the attorney and told James they needed to see him.

A few days later, Carol and James were on their way to Paul Murray's shop to finish going through the unopened boxes still in Paul's storage area when James remembered the call from Attorney Beckwith. He asked Carol if she wanted to swing past the Beckwith office to see what the attorney had for them. Carol agreed. She still seemed a little depressed from all that had happened.

Attorney Beckwith greeted the Days warmly as they were shown into his office by his secretary; little seemed to have changed since their last visit. The piles of files had shifted from one place to another, but the general clutter was still evident. It looked as if the conversion to computerized records was being outpaced by the tortoise.

Stanley Beckwith passed a few words with James about the loss of the mansion and how fortunate it had been that all of the furniture was saved. He asked about the cause of the fire and how the cleanup was proceeding. His solicitous tone changed suddenly, and Carol became more attuned to the conversation.

"I asked the two of you to stop by because of something we found while we were going through files in preparation for their conversion," the attorney said. "In my father's file for Mrs. Carlisle, I found this." Stanley opened the middle drawer of his desk and took out a sealed oversized yellowish mailer. "The instructions that accompanied this envelope state that it was to be opened only in the event of the destruction of the mansion and after the death of Mrs. Carlisle," he said. "I would say that those conditions have now been met." Stanley Beckwith pushed the envelope across his desk to Carol and James.

"What is it?" Carol asked as James picked up the envelope.

"As you can see, it's sealed," Stanley said. "I don't know and, quite honestly, I don't want to know. My connection with the estate is over."

As James and Carol returned to their car, James was pleased with the decision they had made not to tell Beckwith about the discoveries made at the mansion before its loss. They drove to Paul Murray's without much conversation. When they reached the shop, they entered the storage area from the outside door with the key that Carol still had in her possession. James had carried the envelope into the storage area. They had just settled down to work on the boxes they had left unopened when Carol said, "I'm just not ready to do this right now. It's too soon. Do you think Paul would mind if we waited a bit longer?"

James quickly packed up the boxes and returned them to the shelf and he and Carol left hurriedly as she was not feeling well. When they reached their apartment, the envelope from Attorney Beckwith was nowhere to be found.

THIRTY-TWO

SPRING WAS JUST AROUND THE CORNER WHEN Detective Martin Chambers of the Major Case Squad received a phone message from Carol and James Day asking if he would meet with them at the old mansion site. The snow that had fallen often in the early part of the season had become scarce and the January thaw had persisted into what seemed like an early spring. It was rare for people who had dealings with him to request to see him again, so he had returned their call and was now on his way to Rock Cove. Carol had said she had something exciting to share with him.

As Marty drove along, his memory was drawn to the last time he had seen the Days. He had taken a last look at them standing in the cold night air, their images lit by the intensity of the fire and the look of peace on Carol's face. In the swirling wind and smoke caused by the fire, he had seen a young couple who were saying goodbye to something that was not really theirs.

He had been asked for a statement when the fire was investigated. He had confidently stated that none of the people on the premises had had anything to do with it and the Fire Marshal had finally determined the cause to be accidental. There were numerous possible causes because of the ongoing renovations and there had been no injuries. No one really wanted the issue pressed, thanks to a respected member of the Major Case Squad having been present.

When Marty pulled his car into the driveway of the estate, the bright sunshine sparkled off the few remaining mounds of snow the plow had thrown up along the sides of the driveway. He could hear the crunch of the loose stone under the tires of his car. As he turned the curve in the drive where the mansion would have been visible, nothing came into view. It seemed strangely empty without the stately mansion there. Marty pulled his car up in front of the garage, stepped out, and walked toward the charred foundation of what had been the mansion.

He stood for a moment in the warmth of the sun. His thoughts brought him back to the last time he had stood here: the smoke, the sounds, the sight of the flames leaping into the night sky and the heat. Now he could see only the basement walls open to the sky. The debris left from the fire had all been removed and the foundation was showing evidence of some repairs. It looked like construction could be starting any day.

Marty suddenly became aware of footsteps on the loose stones of the driveway approaching him. He turned to see Ben Allen walking toward him.

"How are you, Lieutenant?" Ben said extending his hand to the Detective.

"I'm good, Ben," Marty said taking Ben's hand and smiling. "How have you been?"

"I'm okay," Ben replied. "Good thing we've had a milder- than-expected end to the winter. We were able to get the mess cleaned up."

"So, I see," Marty said.

"Come on up," Ben said, "the Days are upstairs waiting for us."

The two men walked toward the stairs to the rooms over the garage exchanging light conversation about nothing much. They climbed the stairs and Ben opened the door for them at the top. As Marty entered the room, James, and an obviously pregnant Carol, got up from their chairs. James strode across the room and shook Marty's proffered hand warmly.

"Nice to see you, again," James said.

Carol came from behind James and gave Marty an unexpected peck on the cheek.

"Is this the something exciting?" Marty asked with his arms spread apart and an impish look on his face.

"Oh, this is exciting," Carol said in the same light-hearted vein, placing her hands on either side of her distended midsection, "but, we have something we think you may find even more exciting."

She led Marty to the table and offered him the chair he had occupied the last time he had been there. She and James also sat at the table with Ben.

Carol began to relate to Marty what had been happening since the night of the fire. She and James told him about the call from Attorney Beckwith shortly after the fire and how the mysterious sealed envelope had disappeared.

"Do you remember spending a couple of days at Paul Murray's shop going through boxes?" Carol asked Marty.

"Sure, I remember," said Marty.

"What you don't know is that James and I never got through all the boxes," Carol continued. "After the fire, we took a little while to get back on track. With cleaning up the mess left by the fire and the pregnancy and all, we needed to get ourselves working again. We didn't get back to the boxes until Paul reminded us last week that they were still in his storage area." Carol reached into a box that was beside her by the wall and brought out a legal sized envelope in a plastic storage bag.

"When we started going through the boxes last week," she continued, "we opened a box that James had opened earlier that was labeled Nursery."

"I remember that box," Marty said obviously recalling it. "James and I decided it wasn't worth going through at the time."

"We found this in that box. It's the missing envelope from Mr. Beckwith." Carol slid the wrapped envelope across the table toward the Detective. "I took off the outer envelope, but when I realized what it was, I was very careful. I made a photocopy for us. This is the original."

Marty Chambers picked up the package and looked at the writing on the yellowed envelope. The script was faultless and beautifully written by a practiced hand. It read: To Be Read Only If Found After My Death. It had been neatly slit along the top edge. Inside were several folded sheets.

"I was very, very careful, Marty. When I saw it in the box, I got a pair of gloves and the plastic bag," Carol said reassuringly. "James said I was being too careful, but, well, I didn't know for sure."

"You did fine, Carol," Marty said. "Should I read this now?"

"No," Carol replied. "We've all read it. We know what it says." She smiled at Marty. Ben and James exchanged knowing looks and smiled at the detective, as well.

"We think this might answer all the questions about what happened in 1927 and will tell you what happened after," Carol said with a sparkle in her eyes.

"We start rebuilding in a week," said James changing the subject. "It will be a very different style house and we'd like you to come see it when it's done."

"I would like that," Marty said smiling at James. "I would like that very much."

EPILOGUE

I, EDITH MASTERS CARLISLE, DO HEREBY MAKE THIS statement of my own volition and free will. If this statement is being read, I must assume that I am already dead and my home of over sixty years has been demolished in some manner. I am, therefore, finally free to admit to the crimes I have committed since I am no longer able to be prosecuted for them and, even though I stand without being convicted, I have already received my punishment.

In 1927, on the day she was to be wedded, my one and only child, my beautiful daughter, Elisabeth, was murdered by my rival, my social adversary, here in my home. As she had ended my sweet child's short life, so she killed my reason for living. I was consumed by the thought of revenge, blinded by my desire for retribution, and when I saw the opportunity to exact that revenge upon my daughter's murderer, I acted.

I struck Constance Stanhope with the gun she used to kill my daughter. I dragged her, unconscious, to my bedroom where I held her bound and gagged until the room in the attic of my home was completed. I then lied to the authorities and formulated a story that I believed would explain her disappearance. From that day until this, she has been held against her will as my prisoner.

I hired two men from out of town to build a secret room in my home. On a day when I sent my faithful caretaker and housekeeper away on errands, they arrived and completed their work quickly. Neither of my aforementioned employees is guilty of any complicity in my crimes. If they have survived me, they are to be held blameless for the actions I have taken.

I have exacted the punishment I believe befitted the crime committed by Constance Stanhope: a life sentence. I saw my daughter dead on the floor of my home. It was at that moment that I swore her murderer was not going to be convicted of her crime by some unattached, insensitive jury and sentenced to punishment in some distant place. No, she was guilty beyond doubt and the charade of a trial was unnecessary. I would see that she would serve her sentence in a prison cell under my control in the place where she committed her crime.

In the beginning, I was a hard guard. I wanted her to see my face every day and I, hers. I wanted her to know every day my pain and the reason for her imprisonment. I imposed my sentence against her for the crime she had committed against me.

It has been many years now. I and my prisoner have grown old together. Though I have exacted a difficult sentence upon my prisoner, I have, likewise, been served a harsh punishment. And the old anger and petty competitions we once fought each other so bitterly over, and vied to obtain, have long ago lost their glamour. We have both come to realize the price we paid for our pettiness. We have grown old together and she, who was my enemy, has become my only friend.

Last evening, after a few days of not feeling well, my prisoner passed away quietly. I was by her side reading the Bible we had come to read often. I carefully placed her frail form in the chest beneath the bench on which we sat so many times these past few years and spoke of what might have been had we both been better mothers and our daughters been taught to be lesser rivals. Her daughter might have found the love she so desperately needed, and my daughter might have raised her child to be the pride of her grandmother.

Yes, the truth of the matter is that I am as guilty as anyone for the sadness I was forced to endure. Our daughters only played the game my rival and I taught them. My daughter made the foolish mistake of stealing her rival's love, not because she wanted him, but to show she could take him away from one who loved him truer. And I, who knew the central figure within their game better than they did; how worthless he was as a prize, made a deal with the devil. When my daughter got caught in her own game and became pregnant, it was I who confronted the fraud and struck the bargain to keep his secret if he married my beautiful Becky. For, had I exposed the fraud for his fortune-hunting and shallowness of character, both of our daughters would have suffered the social ostracism of their friends. Keeping the cad's secret would give my daughter some chance for happiness and her rival a chance to find a love more worthy of her. The one good deed I ever tried to do for the benefit of my rival, and it cost me everything.

I admit to any and all crimes this statement may make me subject to by its admissions. It no longer matters to me and has not for some years past. As I have imprisoned, so have I been imprisoned. Let me assure you who read this confession that I have already paid the greatest penalty that could ever have been exacted of me.

Edith Masters Carlisle
December 11, 1969

ABOUT THE AUTHOR

Robert B. Stone is a second-time author. He is originally from Long Island, New York and has lived in Rhode Island since 1985. He holds a Bachelor of Science degree from Union College, Schenectady, New York. He comes from a background of having worked for nearly thirty years in the financial services business and holds a CLU and CHFC designation from the American College. He is married to his wife Angela of fifty-three years and resides in East Greenwich, Rhode Island.

Follow the author's Facebook page: *RBS Books*

Made in the USA
Middletown, DE
27 October 2024